SWIFT THUNDER

Tim Champlin

F/S1352l

LEISURE BOOKS NEW YORK CITY

To the memory of
Robert Bungart
(1936-1951)
A true Missouri friend who was
taken away too soon.

SWIFT THUNDER

FOREWORD

We had had a consuming desire, from the beginning, to see a pony-rider, but somehow or other all that passed us and all that met us managed to streak by in the night, and so we heard only a whiz and a hail, and the swift phantom of the desert was gone before we could get our heads out of the windows. But now we were expecting one along every moment, and would see him in broad daylight. Presently the driver exclaims, "Here he comes!"

Every neck is stretched further, and every eye strained wider. Away across the endless dead level of the prairie a black speck appears against the sky, and it is plain that it moves. Well, I should think so! In a second or two it becomes a horse and rider, rising and falling, rising and falling—sweeping toward us nearer and nearer—growing more and more distinct, more and more sharply defined—nearer and nearer, and the flutter of the hoofs comes faintly to the ear—another instant a whoop and a hurrah from our upper deck, a wave of the rider's hand, but no reply, and man and horse burst past our excited faces, and go winging away like a belated fragment of a storm!

> From *Roughing It* by Mark Twain
> describing a Pony Express rider in 1861
> while traveling West by stagecoach.

A special thanks to Dick Davies, Martha Wherry, Suzy Heydel, Charles Hooper, Bob Burnett, and my wife, Ellen, all of whose perceptive suggestions contributed to making this a better novel.

Chapter One

"They're dead, ain't they?"

Joel Rankin looks at me with eyes that're big and scared. His round face is white, making his freckles look like he's got the pox. He's some younger than me, and I ain't but nineteen myself. I'd seen dead men before, but my stomach kind of knots up at the sight of the two bodies lying there in the brush. Their hair's all matted with blood where they been shot in the back of the head.

I swallow a time or two and try to hold back my feelings, as Joel says: "Those are the two prisoners Bill Everard said escaped last night, ain't they? Lance . . . ! Say something!"

"Yeah," I manage to croak. "They're the two Yankee carpenters that was captured."

"Murdered!" Joel says. "They didn't escape, like we were told. Everard or some of our own boys brought 'em out here and shot 'em in the back."

"Looks that way," says I.

"What are we gonna do?"

I'd been wondering the same thing for several seconds, myself. "I'll bring it up to Everard," says I, kind of lame.

I climb back up on my horse.

"Ain't we even gonna bury 'em?"

"No time. No tools. Besides, the general might want proof they was killed." My real reason is, I don't want to touch no dead bodies that've been here since last night and are just swarming with flies.

Me and Joel ride on back to camp from our patrol. I don't say nothing to him, but I'm feeling about half sick. I'd joined this outfit of mounted militia in July, 1859, three months ago, for the adventure of it, but I saw now it was a big mistake. We'd been stopping and searching riverboats for guns that were being run in to the Free-Staters from up North, and we'd captured a goodly number of rifles, too — enough so every man in our company had a Sharps or a musket of some kind with lots of ammunition. This was the kind of adventure I liked, but soon enough I saw these boys along the Missouri-Kansas border were serious about killing one another. It warn't no lark to them. And I didn't want no part of that.

Directly, we hove in sight of the cooking fires and tents of our camp which was strung along Salt Creek, about three miles from Leavenworth City. Most of the boys in the company were Missourians, like me, and the fella that raised the company is a mighty popular man hereabouts. General — he had give himself the rank — Davy Atchison was about fifty-five years old, and a rugged-looking sort. He was a lawyer, planter, and a big slave owner. He was also a senator from the state of Missouri. In his younger days, he'd been an Injun fighter and hunter. A man to be reckoned with, but friendly enough if you didn't cross him.

I dismounted near his tent, and stuck my head inside. Our company warn't long on saluting and military style, so I says: "General, Joel and I're back from patrol." Then I tell him about the bodies we'd found on the way, and what we suspicioned happened to them.

"Misfortunes of war, son," was all he said without batting an eye, when I'm done. "Anything else?"

"No sir." I saw he warn't going to do nothing about it, so I just backed off and left.

After supper, I catch Sergeant Bill Everard alone and brace him about the killings. He don't deny it — just sort of shrugs it off and says: "The Free-Staters are doing it, too. We haven't

8

got any place to keep prisoners, and we sure don't want to turn 'em loose so they can go back to fighting us."

"But that's murder, shooting unarmed prisoners," I say, trying not to sound too righteous.

"Look here," he says, shoving his bearded face at me across the firelight, "that Henry Ward Beecher and his Abolitionist scum keep pushing men and guns down here. They're bound and determined to take the Kansas Territory any way they can get it. They mean to bring it into the Union as a free state. We have to fight fire with fire."

I knew what he said about the Massachusetts Emigrants' Aid Society was true. They did seem to have a pile of money backing their cause. But his casual attitude about killing made me sick, and I shoved off without saying another word. I warn't no pro-slaver by a long shot. Fact is, one my best friends was Shadrack, a nigger who'd been freed by my aunt in her will after she up and died six years ago. Me and Shad'd had some adventures together a few years back after I run off from my drunken pap who'd been thrashing me too regular. I was barely thirteen then, and Shad was about twenty-nine, and he hid me out and give me some food until I could get on my own a few months later.

But I *was* from Missouri, and just naturally resentful of a lot of holier-than-thou New England and Ohio do-gooders who come down here trying to shove us around. When we shoved back, they called us Border Ruffians, which is a lot like the andiron calling the poker black.

But right now I had another problem. And that was how to quit this outfit without getting myself shot as a deserter, which was the common way of dealing with that. We hadn't signed no enlistment papers, but that didn't matter. Everybody knew there was no quitting, once we were aboard.

I thought about it all the next day while we were lazying

9

around camp. But I didn't come up with no solution.

Along about supper time, General Atchison come along and picked me to go with a raiding party of about thirty men to attack the farm of one William Hartz, a well-known Free-Stater who had a place about a dozen miles north of here. There warn't no way I could get out of it, without I begged off sick, which would've sounded phony and made him suspicious. And, being a senator, Atchison naturally had a close acquaintanceship with lying.

A bit later, Joel remarked that I was off my feed some. Truth is, my stomach was churning, and I didn't want nothing to eat at all.

I just wandered over, got my horse off the picket line, and took my time saddling him, while I tried to think things out. I was in a box for sure. I didn't say nothing to Joel, even though I knew he was put off by them murders, too, but I warn't certain if he felt strong enough about it to desert with me. This raid would be mostly after dark, which might give me a chance to slide out and not be missed right away.

While I was cleaning and loading my Sharps, I kept turning the situation over in my head. I didn't have no love for this William Hartz. I'd run across him in Leavenworth City once, and he struck me as an arrogant sort. He didn't make no secret of the fact that he used his farm to arm and shelter Free-Staters. I don't know where he got his money, but he seemed to have plenty of it. But killing Hartz and his family and burning his house warn't going to stop the Free-Staters. The hardest thing I had to do now was to act like I was all full of vinegar to get going on this raid and put a crimp in the Free-Staters.

It didn't seem like no time before we were all mounted and thundering along toward the Hartz farm, with Sergeant Everard leading us. The October sun was sliding down just about the time we got there, but it was still fairly light through the trees.

I don't recollect a lot about the next half hour. It's all just a blur of shooting, yelling, and wild-eyed men with torches. There was a regular flurry of gunfire right off, and one of our men was cut down. Two others were wounded, and three of their men were caught outside and shot down with no mercy. Haystacks and outbuildings was set ablaze, lighting up the dusk. When the shooting started, I didn't take no part, only just rode off quick beyond the firelight, like I was on some urgent business or other.

Mostly the people at the farm were took by surprise when Sergeant Everard busted in the front door. He and several of the boys captured Hartz and his family in short order. When I rode back a few minutes later, Sergeant Everard had got Hartz and his wife and two youngsters, along with three other men, all lined up on the front porch. One of the men has a bloody nose, and they all look like they been roughed up some. Even Hartz has a lump over his eye. He's in a bad fix, but he ain't backing down none, standing with his head up proud. But his wife and kids is 'most frightened to death. His wife is clinging to his arm, and tears are just streaming down her face. It 'most tore my heart out to see it, because I knew they were all going to be killed, and the kids, too. Then the house would be torched.

I couldn't let that happen. I was so scared, I was shaking all over, but directly something just snapped inside me, and I felt so reckless, I didn't care no more what happened to me. Quick like, I worked my horse around so's to be next to Sergeant Everard. He was yelling and waving his carbine at some men who was still out firing the haystacks.

My heart was pounding, but with excitement, not with fear. I'd crossed over the line, and there warn't no going back now.

I eased up so there warn't nobody but me between Everard and the front porch. I thumbed back the hammer of my Sharps and jammed the muzzle into the sergeant's side, grabbing him by the collar with the other hand, yanking him off balance.

"Throw down your gun, Bill!" I yell at him over all the noise and shouting. He tries to twist around to see who it is, but I hold him tight. "Drop it!"

He flips the carbine away. "Dammit! Who . . . ?" He finally gets his head around far enough to see it's me.

"Barlow, you're a dead man!" he hisses.

"There ain't gonna be no more killing or burning here!" says I, still in a blind rage. "Call off the boys! That's enough!"

"Like hell!" He gives another twist, but just chokes himself since I got my fingers locked inside his tight collar.

Of a sudden, he spurs his horse, who jumps forward, and the sarge is yanked right out of his saddle by my grip. He's hanging by his collar, gasping and choking.

I slide off my horse and whop Everard across the head with the barrel of my Sharps to quieten him down. It jars my carbine which goes off with a roar, the slug digging into the ground near the mount of one of our boys who's riding up to see what's going on. The others are beginning to gather. A couple of them take pot shots at the house, busting the glass out of the upstairs windows.

Four or five of our company look at us sort of funny, like me and Everard are having some kind of argument. I got to act quick before they figure out what's going on.

"Get back in the house and get your guns!" I yell over my shoulder at Hartz, and I hear them scrambling to do it. Everard is kind of stunned and don't give me no trouble as I pull him back up onto the porch to get my back against the wall. I still keep the muzzle of the Sharps pressed up against his neck.

Finally, the boys start coming around to what's happening. I don't see Joel Rankin nowhere, so maybe he's already took the chance to slide out.

"The raid's over, boys!" I yell with all the force I can muster. "Get on back to camp!"

"Who the hell are you to be givin' orders, Barlow?" one of the boys says, edging his horse closer.

"Tell 'em to ride out!" I hiss in Everard's ear. He's still groggy and don't say nothing at first. I grip his collar tighter till my fingers begin to lose feeling "Tell them, or I'll blow your head off!"

Normally there ain't no way I'd shoot him, but I was feeling wild and reckless and totally forgot that my Sharps wasn't loaded no more.

Then I hear the clicking of several guns cocking behind me. I glance around and see some gun barrels sticking out the front windows. So Hartz and his people are ready.

Finally Everard kind of shakes himself and straightens up. "Boys," he says, pretty calm, "get on back to camp. I'll catch up with you later."

"Hell, Sarge, we came to burn this damn' Yankee out of here!" one of the men yells.

"Not now!" Everard says, sounding urgent now, as I jam the gun muzzle into his neck. "Ride out now! Or this traitor will shoot me."

The raiders are all milling around, acting uncertain.

"Get moving!" Everard yells, and the men finally pull their horses around and spur away, several at a time.

Just then a gun blast flashes in the dark, and I jump sideways. A man staggers out from the shadows at the end of the porch and falls, his gun clattering on the boards. Another figure slides into the light, holding a smoking pistol. I see the whites of eyes and a flash of teeth.

"He was fixin' t'shoot you from de side. I had to do it," the man says sorrowful like, the gun hanging down at his side. I let go of Everard, I'm so surprised at seeing it's a nigger holding the gun. And it ain't just *any* nigger. It's my old friend, Shadrack. I know my jaw goes slack at seeing him. "What're . . . what're you doin' here, Shad?" I stammer.

Before he can say, Everard jumps away from me, sudden like. But he sees all the guns pointing at him, and he holds out his hands to show he ain't going to try nothing.

"Git!" says I, pointing the Sharps at him and trying to sound mean, which really ain't in me. My desperation is fading, and I begin to feel a little shaky.

"You'll pay for this, you skinny little bastard!" Everard yells at me, red faced, as he swings into the saddle. "We'll be back!" With that, he jerks his horse around and spurs away.

Hartz opens the door and says to me and Shad: "Come inside, young man. You too, Shad. Come in. By God, this calls for a celebration."

He orders the three men to see to the bodies out front and to keep their guns handy in case the raiders come back. Then he ushers us into the big front hall. I'm feeling kind of weak and find a little, fancy chair in a corner and sit down quick, before my knees give out.

"Laura, please bring us some brandy," he says to the woman I figure is his wife. "You boys will have a drink, won't you? My heart cries for those men who died out there tonight, but, by God, your quick action saved our bacon, young man. I don't even know your name."

His wife brings in a decanter of amber-colored liquid and some glasses on a tray and sets it on a table in a room just off the entrance hall. I take a deep breath and finally get up enough strength to wobble into the room and flop down into a bigger, padded chair. I'm kind of stunned and don't know what got into me. All I meant to do was slip away in the dark.

"Lance, it's shore good to see you!" Shadrack is saying, pumping my hand. "You all right, boy? You looks a mite peaked," he says, peering into my face.

I'm feeling sort of green around the gills, but the sight of that worried black face makes me bust into a chuckle, and then he sees I'm O K. "Where'd *you* come from, Shad?" I say. "You saved my life."

"I works for Mister Hartz now. Been here goin' on four months. He pays me good wages to tend the stock."

"You two know each other?" Hartz inquires, looking tall and lean in the lamplight. He's got long, black hair that's going gray. It's swept back from his face, and he's wearing a fine white cotton shirt. He has piercing black eyes under black brows and a hawk-like nose, and has a long pistol stuck under his belt.

"Shore do, Mister Hartz," Shad says. "Lance be about de best friend old Shad evah had, until I met up with you and your family. Lance is de first white man who treat old Shad decent."

I take a good snort of the brandy somebody hands me. I ain't a drinker, and it burns a trail all the way down. But I begin to buck up some after that, and my head clears.

"What's your name, son?" Hartz is asking. He has to repeat himself before I hear.

"Uh . . . Lance Barlow, sir."

"Well, Mister Lance Barlow, here's to you." He raises his glass. "To a very courageous, young man who saved several lives and my home here tonight . . . and to Shadrack who saved *you* from being killed." He takes a sip of the brandy and so do me and Shad. I wonder where his wife and kids have disappeared to.

"I think we should have executed that man," Hartz says.

15

"I'm afraid we'll live to regret letting him go."

"Oh, Sergeant Everard? He ain't the leader," I say. "He was just acting under orders."

"A dangerous man, nonetheless," Hartz says. Then he sets his glass down. "Excuse me a moment." He goes out of the room.

I take another sip of the liquor, letting the fumes go up my nose like smelling salts. I'm beginning to feel some better. I feel the blood coming back to my face.

Hartz returns directly, with two small packets in his hand. "Courage such as you two showed tonight deserves to be rewarded," he announces, handing me and Shad each one of the paper packets that's tied with string. "We owe you our lives, and nothing can repay that."

"I didn't do it for no reward," says I, not wanting whatever it is. Fact is, I don't want nothing from this man. I just want to get away from here as soon as I can.

"I insist," he says, those eyes boring into me. So I take the packet, not looking for no more trouble tonight. When I slip the string off the paper and unwrap it, my eyes 'most bug out of my head. There's a stack of greenbacks. I flip through and see they're all twenties and fifties.

"There's five-hundred apiece for you," Hartz says. "That's only a token of the gratitude I feel."

I figure Shadrack must be used to this man by now, but he looks as surprised as me, just gawking at the money, then at me and Hartz, opening and closing his mouth, but not saying nothing.

"I'm afraid this means you won't be able to continue working for me," Hartz says to Shad. "As a Negro who's shot a white man, you'd be marked for lynching for sure if they catch you. I could try to protect you, but I think you'd be better off by going into hiding or fleeing to another part of the coun-

16

try. This money will give you a good start." Then he turns to me. "I won't ask what qualms of conscience prompted you to act as you did. But you have my eternal gratitude. Rest assured we won't be caught off guard again when those Border Ruffians return. If you would care to join the Free-Staters, you've certainly proven your loyalty. . . ."

"Thank you, sir," I bust in, before he gets any more ideas, "but after tonight I'm done with all this fighting for now." I try not to rile this man, because he's got a reputation as a hot-head.

"What will you do now?" he asks.

"I been thinking of going back to Washington and getting a job with the government." Of course, I don't have no such notion, but I just come out with the first thing that popped into my head, and even I'm surprised at what a stretcher it is.

"Well, I wish you much good fortune in our nation's capital," he says, gulping the rest of his brandy and sticking out a big hand to me. "Put in a good word for those of us who're trying to wipe out the poison of slavery."

"I'll do that, sir," says I, taking his hand. I don't have no trouble sounding relieved and grateful.

"Mister Hartz, I be goin' with him," Shad speaks up.

"I'll miss having you here, Shadrack," he says. "Just be careful traveling together until you get east of Missouri," he says. "If you're going, you'd best be off tonight. These raiders may be back for revenge. And, to speed your journey, pick out two good saddle horses from my stock, Shadrack. You know them better than I. I'll have the cook pack some food. You'll need to put some miles behind you before daylight."

"Sir, my own horse is still out front," says I, not wanting to be beholden no more than necessary to this man.

Through the busted front window I hear Hartz's men laying out the dead bodies on the wooden porch, and shiver, knowing one of them could have been me. The light from the burning sheds and haystacks is wavering on the walls and glittering off the glass decanter, and I think how luck has been riding with me today. When I woke up this morning, I never suspicioned the day would wind up like this. Things are working out so good, it's almost scary.

Chapter Two

Shadrack and me rode most of the night and come to the village of Elmwood on the Kansas side of the Missouri River, just across from St. Joseph, Missouri. We were pretty well wore out, so we just hunted us a spot in a thick patch of timber down along the river, unsaddled, watered, and hobbled our horses, then turned in and slept like dead men.

We woke up along about supper time, hungry as wolves, and dug into our saddlebags for the ham sandwiches Hartz's cook had put up for us. I felt a good bit better after that sleep and food, and was all for pushing along to town to see if there was any sign of Everard or some of the boys from my militia company after us. But Shad didn't think nothing of that idea.

"No suh, Lance. I be de one who shot one o' dem raiders. I ain't stickin' my nose outta dese woods in daylight. Dey catch me, dey hang me, sure."

I studied on that a minute or two, then says: "I reckon you're right. I'll slip into town. Let's find a place for you to stay out of sight, and I'll be back before dark."

We saddled our horses and led them through the woods along near the river. I hear a steamboat blowing for a crossing, and the late afternoon sun picks up the white expanse of a big side-wheeler steaming upstream from a bend a mile below us. She's all gingerbread and gilt, a mighty grand sight with the smoke streaming from her tall stacks as she bulls up ahead against the current. I reckon the Missouri's too dangerous with bars and snags in low water season for her to hunt easy water under the banks.

Directly, through the trees, we spot a log cabin. I see right off it's empty. We come up and push inside. It's been flooded out a time or two and the roof's partly caved in, but Shad allows as this is a good place for him to hide out and wait for me. I give him my Sharps, and I take his old pistol, and shove for town about two miles away.

Elmwood ain't what you'd call a regular town. It's just one of them ramshackle river towns that sprung up on the Kansas side about ten years ago when swarms of gold rushers was busting to get across the river here and take off for the California gold fields. Now it's just a sad collection of wooden buildings, mostly without no paint, and leaning on one another for support. It's late in the season, but there's still a pretty steady trickle of gold rushers coming through again, but now they're headed for the new diggings in the Rocky Mountains, up near the new settlement of Denver City.

There warn't nothing much to see in Elmwood, and I kind of slouch around from the hotel to the three saloons to the mercantile. I keep my hat pulled low, but my eyes are darting here and there. There ain't no sign of the boys. I lounge around on the wooden board walk in front of the Argonaut Hotel, lending cuts of my plug tobacco which I'd just bought for that purpose, 'cause I don't chew. The conversation works around, easy like, to the border war, and I discover there ain't been none of the raiders in Elmwood in more than a week. I go away satisfied we're safe for now, 'cause the loafers in any small village know durn near everything that goes on in public, and a lot of what's private, too. It's their job, and they're good at it.

I make sure it's good and dark before I head back to the cabin, and I mighty near couldn't find it, 'cause Shad warn't showing no light. When I finally come up to the cabin, I call out his name, soft, a couple times, and he came out.

"I's here, Lance. Step down and come on inside. I got a fire goin'."

I didn't waste no time. The night was getting chilly. He'd gathered up a considerable pile of dead wood, and, when he swung open the rusty iron grate on a little stove, there was some cheery flames crackling. He'd straightened up the place a good deal, though there warn't much he could do. There was the empty wood frames of two bunks and one busted chair and a table with only three legs. But it was shelter for the night, even though it had a dirt floor, and the sky was showing through the roof here and there.

I hadn't thought to buy no food in town, so we just finished up what little was left of our sandwiches while I tell him there ain't no sign of anyone chasing us.

After that, not being sleepy, we sat and talked, breaking up dead branches and feeding the fire through the open grate. I got out my corncob pipe and lit up, and Shad did the same, only he was smoking a cheroot that William Hartz had give him.

We sat and jawed about old times, and I brung him up to scratch on what I'd been doing, and he done the same. He'd come to the territory from Cape Girardeau to work, he said, because he couldn't get no decent job there as a free nigger.

"Why didn't you go across to Illinois or Ohio or one o' them free states?" I ask.

"I tried dat for a while. But dem free states ain't what dey cracked up to be," he says. "Dey don't own no slaves, but mostly dey don't treat niggers no different, slave or free. Besides, I don't have no kinfolk or friends dere."

"Where'd you meet up with William Hartz?"

"I come out to de territory 'cause I hear dey lookin' for hands on de farms and ranches, and I figure maybe I get a fresh start. But looks like I just winds up in de middle of a war," he says, kind of glum, taking a puff on his cigar and staring into the fire.

21

"I reckon you didn't go far enough West," I says.

"But dey's wild Injuns out dere, I hear," he says. "I just don't have no luck, Lance. Dey ain't no place fo' me."

"They's some good people in Cape Girardeau who'll give you work," says I, trying to cheer him up some. "And you'd be near your wife and son." I figured they was still slaves there.

"I reckon I'll just lay low for a while and den go home later on."

"You may be right at that. Let's stay here for a spell to see if anybody comes after us. These woods are thick, and it don't appear nobody comes around here much. We'll keep a good lookout. If somebody comes after us, the river's right close. I'll get us a skiff or a canoe, if we have to make a fast getaway. I reckon we'll be safer here than traveling just now."

Elmwood warn't near as grand as the big, brick town of St. Joe across the way, but Shad says he dasn't live over there. St. Joe is full of hardcases who wouldn't think nothing of grabbing Shad, burning his papers that shows he's freed, and selling him back into slavery. Our cabin suits me, and I ain't partial to big towns anyhow.

Well, our few days turned into weeks. At first we were very cautious. Shad stayed hid, and I went to town every day, watching and listening, but I reckon General Atchison and Sergeant Everard didn't think we was worth going after. We was just small fry compared to Hartz and the other big Free-Staters. By the time we figured we was pretty safe, cold weather begun to set in, and we decided to settle into that cabin for the winter. Without attracting no attention, I got some boards, a few at a time, a hammer, nails, and rope, and me and Shad fixed up the roof and door of the cabin, rigged some rope springs on the bunks, and generally made it livable. When the first snow came in late November, me and Shad

22

had been snugged in for some time, and Shad was getting uneasy. One morning he says: "Lazyin' around'll do a body good for a while, Lance, but I's got to be busy."

That day, while I was off in town, he walked over to a farm that's two miles away and got himself hired to tend the stock, just like he done for Hartz. But this time he gets paid only two dollars a week. He didn't ride his horse over there for fear the farmer would recognize the Hartz brand and think he stole him.

What with buying stuff to fix up the cabin, along with some new clothes that warn't ragged and wore out, winter coats, an axe to chop firewood, food, a skiff to fish out of, grain and hay for the horses, and other odds and ends we needed, my reward money from Hartz got drained down to less than four hundred dollars. But it was still plenty to see us through to spring, even if I didn't get a job.

I didn't know how long Shad and me were going to be here, but time was beginning to hang heavy on me, too, during these cold, dreary days. I figured we'd probably move on in a few weeks, but for now fishing, tromping through the woods, fixing up the cabin, or just lazying around was getting mighty tiresome. We'd been here about a month now, and I'd almost quit jumping and looking over my shoulder at every strange noise or voice. If any of my old militia company was going to come after us, they would've been here by now. I reckon they'd either not bothered, or we had give 'em the slip for sure.

One raw November day I was in Elmwood, just killing time and wondering if maybe I should try to find a job. Since I didn't drink or gamble, I didn't spend much time in the saloons where most of the men in the village seemed to gather. I'd wandered into the mercantile to look for a pair of leather gloves. I had just slipped one hand into a glove for size when

I looked up and there, looking right at me across a counter piled with canvas pants, was Sergeant Everard! My heart jumped up into my throat and mighty near choked me. We stared at each other for a long second or three. I could see the surprise on his face change to hate. Just as his hand went down for his gun, I was around the counter and streaking toward the door. Trouble was, he was between me and the front door. Fear gave wings to my feet, and his gun blasted as I whipped past him. He missed, and I slammed open the door and dodged to the left down the sidewalk. His gun barked again, and one of the panes in the front window exploded behind me. Thank God he warn't no pistoleer.

I'd never moved as fast as I did then. I was wearing only a light coat, and my hat blew off as I raced around a corner and cut down between two buildings. I ran like the devil was after me — a devil with hellfire blazing from his Colt. I was unarmed and had only my own speed and trickery to help me. I couldn't let him catch me in the open, so I quick like dodged into a big privy behind a saloon and slammed the door, sliding the wooden latch into place. I know he's seen me and thinks he has me trapped, but I drop to the floor just as a slug comes tearing through the thin wall. Then another. My heart's pounding, fit to bust, but I've counted at least four shots. I crouch to one side of the door as he hits it with his weight. It don't give, so he backs up and slams it with his boot. The door begins to split. Then I notice there's another man in the four-holer, who has stopped buttoning up, and is plastered against the end wall, his eyes big. There ain't nowhere for me to go, 'cause there's only one way out. And there ain't nothing in here to use as a weapon. The other man ain't wearing no pistol I can see. This here privy is one of them fancy ones that has one, long, hinged lid so they can lift it to pour lime into the trench, I reckon. I yank up the hinged top and tilt it back against the wall.

Three more hard kicks rips the door open, and Everard staggers through the splintered wood. I grab the man in the corner and sling him as hard as I can into the sergeant, and the momentum carries the two of them headfirst into the open pit.

There's yelling and cussing, but I don't stay to see more. I bolt out of there like a scared jackrabbit, and it ain't but a few seconds until the village sees the last of me. I'm thinking clear enough to run into the woods just opposite the way I really want to go in case Everard should ask if anybody saw where I headed. I must have run, flat out, for near two miles, 'cause then I just collapsed in the bushes right near the river-bank and panted for about ten minutes, hoping he ain't still behind me.

When I'm finally able to hear something besides my heart pounding in my ears and my heavy gasping, I sit up and look around. Nobody in sight. Then I sneak down along the river until I'm below the cabin about a half mile before I come creeping back through the woods. There warn't no leaves on the trees to hide me so I was mighty careful. Cold as I was, I set there, watching our log cabin from a ways off for the rest of the day.

Finally, along about dusk, I see Shad come walking up, whistling soft to himself, and go inside. I wait until it's full dark, then ease up to the cabin and slip in.

"Shad, I gotta tell you somethin'."

"What's de matter?" he asks, looking at my scared face.

I tell him what happened in the village, and he takes it pretty calm. Fact is, he sort of grins and says: "Dat must've been a sight . . . two of 'em wif dere heads stuck down in all dat shit."

I had to bust out laughing at that picture myself. "Tell you the truth, I didn't wait around to look."

"If he was mad befo', he *really* be mad now," Shad says, still chuckling.

I felt some better after a good laugh, but I was still scared Everard would somehow find us.

Shad didn't go to work for a few days, and we just laid low, keeping my Sharps and the pistol loaded and handy.

Finally Shad went into town by himself and found out from some of the black servants at the hotel that Everard had been laughed out of town and hadn't been seen again, and the other man I'd shoved into him was a stranger in town who'd left shortly after.

Shad returned to work at the farm, and I stayed away from the village for a good while, and gradually my fear of pursuit went away, 'though I was still mighty cautious when I went to town, always wearing a loaded pistol. I bought a new hat to replace the one I'd lost in that wild chase, and kept it pulled low over my face whenever I was out of our cabin.

Things run along this way through December. Wreaths and such decorations begun to appear in the store windows of the village, so I knew Christmas was coming. I hadn't planned to take no notice of it, but I got to thinking what my Aunt Martha would've said about that. She was the widow woman who'd owned Shad, and the one I'd lived with off and on until my drunken pap would come and get me. Anyway, she was a stickler for going to church, especially on Christmas and Easter, and 'most every Sunday. When I whined and said it was too much, she allowed she'd never heard of anybody getting hurt by attending church. In fact, she'd known lots of cases where it'd helped, she said. Where she dragged me, the preaching was mostly hellfire and damnation or was almighty long and tiresome, so I never got too fond of it. I didn't want to be no slave, but Shad'd got out of going for that reason.

The slaves had their own services.

But when I set in the cabin one night, thinking on all this, I said: "Shad, Christmas is coming up in three days. Do you reckon we ought to go over to St. Joe to church?"

I don't know what made me say it, except maybe I was feeling a mite homesick for the old days. I did owe a lot to my poor, dead Aunt Martha. She'd sent me to school long enough so that I learned to read and write and cipher a little. She might be looking down from heaven and be proud of me for going to church.

Shad rolls his eyes at me and says: "I don't reckon they'd let me in a white folks church, Lance."

"If anybody asks, I'll tell 'em you're my slave . . . my personal manservant, and I can't do without you."

He nods, still not convinced, I can see.

"Look here, you got one o' them Biblical names from the Old Testament . . . Shadrack."

"Lance, de Lawd done delivered me outen de fiery furnace once back at de Hartz place. I don't want to go to workin' Him too hard."

We hashed it over while I set on my bunk, smoking my pipe, and he set at the table, sipping coffee. The more he drug his feet on the matter, the more I pushed it until I begun to sound like my Aunt Martha.

"Lance, I kin stay here in de cabin and you kin read de Bible to me," he says.

"It ain't the same thing," says I. "We can do that any time. Christmas don't come but once a year. It's special."

He finally agrees to go, but he ain't thrilled about the idea. "All right," he says. "Which one we goin' to? They must be a dozen churches in St. Joe."

Well, I hadn't give that no consideration. "All I know is, it won't be one o' them hellfire and brimstone places. Let's go to one that has lots o' ceremonies and candles and good-smellin incense."

He was agreeable, so, come Christmas morning, we put on our best clothes and heavy coats and saddled up the horses and started toward the ferry landing. It was just after sunup, and there was only a few inches of snow on the ground, which was crunching under the horses' hoofs. A bitter north wind numbed our faces and cut right through our heavy woolen coats. It was the kind of morning that makes a body believe there ain't no hell with everlasting fire. I couldn't imagine no place so hot it couldn't be snuffed out by a Kansas winter.

On board the ferry, I struck up a conversation with a well-dressed couple who directed me to a church about five blocks from the river.

There was a gang of people at the big, brick church, and nobody hardly give Shad a second look when we went in. Well, they had ceremony and chanting enough to suit anybody, and beautiful white garments and incense and everything. I didn't much know what was going on, but I just soaked it all in and was glad I come. Even the sermon was tolerably short, all about Jesus being born in a stable, which I figured was a lot tougher on Him than living in our cabin would've been.

I was feeling good when we come out an hour later and everybody commenced to riding off on horseback and in buggies. But my good feelings fade quick when we discover our horses are gone.

"Maybe they just pulled loose from the hitching rail and wandered off," I say to Shad. But the bottom has dropped out of my stomach.

We ask around, but nobody's seen them. Then the crowd thins out and disappears, and we look and look for several blocks around, but there ain't no sign of the horses. The snow has been tromped on all around the church and packed down in the street, so there ain't no hope of tracking them.

"Somebody's stole 'em, Shad. Drat the luck! But why steal these two?"

"Dey was the best two saddle horses out here," he says. "Most o' de other folks come in buggies and wagons, mostly wif plow horses or mules pullin 'em."

As usual, Shad was right. Somebody'd just come along and seen two nice horses, saddled and waiting, and took them. I didn't figure it'd do no good to report this to the police, since we couldn't prove we owned them, even if they was found. Besides, we didn't want to call no attention to ourselves.

We trudged off toward the ferry landing, pretty disgusted.

"I wish Aunt Martha was here. She said going to church had never hurt nobody," says I, pressing my coat collar up around my ears.

"De Lawd gives and de Lawd takes away," Shad says. "I just gives thanks dat I's a free man."

Shad had a way of looking on the bright side of everything. Maybe I ought to try that. It didn't cheer me much, but I remembered the box of cigars I'd bought him for Christmas is safe in my saddlebags at the cabin. And there was some comfort in knowing we still had our money and guns.

Things drug along pretty quiet after that. The month of January was long and cold, with lots of snow, and the wind moaning around the cabin and through the bare trees at night. We were protected from most of the drifts being down in the trees, but it was still mighty drafty in there, even with the stove going full blast. It kept me busy almost full time collecting and chopping firewood to stay warm.

We had some good discussions, me and Shad, whilst we

29

were setting by the glow of the open stove door on those long winter evenings. We talked about people we'd known back in Cape Girardeau, some who'd died and what the others were doing, since the boys and girls I'd known had pretty much grown up by now. We talked about whether there was going to be a war, about all the things we'd been doing since we last saw each other a few years before. And we even rehashed that awful night at the Hartz farm. My mind had kind of blocked out some of the particulars, and I couldn't recollect it all too clear. But certain details stuck in my memory, like the burning haystacks, and those dead men laid out on the front porch, and Mr. Hartz with those glittering black eyes, handing us all that money that was now pinned inside my pocket.

"Lance, I know we's got all dis money now," Shad says when I pulled out the wad and begun to count it. "But you be mighty careful 'bout flashin' dat roll around where everybody can see it. Dey's plenty o' folks who'd do 'most anything to get dere hands on dat kinda money. Why, each of us has got mo' den most men make in a year."

"You're right," I say. "Ain't it great? I could buy me some new clothes and a nice horse and really make a show for the girls over in St. Joe."

He looks at me kind of funny, then turns away to shove another hunk of wood into the stove. "Lance, I ain't yo' daddy, but I got to tell you t'be careful o' dem girls over in St. Joe. You's about a grown man now, and some o' dem saloon girls be lookin' mighty good to you. But dem whores be whited sepulchers. Dey's gonna tempt you sumpin' fierce, and tell you what a good-lookin' young fella you is, and invite you to come and have a good time and a drink, and de next thing you know dey's done laid wif you and taken all yo' money and gone, leavin' you wif empty pockets and a bad head. I know you don't drink, so you ain't got no business hangin' around dem water-front saloons where dose girls carry on deir trade."

Shad warn't prone to long speeches, and this was about as much as I'd heard him say at one stretch. It was almost like a sermon, but on a subject that my Aunt Martha would never have brought up, even if I'd been older when I lived with her.

"Shad, don't worry about me. Ain't nobody gonna get their hands on this stash. I'm gonna make this last me a long time. Or I might invest it in something that'll make me more."

I didn't know why he was so worried about whores taking advantage of me. I'd been on my own for several years now, and knew how to take care of myself. At least I thought so.

By the end of February or the first week of March, I was plumb sick of cold weather when we finally got a thaw. A warm wind out of the south begun to blow, and our frozen world begun to loosen up and thaw out a bit.

Shad'd kept on working right along, walking to that farm every day when the weather warn't too vicious. We hadn't gone to the expense of replacing our horses, since we didn't really need them through the winter.

I reckon it was mostly the weather, but I was feeling kind of low and miserable that day when I went into town. Deep down, I knew I'd got to decide what I was going to do with myself. Shad was right. A body has to stay busy. But all my jobs put together hadn't amounted to nothing. I wondered if I should maybe go back to working on the river. At least a riverboat warn't as deadly dull as clerking in a store, which is what I'd been doing off and on, except for that three months with the mounted militia, which was a big mistake.

It was a cold, wet day in early spring, with melting snow in piles, and the main street just a regular, churned-up swamp

31

of mud, sucking at wagon wheels and hoofs. I bought a newspaper, scraped the mud off my boots, and went into the Argonaut Hotel — the only place in town I could get fresh-caught catfish and corn bread, without I fixed it myself. They warn't partial to serving niggers, so I only ate there now and again when Shad wasn't with me.

While I was waiting for my food, I folded out my copy of the *St. Joseph Daily Gazette* that was brought across the river on the ferry every day. When there was lots of news, the paper had two pages, but mostly it was just a one-page affair that tried to act like a big St. Louis paper.

But I reckon learning to read warn't no great thing when the paper was full of news about all the feuding in the Congress about admitting new states to the Union as slave or free. It looked like there was going to be a war if things warn't settled peaceable pretty quick. Generally, folks said senators and such men were to be looked up to, but blamed if I could see if most of them didn't act just like a bunch of riverboat bullies, hitting one another with their walking sticks and forever wanting to fight duels. It almost made me ashamed to be a member of the human race. Maybe there'd be a good President elected later this year who could set things straight again. But with that stumpy, little windbag, Stephen Douglas, and that skinny, joke-telling Abraham Lincoln fighting for the job, I didn't reckon I could set much store by that hope. There was some others like Salmon Chase and William Seward that were scrapping to be nominated, too, but they all liked to puff out their chests and make long speeches that would almost put a body to sleep. I figure men like that generally want to be king instead of President.

I was just laying the paper aside, feeling bluer than before, when I caught sight of an announcement. I picked up the paper again and took a good look.

WANTED
Young Skinny Wiry Fellows
not over eighteen. Must be expert riders
willing to risk death daily. Orphans preferred.
Wages $25 per week.
Apply Central Overland Express
Patee House, 12th & Penn Sts., St. Joe

Well, I tell you, it hit me like a thunderbolt. Here was my chance to be something at last, just laid out right in front of me. I'd been hearing talk for months about some rich men trying to start a company to carry the mail to California with a string of fast horses and light riders. They even bragged they could do it from St. Joe to San Francisco in ten days, which sounded like the worst kind of foolishness to me. But I reckon they were trying to impress all those senators and congressmen to give them money to try it, anyway. It would take a heap of money to get started. But that warn't no concern of mine. Russell, Majors, and Waddell were the men behind it, and they'd been operating a freight business for a few years, so I reckon they had the experience of hauling stuff.

My heart begun to pound when I read that announcement again. Talk about adventure! This was the kind of thing I'd been looking for that wouldn't hurt nobody else, but was still plenty exciting. I had to tell Shad. I was out the door and halfway down the street before I remembered Shad was at work on the farm, and not at our cabin. Oh, well, I'd lost my appetite for catfish or anything else, and I just kept on going.

"Lance, you sure you wanta try dis?" Shad says to me that night while he's frying up some bacon for supper. "You set a hoss pretty good, but you ain't no expert, like them circus riders. Dese bound to be half-broke mustangs and racin' ponies."

"Don't matter, Shad. I reckon I'll just lie about it. I know I can do it. I'll make 'em think so, anyway. Besides, I'm about the right age, and I'm an orphan."

"Yeah, and I s'pose you's skinny enough, too," Shad said, setting a mess of beans on the stove to boil.

I got up and paced to the door that was open a crack to let out some of the smoke. I was too nervous to sit still. Shad was right. In spite of being older, I was still mighty slight of build. I reckon Aunt Martha knew what she was talking about when she told me smoking would stunt my growth. But then, maybe I just took after my pap. He was skinny, too. But I reckon his was from sucking at the jug all the time and not eating regular.

"Shad, why don't you quit that farm job and come along with me in the morning. We'll go over to St. Joe and sign on."

"Lance, you know I's too big for a pony rider."

"No, no. Not a rider. I'll do that. You can get a job as one of the station keepers. They'll need a bunch of them. About two years ago I made a trip all the way to Santa Fé as a bullwhacker's helper with a wagon train that was run by Russell, Majors, and Waddell. It about wore me out, but I saw lots of country. That was a good outfit to work for. Treated me square."

Shad doesn't say nothing for a minute. Then he says: "Lance, you knows they ain't gwine t'hire no nigger for one o' dem jobs. I might as well go on back to Cape Girardeau. I think I knows a man dere who'd hire me at a lumber yard so's I could be near my wife and child. I miss 'em sumpin' awful."

"You could be a stock tender at one of them stations," I say, kind of lame like.

"I reckon maybe I could," he says, none too pert. "How

34

long you reckon de job gonna last?"

Well, it was something I hadn't give no consideration. "I
. . . uh . . . don't rightly know. You could quit anytime and
go on back if you get homesick."

Neither one of us said nothing for a few minutes, while
Shad stirred the beans and turned the bacon, and I come back
from the door and set down at the table.

He dishes up two tin plates, puts a piece of corn pone on
each one, and we set down to eat.

He didn't say nothing more for a bit, then he says: "I
reckon I'll go over to de farm in da mornin' and collect
m'wages. Maybe it won't hurt none to be a stock tender for
a spell. De pay got to be better'an two dollars a week. But I
don't care 'bout de pay. I's richer den I ever been since I got
dat five hundred dollars reward money. Blamed if I know
what I's gwine to do wif all dat money." He give me a grin.
"What time do de ferry go over to St. Joe in da mornin'?"

Chapter Three

Later that night it come on to rain, and it just poured down. I lay awake in my bunk a long time, wondering if I could get hired as a pony rider. There was liable to be lots of fellas wanting those jobs, most of them probably better riders than me. That didn't matter none. I didn't have no time or horse to practice, but I figured to get hired somehow.

It was getting late, and Shad was snoring in his bunk across the room. I finally wore myself out thinking and planning and dozed off to sleep with the fire burning low in the stove, and the rain drumming on the cabin roof.

It felt late when I woke, and Shad was up and gone. He had stirred up the fire and left me some coffee in the pot. It would have been a good morning just to lazy around in bed, but I jumped out and dressed and had some coffee with a cold hunk of corn pone for breakfast. Shad would likely be back from the farm directly, and I wanted to be ready. I judged we had at least two more hours before the ferry run, about mid-morning.

It was windy outside when I went out to use nature's facilities, but the rain had stopped, and the clouds was scudding in low from the west. I was itching for Shad to get back so we could be off to the ferry landing that was about a mile away through the woods. But it got later and later, and Shad never showed. Finally I judged it was nearly time for the boat to be putting in. There warn't no sign of Shad, so I lit out on my own. There was two more ferry crossings in the afternoon, but I was all of a sweat to get over the river and put in my bid to be a pony rider, 'cause I warn't sure how long that announcement had been in the paper before I saw it.

Shad had either got delayed somehow, or had changed his mind about going with me. I judged he'd be along directly and know I'd gone on ahead. I'd catch up with him later.

I ran most of the way through the woods, and got to the landing all out of breath. What was left of my reward money was folded up in bills and pinned inside my pants pocket, but I already had a bill out when I run up the gangway to buy my ticket. They had kept steam up, and the way the pilot was pacing around the wheelhouse, it looked like he was in a mighty big hurry to be off. I could see why. The river was high and rising every minute. Logs and all kinds of driftwood was sweeping along and swirling around in the eddies, sometimes even bumping the steamboat's sides. They must've had a powerful lot of spring rain upstream. The Missouri was big and brown and treacherous.

I had just got aboard the main deck when the hands was hauling up the gangway and the pilot give a long blast on his steam whistle and the paddlewheel begun to churn, backing us off and swinging us into the current.

I climbed up to the hurricane deck for a better look around. Most of the other passengers — there warn't but a handful crossing to the east side — were inside keeping warm. I pulled my head down into my jacket collar and kept to the leeward side till the wind got astern of us. We plowed up into the force of that current for a time, making slow headway, until we got a ways above town. Then the pilot eased her back, pointed the jackstaff at the far shore, and let the river do some of the work pushing us across toward St. Joe.

By the time the ferry nosed up to the landing, I was waiting for the gangway. I ran up those slick cobblestones and kept right on going along the brick and mud streets to the Patee House, the big, brick hotel. It was an uphill grade the last block, so I slowed down and walked to catch my breath. I didn't want to seem like I was in too big a sweat to apply. I had found, when trying for a job, not to look too eager. More than once I had been took advantage of by trying too hard.

By the time I reached the front porch that ran all the way across the front of the building, I was calm and collected.

There was probably a dozen or more men lounging around and perched on the porch railing. I knew they were after the pony riders jobs, because they were all small, wiry-looking, young fellas, and they eyed me kind of suspicious like. I knew they warn't too thrilled to see another one show up, but I pushed open the front door and went on in, big as life.

There was a bunch of men and women milling around the front desk. A table was set up on the right side of the lobby near the big front window to let in some light. Two men sat behind the table talking to four young men standing in front of them. Two of them were just finishing up, and shook hands with the man behind the table.

"What can I do for you, son?" the big man says as the others walked away.

"Where do I sign up for the Pony Express?" I says, brash as I could, stepping up.

"Can you ride?" the big, bearded man behind the table asks me.

"Sure can."

He looks me up and down, careful like. "You a good rider?"

"Good as most," I says, trying to look him in the eye. He had a most penetrating eye.

"Well, I'll take your word for it, since we haven't got time to give you a try. Besides," he says, glancing out the big window, "it's beginning to storm again. What's your name?"

"Lance Barlow," I answer, relieved to be off the subject of riding.

"Where you from, Barlow?"

"Right now, I'm living just across the river near Elmwood," says I, not wanting to give my whole history.

"How old are you?"

"Nineteen," I say, giving myself the benefit of the doubt. But I take heart because I see him writing all this down on a long sheet of paper, so I think maybe I'm hired.

"You got any folks or family, Barlow?" he asks, more curious than gruff now.

"No, sir. I'm an orphan. Been on my own for a few years."

"Not married?"

I shake my head.

"Why do you want to be a pony rider?" he asks, leaning back in his chair, his eyes kind of twinkling as he looks me over.

The question makes me back water some, and I have to think quick to figure out what he wants to hear. So I say something about wanting to be part of history while working for a good company and wind up mentioning off hand that it'll all be a great adventure.

He grunts, and then says: "How much do you weigh, son?"

"I don't rightly know, sir," says I honestly. "I always been slight for my age."

He sizes me up. "About a hundred and thirty-five, I'd judge." He writes that number down.

"You sure you're not maybe fifteen years old?"

"No, sir. I mean, yes, sir. I'm not exactly sure of my age, but I know I'm at least nineteen."

He smiled. "Okay. You're hired. Wages are twenty-five dollars a week. Sign here." He shoves a thick ledger book toward me. I take the pen, dip it in the inkstand, and sign.

"Can you read?"

"Yes, sir." I pull myself up, puffing my chest out the slightest bit.

"I require all my employees to sign this pledge." He hands me a sheet of paper with some printing on it. I take and hold it to the light. It reads the same as the one I had signed when I was a bullwhacker's helper two years before.

When I am in the employ of A. Majors, I agree not to use profane language, not to get drunk, not to gamble, nor to treat the animals cruelly, and not to do anything incompatible with the conduct of a gentleman. I agree if I violate any of the above conditions to accept my discharge without any pay for my services.

It don't say nothing about lying, so I reckon I'm safe, since I don't do none of them other things.

While I'm signing my name at the bottom, the other man sitting behind the table leans over and says something to my man, addressing him as Mr. Majors, and it's then it hits me who I'm talking to. It's Alexander Majors himself, one of the three men who own the company. The big man is wearing a wool tweed suit and a starched shirt, but he has the reputation of being a real frontiersman.

"Mister Majors," I say, handing back the pledge. "I was a bullwhacker's helper on one of your wagon trains to Santa Fé two years ago."

"Then you've already proven yourself, young man," he says. "And no doubt you've already received one of the Bibles I give to all my new employees."

"Yes, sir," I say. "And I appreciate it, too. I read a good deal of it on that long trip to Santa Fé." For the life of me, I couldn't remember where that book had disappeared to, but

I warn't about to tell him that.

"You'll be under the direction of my Eastern Division superintendent, Mister Albert Lewis. He'll assign you to a leg of the route that could be anywhere between here and the Rocky Mountains," he says, all business.

But I was only half listening, I'm so busy giving thanks that it's storming to beat the band outside, so I don't have to show nobody I can stick to the wet back of a racing pony before I'm hired.

"There's one other thing the company furnishes on this job," he says, reaching into a wooden box under the table, and he hands me a new Colt revolver. "You'll furnish your own powder and caps, and a holster, if you want one," he says, as I take the smooth walnut grip. It's a .36 caliber Navy model, all gleaming and blue-black.

"You know how to use one of these?" he asks.

"Yes, sir," I say, hefting it and feeling the balance in my hand.

"Not likely you'll have to," he goes on, "but I want every rider to carry one as a precaution, nonetheless."

"Yes, sir," I say, glancing toward the rain that's slashing like fury at the front windows. I wonder again about Shad.

"If you should lose that gun, or damage it, forty dollars will be deducted from your wages to pay for it," he says.

"Yes, sir," I say again, figuring this sounds fair enough.

Finally, Mr. Majors grins and sticks out a big hand. "Welcome to the Pony Express," he says, giving me a strong handshake.

I suddenly remember about Shad and say: "Sir, I have a friend who wants to be a stock tender at one o' the relay stations."

"By all means," he says. "Where is he?"

"He's not here just now."

41

"Well, tell him to apply to Mister Lewis as soon as possible." He points at someone behind me. "That's him over there. He'll be having a meeting with you new boys shortly."

I look and see a man's head in the middle of the lobby, but I can't see nothing else of him, there's so many men jammed up around him.

"Thank you, sir."

I slip the revolver into my coat pocket and push off into the crowd that's growing all the time. I don't like crowds, so I shove on out the front door. The bunch that was on the porch when I come in is mostly gone inside, just one or two older men smoking cigars and trying to stay back out of the rain that's blowing around.

About a dozen horses are still hitched to the rail out front, their heads down, looking wet and miserable, saddles and gear all soaked.

I judged it to be about noon. Sure enough, the clock above the desk in the lobby says it's 12:15.

I hear a man's voice, louder than the rest, making some announcement, and I slip back into the crowded lobby.

"All right, gents, just hold your questions and follow me," Mr. Lewis yells, waving his arms. "In here." He points over his head at a room off the lobby.

There's a general rumble of noise, and I just fall in behind the crowd of men flowing that way, and directly we're all standing inside a big room. Lewis had climbed up on a platform and was trying to quiet the crowd that's still jawing.

I keep one hand in my pocket on that new pistol, in case of pickpockets.

"Okay, fellas," he shouts, "my name's Albert Lewis. You've all been hired as pony riders. Before we go any further, let me tell you that the correct name of this company, in spite of anything else you've heard, is the Central Overland California and Pike's Peak Express Company. That's a mouthful, but just so you'll know."

There's a general ripple of laughter.

"Now, then, most of you are pony riders. Those of you here who were hired as station keepers and stock tenders will get your assignments and detailed instructions from Mister Benjamin Ficklin who is my boss and the general superintendent of the entire route. He's here in St. Joseph today and will meet with you this afternoon. . . ."

"Do you figure Mister Majors, Mister Ficklin, Mister Lewis, and the station master are enough bosses for us riders? Seems like I might need a couple more supervisors just to make sure I get the job done. Hell, riding a fast horse is pretty complicated work!" one of the men yells.

There's some heads twisted around to look at him, and a few of the men laugh, then somebody yells: "Shut up and let the man talk, Charlie!"

"Pipe down or get outta here!" a third man roars. He's big and rough looking and nobody gives him any guff.

When they quit hollering and settle down, Mr. Lewis takes a deep breath and continues. "There're other men being hired right now at the California end of the run. Many of the stations have already been built, and more are being constructed as we speak. We'll be ready to go in less than a month. These stations are fifteen to twenty-five miles apart. Riders will start from East and West at the same time. Each of you will be assigned to a section of the route that's forty to one hundred miles long. You will ride back and forth over the same section, so you'll get to know it well. Some of you are already familiar with certain areas because you live near there. But most of you have come from a good distance away, so the company will put you up here at the hotel for a few days until all this is sorted out, and you get all your instructions. I'll have a chance to meet with each of you personally. Once you know your assignment, it's up to you to get to your station on your own, and be ready the day we start, which will be April third."

There were a couple of questions, then the meeting broke up, and I slid out and headed for the ferry. I figure when I get back with Shad, I'll get with Mr. Lewis and find out my assignment.

But my heart sunk when I got to the river. There's a big sign on the ferry that says **CLOSED**. There's a deckhand lounging up forward by the guards.

"When does she go across?" I yell at him.

"She ain't goin' nowhere," he says. "Can't you read?" he adds, kind of sassy, pointing at the sign. He ain't no older than me, but he wants to act big.

"Boilers down?" I ask, knowing all the time that ain't the reason.

"Naw. River's floodin'. Too dangerous."

"You ain't afraid of a little driftwood, are you?" I taunt him.

His face reddens up, and he says: "Ain't my decision."

"Where's the captain? I mean to get across."

"He's ashore. You're welcome to swim if you've a mind," he kind of sneers. "But this boat ain't goin' nowhere today."

With that, he turns and walks aft, and I'm standing there in the rain, getting chilled through with water dribbling off my hat brim.

I knew I was stuck. I was shocked at how much higher the water was than when I come across only a few hours before. The brown water was just booming along, carrying big snags that used to be sawyers and planters, the snaggled roots sticking up, ready to tear up a paddlewheel or cave in a hull. While I looked, I even saw part of a house float by, canted over on her side. Somebody's home that's fallen in from an undercut bank upstream. Big chunks of ice was drifting along, too, looking dirty and mean.

What to do? Shad'd likely know I was stuck on this side, but I didn't have no hankering to stay at the Patee House. If the rain stopped, maybe the river would start dropping in a day or two, but I warn't hopeful. I knew it'd likely take as much as a week or more.

I walked off along the bank about a half mile until I saw a man bailing water out of a skiff. I hailed him.

"Hello, yourself," he answers, looking up quick and then going back to work.

"How much to row me across?" I ask.

He takes a gander at the river, then at me. "Can't do it. Too dangerous."

"I'll give you five dollars."

"Nope." He grabs the skiff by the stem post and drags her up a few feet.

"I'll give you ten dollars to land me on the other side," I say, reaching into my pocket.

He hesitates, looking at me like he don't believe I got ten dollars. I slip the pin out and turn my back to peel off a five-dollar bill so's not to show him my roll. Then I hold out the note.

"Okay, let's go," he says, quick like, reaching for the money.

"Here's five now, and I'll give you five when we land over there," says I, handing over the bill.

We push the skiff back to the water, and he takes a seat at the oars, with me in the stern. This man's big and powerful in the arms and shoulders, but I see before we're fifty yards out that it warn't no use. At the rate that current was carrying us downstream, we'd be in Westport Landing before we got half-way across, if we warn't hit by something and drowned first.

Finally, he lays on his oars and blows a minute. "Can't make it, kid," he pants, pulling one oar to keep the bow across the current. "Much as I'd like to have the money, my life ain't worth it." Then he looks up and, quick as a cat, jerks an oar loose and fends off from the roots of a huge, half-submerged tree we was drifting down on.

He slips the oar back into its oarlock on the gunwale. Then he gives the oars an expert twist, and the skiff swivels around. The pull back was mighty nearly as hard until we got into slack water near the bank, and he rows us back up a mile or more to where we started. He was 'most done in as he hands back my five.

"Keep it," says I, stepping out. "You earned it."

I trudged back uptown to the Patee House, knowing there was no way I could contact Shad. Not having somebody to share the news with sure took some of the excitement out of being hired on as a pony rider.

Chapter Four

As it turned out, I had to stay at the Patee House for five days. The accommodations was prime, and I didn't have no complaints along that line, especially since my new company was paying for it. I even got the porter to carry the tin bathtub up from the lobby to my room and fill it with hot water. This was a mighty big hotel and my room was away up on the fourth floor, so I felt obliged to tip the porter a dollar. It was a good deal of money, because most working men didn't even earn that much in a day. I don't mind spending money when I got it, but I don't fancy throwing it around like royalty. Anyway, I took a good soak and scrubbed until I was all over tingly. It warmed me up good, and I even sent my clothes to be washed. I warn't too partial to bathing when I was a kid, but I'd long since had my fill of lice and fleas and such varmints, so these later times I'd took to bathing as regular as I could. But living in a cabin with a dirt floor and no tub didn't allow for keeping too clean.

Every day I took a walk down to the river, but the weather was still bad and the river just as high and wild.

The second day Mr. Lewis sends for me, and we set down at the little table near the front window off the lobby where I'd first talked to Alexander Majors.

Mr. Lewis is friendly and tells me how lucky I am to be hired on as a pony rider, 'cause there's lots of fellas that got turned away. He don't have to impress me, since I already know how lucky I am. Of course, there's a goodly number that got turned down 'cause they was too big or too old, or had some other problem. But I let on how grateful I am, which is the truth.

"Barlow," he says, friendly like, "you'll be part of history. The whole country's excited about this new venture. I'm getting around to talking individually to every man on my division, and giving them their assignments. I've decided to put you on the run between the two home relay stations of Marysville in the northern Kansas Territory and Liberty Farm in Nebraska Territory, a distance of about a hundred miles. If it's not winter or raining, it's a fairly easy run, compared to some of the others. The route runs along the valley of the Little Blue River, so you can't get lost."

He pauses, and I nod, trying to look serious and wise.

"O K, now, the swing stations are from ten to twenty miles apart where you'll change horses. At the home stations, you'll eat and sleep and be ready to carry the mail back over that same route, night or day, as soon as a rider comes in going the other way. Got it?"

"Yes, sir."

"It won't be long before you know your route so well you'll be able to ride it in pitch dark, which you'll have to do. You'll be expected to ride flat out, when conditions permit. You'll have to switch horses in under two minutes. In order to maintain our proposed schedule of ten days each way, we calculate we'll have to average at least ten miles an hour. Now, that may not sound like much, but there will be delays for various reasons, so you've got to push to the limit all the time. Of course, you'll be expected to use your best judgment when it comes to getting the most out of your mount without injuring the animal in any way. The care of your horse and the swift delivery of that mail pouch to the next rider are the only two things you have to concentrate on."

"Yes, sir."

"Mister Majors has set the beginning date as April third. It would be wise for you to get on out to your first station at

Marysville and be ready. Wouldn't hurt to ride over your route a time or two to get familiar with it. Any questions?"

I didn't have a horse, but figured to buy one for my own use, anyhow. Then I remembered about Shad, and I say: "Are all the stock tender jobs full?"

He looks kind of startled that I'm asking. "Why, no, I don't believe they are. We can always use a good man to handle the horses. Why?"

"I got a nigger friend who's good with animals."

"He's not a slave, is he?"

"No. A free man."

"Fine. Don't matter to me what color he is. Send him along to see me. I'll put him to work."

His answer is reliefsome to me. "I'll do that, sir."

I'm squirming some to be up and off. This reminds me of being lectured at by my Aunt Martha, even though I know what all he's telling me I've got to know, but I always get edgy when I set still too long at a stretch.

"Where's Marysville?" I ask.

"Across the river and nearly straight west a hundred and twelve miles. You might check the relay stations along the way, starting with Troy, about ten miles from here. I'll give you a list. Never hurts to know 'em in case you're ever called on to ride that leg."

He gives me a couple more pointers about the job, then I get loose and go to eat some lunch in the hotel dining room. If Mr. Lewis knows I got over three hundred and fifty dollars reward money in my pocket, he never lets on. But he don't ask me if I need an advance to get a horse. I reckon he figures getting to Marysville is my problem.

It's about two hours after lunch time, and there's only one other person in the dining room — a young fella eating by himself. Now, growing up, I'd learned to steer clear of strangers because generally they meant trouble for me. And I'd found out that taking care of myself was about as big a job as I could handle, without no outside complications.

But I'd sort of got over that, and this fella looked kind of forlorn, so I pick up my plate and walk over. "Mind if I sit down?"

"No. Help yourself."

He looks to be at least four years younger than me, slim and dark haired.

"You a pony rider, too?"

"Yeah." He puts down his spoon and sticks out his hand. "Bill Cody."

"Lance Barlow."

He has a strong grip and an honest look, so I take to him right off. I notice he's eating some kind of broth and a little hunk of corn bread. He looks to be skinnier than he should be for his general size.

"Trying to keep your weight down?" I venture, digging into my potatoes and steak.

He doesn't answer at first, and then I could've bit my tongue because I see his clothes are thin and shabby, and he probably don't have no money.

"Yeah," he finally says, looking down at his bowl.

We don't talk for a minute or two. Then I says: "Where you from?"

"Kansas," he says, without giving no particulars. "But I been driving horses and tending stock for a freight outfit."

"Got any kin? I think it'd be nice to have family. I'm an orphan myself," I say, trying to make him feel easier.

"My mom and two sisters. They're the ones I'll be working for. I'm the man of the family."

He tilts his chin up, proud like, when he says it. We're not getting any money up front, so it'll be a good while before we see any pay. I'm trying to figure out a way to offer him a stake until we get going, when he slurps down the last of his soup and gets up, sudden.

"Nice to make your acquaintance, Barlow. I've got to go."

"See you later?"

"Sure," he nods, and strides off before I can say more.

Later that afternoon I get me an envelope from the front desk and ask the clerk for Cody's room number. I put two gold double eagles in the envelope with a note that says:

Use this until you get paid. A friend.

I seal the envelope and slip it under his door after I see him go out. I'd got a boost or two along the way from other folks, and I figured this skinny boy needed one now before he starved himself out of a job.

The next day the sun finally busted through the clouds, and things begun to dry out. I walked down to the ferry landing which is all under water clear up past First Street, flooding a lot of buildings. But I can see from the water marks on the bricks that the river has begun to drop.

But I had to fidget around two more days before the water went down far enough for the ferry to start running again. I spent a good deal of that time meeting other pony riders at the hotel. I made a point to eat with young Bill Cody and pushed him into letting me buy him a few meals, because I expected he'd probably sent most of that forty dollars I slipped him back home to his mother and sisters. I knew what it was like not to have a pap to take care of things.

When the ferry started running again, there's a gang of people backed up, waiting to cross. I just shoved into the crowd and finally got aboard for the boat's second trip over. It was still a mighty fearsome river, but we made it with no trouble. The Kansas shoreline is bordered by a thick stand of timber, about a quarter mile deep and two miles long. Because the water was so high, the ferry had to poke her nose 'way up amongst the trees at the foot of a muddy road, nearly on the far side of the timber. I didn't envy the pilot none having to pick and feel his way up in there, but he done it without so much as scratching the hull.

As soon as the gangway was down, I was off and dodging through the wagons and mules, slipping and sliding in the mud. When I saw how high the water was, I had to circle 'way around and come at our cabin from the shore side, instead of going straight through the woods. I knew the river had got our place. But it still took my breath when I finally saw it. Only about three feet of the walls and the roof was sticking up out of the water, 'way off there amongst the trees. Everything had been washed out. There warn't nothing of value in there. Just a little food, a couple of blankets, and an extra shirt — stuff that could be replaced easy enough. And the same for Shadrack's things. But where was Shad? The cabin had probably been under water for at least three days. Shad always carried his money on him. He could take care of himself, but I'm feeling mighty uneasy, just the same. Supposing he'd been caught asleep and drowned? Was his body in that cabin even now? The water had come up mighty quick. And if he turned up missing, who would go looking for a nigger they didn't own, or didn't even know?

My mouth was so dry I couldn't seem to get no spit going to swallow. Maybe Shad was in town or some place close by, waiting for me. Maybe he was at the hotel in town. But I knew that warn't true, without he was sleeping in the stable.

Then I remembered the farm where he'd been working. That was it. When he saw the cabin was going to flood, he lit out to stay at the farm. That thought should've started me feeling better right off, but it didn't. Somehow, I couldn't shake the feeling down in my innards that something was wrong.

I turned away and started toward the farm with a weight in my stomach as big as a cannonball.

"No, I ain't seen your nigger," says the farmer who gives his name as Abner Johnstone. I'd caught up with him in his barn yard an hour later. He scatters a bucket of chicken feed while he talks, and a bunch of hens come running, clucking and pecking around our feet.

"Shad ain't my nigger," says I. "Just a friend. When was he here last?"

Johnstone's a big, slow-moving man with a round face that's red from whiskey and cold weather. He has a floppy hat pulled down over brown, curly hair, and is wearing an old canvas coat. He slogs through the mud, swinging the empty bucket, and climbs over the stile, not saying nothing. I follow along.

Finally he says: "I think it was four or five days ago. He came one morning, asking for his pay. No notice or nothing. Just quit. I paid him off, and he left. He was a good worker while he was here, but I reckon you got to own a nigger if you want to keep him on the job."

I start to say that paying two dollars a week wages is about as close as he's going to get to owning a slave. But I hold my tongue. No use in getting him riled.

"He left me needing a hand." He turns them watery blue eyes on me as he stops by the porch. "You wouldn't be looking for a job, now, would you?"

"No, sir. I got a job. You don't have no idea where he went, do you?"

"Nope. Ain't seen hide nor hair of him since."

"Did he say anything?" I begun to feel nervous again.

"Just said he was quitting to get another job. That's all I know." He scrapes mud off his shoes on the lowest porch step. "I can't stand around jawin' all day, kid. I got work to do."

With that he goes on into the house and I head out on the road toward Elmwood. I didn't have much hope he'd be there, and sure enough, he warn't. I ask around at the hotel and the saloons, and even amongst the loafers along the street. Ain't nobody admits to seeing him. He'd been around enough where somebody would've recognized him. There's a few other niggers around, but they're usually free men that're working the steamboats, or they're slaves just passing through with their masters.

I stop in front of the Union Brewery Saloon and wonder what to do next. Shad was a grown man and didn't need me, but I somehow felt responsible for him. Truth was, I probably needed him more than he needed me. I'd met lots of people in these last years, but Shad was still the truest friend I ever had. He would likely go home in a few months, even if he took that stock-tender job. But it warn't like Shad just to disappear without he had a good reason, or was in some kind of trouble. A free nigger with five hundred dollars in his pocket could be mighty tempting to some of these Border Ruffians. I just stood there on the street trying to puzzle it out. Could be we'd missed each other if Shad had took one of the first ferries to St. Joe just after I come across. Maybe that was it. I'd go back and check. If he warn't there, I'd just have to sit tight at the Patee House and let him find me. I didn't know what else to do.

Chapter Five

I rented a room at the Argonaut Hotel that night but didn't sleep none too good. I looked for Shad the next day, and then took the ferry back to St. Joe the next afternoon. But there warn't no trace of him over there, either.

Since our cabin was flooded, and I didn't have no place to stay, I checked back into the Patee House. Then I roamed around St. Joe, meeting every ferry and asking questions of mighty near everybody I come across. I even wrote a description of Shad, down to the burn scar on his right arm, got me some handbills printed up, and begun passing them out and putting them up on walls. The handbills say he's a runaway slave and offers a two hundred dollar reward, which is about all I can afford. That's a dirty trick to play on Shad, but I figure if that don't fetch him, then he ain't nowhere around here, or he's dead. I don't like to think about that, but a week later when the river goes down, I go back over to the cabin. I'm relieved to see Shad's body ain't there. The inside of the cabin is just all over muck and slime and stinks near as bad as a pig farm. 'Course, Shad could've been drowned and washed away. And, in the next few days, I begun to think more and more that he has somehow been killed by the river since nobody has come forward trying to claim the reward money.

But, bad as I felt, time was running on, and I had to get ready to ride. The company give us each a new pair of Levi denim pants and a red flannel shirt. I reckon they wanted us all to look alike, or else they wanted the station keepers to recognize us at a distance in daytime. One of the bosses even had the idea of giving us each a brass horn to blow when we was a ways off to let the station keepers know we was coming in, sort of like some stagecoaches did in England away back when. But I was glad when somebody figured out that warn't needed. And they didn't want us carrying no more weight than we had to. For the same reason, they took back the few carbines they'd issued to some of the riders at first.

What with one thing and another, it didn't seem like no time before March was nearly gone, and spring had begun to bust out all along the Missouri. The sun come out and dried up the everlasting mud, while the river dropped back into her banks. Things took on a brighter look, all around, with green grass and leaves beginning to sprout, and the birds singing, fit to burst. I reckon of all times of year, spring is my most favorite. It's like nature is trying to say she's sorry for all the bad things she did during the winter.

I got myself a haircut in the hotel barber shop, and had my boots cleaned up and blacked. I bought myself a belt and holster with a flap for the Colt revolver, and laid in a supply of balls and caps and powder. I even sprung for ten dollars to buy a fringed buckskin jacket I saw in a St. Joe store. It was soft and comfortable and saved wear and tear on my clothes. But, best of all, I felt more like a pony rider when I was wearing it.

One day I was at the ferry landing, watching the passengers file off, still halfway hoping I'll see Shad come down the gangway, when Bill Cody comes up behind me.

"There you are," he says. "I wanted to tell you good bye."

"Where you headed, Bill?" I ask, seeing he's got a small satchel in his hand.

"I asked Mister Lewis to assign me to Julesburg. I worked out that way, and I like the country."

"Ain't there Injuns out there?"

"Oh, sure . . . Sioux, Cheyenne, Arapaho . . . maybe some

others," he grins at me. "That just makes it more exciting."

"Well, good luck to you. Hope to see you again." I stick out my hand, and we shake. We ain't known each other long, but he's a good kid, and I'll miss him. Seems like my friends are always leaving. To take my mind away from this, I go off to spend the next four hours shopping for a horse of my own. But I come back to the hotel late in the afternoon with nothing. It seems that the few horses in this town still for sale are fetching more money than I got to spend. I reckon the horse traders are digging into the pockets of them gold-crazy fools that are itching to get to the Pike's Peak region. 'Course, good horseflesh is scarce hereabouts on account of Russell, Majors, and Waddell has bought up the best ones, paying up to two hundred apiece for them. The newspaper says the rest of the company horses come from ranches in California. Any decent animals that's left has been snagged by people on wagon trains passing through, headed West.

I can't be paying out the rest of my stake for a horse, so the next day I go across to Elmwood and scout around for something to ride. But it's the same story there. Then I recollect seeing some mules on Abner Johnstone's farm, so I walk out there to see if he'll sell one. I don't much like the looks of that man, but I reckon I know enough to deal with him without getting cheated.

"You back again?" Johnstone says, kind of snappy, but curious, too. "What d'you want this time?" He leans on a spade he's digging post holes with, and wipes his face with his shirt sleeve. "You ever find your nigger?"

"I'm lookin' to buy a riding mule," I say, not giving him the satisfaction of knowing if I found Shad or not. "I saw you had some mules."

"Yeah, I reckon I could spare one, if the price is right." He squints at me, and slaps his hat back on his head. "How much you willing to spend?"

"Lemme see the mules," I say, not taking his bait. "You ain't got any horses to sell, have you?"

"Nope. The mules are over there in the pasture behind the barn." He stabs the spade into a fresh pile of dirt and heads that way.

He's got only four mules, and I eyeball them from a distance before walking toward the likeliest looking one. He ain't as big as the others, and is a lighter brown. Johnstone helps me corner him against the fence, easy like, so I can look at his big, yaller teeth. They don't seem to be worn down much. Then I feel of his tendons, and bump up his feet, one at a time, to check his hoofs. I really don't know a lot about livestock, but I ain't about to let him know that. I judge this mule ain't over five or six years old, though, and seems to be in good shape. There ain't no galls on him that I can see.

"How much for him?" I ask.

"A hundred twenty. He's the best of the lot."

"You'd say that no matter which one I picked," says I, bold as brass, looking him in the eye. "I'll give you forty."

"What? Why are you coming around here wasting my time, boy?" He starts to walk away, acting disgusted, but I know it's all bluff.

Anyway, we haggle around a while, and I finally wind up buying the mule for ninety dollars, which is the best I can do. But he throws in a ratty old saddle and bridle. I pay him in greenbacks, without letting him see how much money I got. It's put a good dent in my poke, but I'm relieved not to have to walk no more. Johnstone helps me get saddled up, and I ride out, glad to see the last of him. There's something about that man that gives me the willies. Them watery blue eyes, that whiskey nose. I don't know. But I'm shut of him, and I got me a decent mule to ride. He don't much like to run, but he trots good, even if it about jars my teeth loose.

I name him Hammer because of the way his favorite gait pounds me. When we get to Elmwood, I put him up at the livery and make one last trip back to St. Joe to check out of the hotel and fetch my traps.

The sap of spring is rising, and right now I'm feeling the best I've felt in years. I got me an exciting new job and a new riding mule and plenty of money in my pocket. I know nothing's ever perfect, but the loss of Shad is the only shadow on my soul on this sunny day.

I got a couple hours to kill before the ferry crosses back over to Elmwood, so I figure to give St. Joe one last look before I head out to my home station in Kansas. Not wanting to go too far, I just stroll along near the waterfront. I'd been down here before and seen most of these saloons and warehouses that lined First and Second Streets. It was just past noon, and I hadn't eaten nothing today, so I go into Grundy's Saloon where they have the best free lunch. Besides that, they're known to have right good corned beef sandwiches.

I'm just finishing off a corned beef on rye with hot mustard, when a girl kind of sidles over with a glass of beer in her hand and says — "Anybody sitting here?" — pointing at two empty chairs at my table.

"Help yourself," says I, not wanting no company. But I'm wiping my mouth and getting ready to leave anyway.

I can feel her eyes giving me the once-over. I look at her. She's not any older than me and has pretty features, but her eyes look sad. Maybe it's just the dark circles under them, like she ain't had much sleep.

She sees I'm leaving, and says, quick like: "Would you like to buy me a drink?"

I ain't used to women being this bold, and it makes me uneasy. "Sorry, I gotta go," I say, getting up. It ain't my nature to be blunt with people who ask me for handouts, and I feel a stab of guilt, but then she slides up and just rubs herself up against me so I can feel her body through the fancy dress she's wearing. I catch my breath as she slips her hands over me. I know what she is, but the nearness of a woman who smells this good and looks this good makes my heart begin to pound. I feel all smothery like I can't get my breath.

"You're really handsome," she murmurs kind of soft. "Let's go up to my room," she adds, so low only I can hear.

What's to stop me? thinks I. My throat feels so dry I can hardly swallow. I have plenty of time before the ferry.

But, sudden like, from somewhere in the back of my head, I hear Shad's voice: *Lance, dem whores be mighty temptin', but dey's whited sepulchers wif all corruption inside.*

I look down at this wonderful creature I've slipped both arms around and don't see nothing but a woman that's very beautiful and exciting. Then comes Shad's voice again, as clear as if he's standing behind me. *She get you to take a drink, den lay wif you and take yo money.* The voice sounds so real, I twist around to see if anybody's there. But there ain't.

"My name's Greta," says the woman, taking my hesitation for a yes. "I'll get us a bottle, and we'll go upstairs." She slips out of my arms and signals the bartender.

You be breaking one o' de Lawd's commandments, the voice says, right in my ear. I jump at the sound and bolt out the door into the street, while the girl's busy getting the whiskey.

I don't stop running until I finally get near the ferry landing, all sweaty and out of breath. Where was that voice coming from? I must be losing my mind. My pap used to hear voices and see things when he'd been drinking heavy, but I ain't had nothing to drink but a small draft beer to wash down my sandwich. I guess it was just some of Shad's warnings from those winter discussions in the cabin coming back to me. But

60

why now? I shake my head. I guess I'm the only white man in Missouri with a black conscience. The idea makes me grin. But then a cloud passes across the sun, sending a shiver over me, and I wonder if maybe Shad was talking to me from the other side of the grave. What a stupid notion! I shove the whole thing out of my head and sit down on a piling in the sunshine to wait for the ferry.

That night I stay at the Argonaut Hotel in Elmwood and the next morning saddle up and start for Marysville. It's a two-day trip, so I ain't in no hurry. Hammer and me cross the Missouri River bottomlands past the little village of Troy, under the river valley's west bluffs, and then up the winding, timbered valleys to the high, rolling plains. It's one of them bright spring days when the air's kind of soft and fresh, and you can't seem to get enough of it into your lungs. The prairie flowers are blooming, and the grass is greening up the gentle swells of land. The trees has thinned out, and you can see a pretty good distance. There's just lines of trees in the bottoms, along the streams every now and then. I'd been out this way before when I went up into the Nebraska Territory, but I didn't go this same route. It ain't hard to follow, because a bunch of the wagon trains have been this way, and the path is pounded down and rutted pretty wide.

The first evening I stop at a swing station called Log Chain. There ain't no indication on the map Mr. Lewis give me how it got that name, but I don't really care. I'm tired after a long day in the saddle. It looks about like the other four stations I'd passed that day — low log hut with a sod roof and a pole corral holding three of the sleekest-looking ponies I ever saw. The hut ain't nothing I'd let my dog live in, if I had a dog.

A man's sitting on the log step, whittling, when I ride up just after sundown.

"Howdy," I say, not dismounting. "You the station keeper?"

"Not hardly. He's inside." He looks me over. "We don't allow no saddle tramps here. Better move on." He puts his hand on a big pistol he's wearing at his hip.

"I ain't no saddle tramp," says I, stepping down and stretching the kinks out of my back and legs. "I'm a pony rider. Heading for my station at Marysville. Name's Lance Barlow." I stick out my hand, and he softens up some. "Ned Franklin," he says, shaking my hand. He's whip thin and has skin the color of walnut, so I reckon he's a half-breed of some kind. "We got plenty of grub if you're hungry. But there's no room to sleep inside."

I see there's smoke coming out of the stove pipe chimney. Another man steps out of the log hut. He's a big one, wearing a roundabout that's struggling to hold up both his britches and a bulging belly. His hair's thick and black and so is his mustache. "Got some coffee on. C'mon in. I'm Blather Murphy."

"Nice to know you. Lance Barlow."

"Lance? Like a spear? And Barlow? Like the pocket knife?" He gives a laugh. "That's a funny name."

"No funnier than Blather," says I, feeling a mite warm.

"I reckon not," he says, still chuckling. "Actually, Ed's my real name. But I been called Blather so long, I don't answer to anything else." He slaps me on the shoulder, and I relax. I peg him as a gruff Irishman who don't mean no harm.

"I'll take care o' your mule," Franklin says.

"Thanks." I step inside the hut. There's two narrow bunks built, one atop the other, against the back wall, one tiny table and two chairs, and a potbellied stove that serves for heat and cooking, all of it setting on a dirt floor. One of Mr. Majors's Bibles is lying on the lower bunk — open. I reckon they don't have nothing else to read except maybe the writing on corn meal sacks.

The place is too new to smell bad. It's got an odor like pine sap and, just now, boiling beans and bacon.

"Sit down. Supper'll be ready in a minute."

I pull up one of the barrels that's been cut down to make a chair.

"So you're a pony rider," Murphy booms over his shoulder. "Only three things keeping me from being a rider . . . too big, too old, and can't sit a horse worth a hoot." A deep laugh rumbles out of his chest. "But this is good enough. Pay is decent, and I don't have to be out in all kinds of weather." He turns around and sets a tin plate in front of me with some smoking bacon and beans "But damn! If I was younger, I'd love to give it a try," he says.

The half-breed, Franklin, came in then and sat down at the table, and I started to dig in. But Blather Murphy commenced to giving a blessing that rambled till I didn't have no fear of burning my mouth on the food.

"This Pony Express is a great thing," Murphy says. "Going to cut the mail run to California down from fifty or sixty days to ten." Murphy doesn't sound happy about it, though. He shoves a hunk of bread into his mouth and shakes his head. "But Russell, Majors, and Waddell won't be getting no contract from the government to haul the U. S. Mail. And without that extra seven hundred thousand dollars, this whole operation won't last any time at all."

"Why's that?" I ask, thinking more about how hungry I am than about conversation.

"Because without that contract they won't be able to haul enough privately posted letters, even at five dollars an ounce, to meet expenses."

"If the company shows it can haul mail that much faster,

why can't they get the government contract?"

It appears he was just waiting for me to ask.

Franklin looks bored, like he's heard all this before.

"It's all political," Murphy says, wiping his mustache with an honest-to-gosh cloth napkin. From the looks of his belly, Murphy likes his victuals and ain't sparing no expenses where eating is concerned, since I don't figure cloth napkins are part of the company supplies.

"Yes. The Postmaster General is a Southerner, and so are several other men in high positions in the Congress. They want the mail to keep going the long, ox-bow route on the Butterfield stages down through El Paso and New Mexico to Los Angeles and then up to San Francisco. So, what if it's a lot longer? It's in Southern territory. They don't want to fund the Pony Express to take it straight West across the Northern route — even if the company shows it's a practical route, year around."

"So that's it," says I, when he hauls up for breathing and chewing.

"Darn right. And with the country about to split wide open, it's not likely there's going to be any compromise on something like a mail contract. Both factions want that California and Colorado gold, and the mail is the way right now to keep in close contact with those far regions."

He lets up a spell to shovel in some bacon and take a sip of coffee. Then he says: "But it really won't matter if the company gets the U. S. Mail contract or not, because I'm afraid the Pony Express is doomed before a few years have passed."

"Why's that?"

"Progress, my boy," he says, waving his fork at me. "The telegraph will span this country before long, and so will the railroad. The only thing that might hold up those two marvelous inventions will be war. God help us all if the Southern states vote to secede. There'll be civil war for certain. Then we won't have to worry about the Pony Express, or much else, either, except keeping ourselves or this country alive. Any of these things will put the company out of business."

The way this Murphy eats, the company may be out of business before that, thinks I. "What would you do then?" I ask, figuring the big man to be about forty years old, and not in condition for no hard labor.

"The Lord will provide," says he, without batting an eye.

"Mister Majors figures the Lord will provide that mail contract, then, if he and his partners are going ahead with this operation."

"You've met Mister Majors?" he asks, all eager.

"He hired me in St. Joe."

"I just missed him. He'd gone when I got there to hire on. He's a God-fearing man, too, I hear. He's the one who supplies those Bibles to all his people."

"I know," says I. Then, to change the subject, I say: "Those are some mighty fine-looking horses out in your corral."

"Best money can buy," Murphy says. "Speed and endurance. That's what the company was looking for. And the Lord provided them."

I tell him about the trouble I had finding a horse in St. Joe.

"Not surprising," he says. "We got the saddles and other tack all ready to go, too. Special-made, light saddles that only weigh about thirteen pounds. Have you seen one of those mochilas?"

I nod.

"What's it look like?"

"Mister Lewis showed us one in St. Joe," I say. "It's a big, square piece of leather with slots cut in front and back, so it'll fit down over the horn and cantle of the saddle. The rider sits on it. Near each of the corners is a pocket attached for mail. Three of 'em have locks. The fourth one is left unlocked to add letters along the way. When we're changing horses, all we have to do is yank it off and sling it on the other saddle. Won't take no time at all."

"I don't know who came up with that idea, but it's a good one."

I notice Franklin ain't said a word. Maybe he's just naturally quiet, which is good, because I'm beginning to see why Murphy has his nickname.

The big man scoops out another helping of beans from the pot, then slaps some butter on another hunk of corn bread. "Anybody want a refill while I'm up?" he asks.

Me and Franklin decline and, shortly after, Franklin says: " 'Scuse me. Think I'll step outside for a pipe." He goes out, leaving me with Murphy.

After a bit, even with a second cup of coffee, my eyelids begun to get heavy, and Murphy's voice is just a steady noise somewhere, like the churning of a paddlewheel.

I shake myself and stand up. "Mister Murphy. . . ."

"Call me Blather."

"Blather, I got to get me some shut-eye. I'm done in. Thanks for the grub. I'll get my bedroll and sleep in your stable, if that suits you."

"Perfectly all right, lad."

"You don't post no guard, do you?"

"Not necessary, this far East. What Indians that haven't been run out a few years ago are peaceable. I just have the Lord watch over us and the horses in case of road agents or Jayhawkers or wolves."

The way Murphy was calling on God Almighty like he had

Him on wages, I reckoned we were all safe.

I get my gear and haul it into a lean-to stable that's built against the side of a slope, facing south, away from the winter wind. The nights this time of year are still cold, and I wrap up in my blanket and burrow down into the hay that's fresh smelling. It feels like a featherbed. I'm beginning to nod off when a thought of Shad comes into my head. Maybe I should have asked Blather Murphy to pray for him if he's still alive somewhere. It's the last thing I remember before sleep takes me.

Chapter Six

I'm up early next morning and saddle up Hammer in the frosty air. He's all frisky and ready to get going. My ears are still tired from Blather's talking, so I don't wait for breakfast. I would have liked a cup of coffee, but I settle for a swig of water from my canteen. I thank Murphy and Franklin and ride off just as the red ball of sun is easing up over the rim of the world behind me.

The day warms up fast, and I shed my coat by noon. I'm following an old military road that leads across the Kickapoo Reservation, but there ain't nothing to fear since they been peaceable farmers for a few years.

In early afternoon I come up with a wagon train of emigrants that's moving slow. There's only four wagons. We wave at each other and I pass by, wondering if they're bound for the gold fields, or maybe Oregon. An hour later they disappear behind a swell in the prairie.

Shortly after, we come to the town of Seneca, Kansas, which has the only inn for miles around — the Smith Hotel. Some of the boys back in St. Joe said this was a mighty good place to stay or to eat, so I stop for an early supper. I ain't disappointed when I come out a while later still tasting the apple pie I'd finished off my meal with.

Me and Hammer go on and finally come to the Pony Express home station and barn a couple miles north of Marysville. It's some bigger than the swing station of Log Chain, but it warn't no Patee House, not by a long shot. The station keeper, a man named Nathan Rising, was as far removed from Blather Murphy as a body could be. He was lean as a hoe handle, dressed in white shirt and string tie every day, had very little to say to me, and spent most of his time, the stock tender said, in the town of Marysville where he was part owner of a general merchandise emporium. The stock tender, Ephraim Hanks, a part-time Kansas farmer, said Rising had got the job because he knows William H. Russell, one of the company owners. Rising don't really need the money, Hanks says. "Figures if he's part of a history-making company, he might get better known himself so he can make some speeches and maybe run for office some day," Hanks tells me, kind of snorting when he says it. But he don't say nothing directly against his boss.

I settle into my new digs, which ain't nothing more than a little frame farmhouse the company has bought and fixed up some. It's only got four rooms, counting the kitchen, but one of the rooms is mine, and it's got a puncheon floor, and real glass in the windows.

I don't waste no time, since Hanks tells me the date is March 30th. The next morning, I saddle up Hammer to ride over my leg of the route. I ask Hanks about taking one of the company mounts, which are sleek and well-muscled and carry the brand X P on a hip. It'll be my only chance to see if I can stick on one of these ponies when it's running, flat out, before I have to do it for real come next week.

But Hanks shakes his head and says: "Sorry. I've got strict orders that these horses are not to do anything but a little careful exercise until they have to run with the mail. That won't be for about five days yet."

I don't relish the thought of Hammer's trot jarring my backbone for about two hundred miles, up and back to Liberty Farm, Nebraska Territory, but I ain't got no choice. With a little convincing talk, I get Hanks to lend me a pony rider's saddle, and I leave my old one with him to get the split seams stitched up at the harness maker's shop in town.

Hammer and me make the run up to Liberty Farm in two days, following the Oregon Trail that's about cut a trench alongside the Little Blue River. Like Mr. Lewis said, it warn't no problem finding my way. I stopped in at each of the swing stations along the route — Holland Ranch, Rock House, Rock Creek, Big Sandy, Millersville, Kiowa, Oak Grove, and Little Blue. They was mostly crude affairs, except for Holland Ranch, which was the home of Henry Holland, his wife and son and daughter, Hanks told me. Holland had built a stout-looking house of two stories, the second floor up under the eaves. The place was clapboard, made of sawn walnut logs, and the whole thing on a rock foundation and set in a little grove of trees for a windbreak. This place was only a few miles from my home station at Marysville, and I stopped here for a few hours on the way back when Mrs. Holland invited me to have some fresh-baked, dried-apple cobbler — she called it strudel.

Even without the cobbler, I wouldn't have needed no convincing to lay over a bit once I set eyes on daughter Jane. She almost took my breath for a minute or two when she come into the kitchen where I was eating and talking. Mrs. Holland introduces us, and I mumble something as I get up and take her hand. She's about my own age or a tad younger maybe, a few inches shorter, has dark blonde hair and brown eyes.

"Pleased to meet you," she says, all bouncy and bright eyed, giving me a quick once over.

"Lance is a Pony Express rider," Mrs. Holland says. "So the next time we see him, he'll be passing through here in a big hurry."

Jane gives me a friendly smile and then says: "Momma, I'm off to town to meet Olive. I won't be late."

"Aren't you going to eat supper?"

"Not hungry," she says, lifting a drumstick off the platter

of fried chicken on the counter as she goes out the door. "Nice to meet you, Lance," she throws over her shoulder. And the door slams behind her.

"That girl," her mother says, shaking her head. "I hope Greg is staying to supper, or their father is going to be very upset."

"Who's Greg?"

"Her older brother. He doesn't actually live here any more, but he comes out from town most evenings to eat with us and visit."

"Does he have a job in town?" I ask, trying to be polite.

She kind of tucks her head at this, and gets busy checking the bread in the oven. Then she mumbles: "He's an officer in the Mounted Rangers."

She don't seem too proud of it, so I let it drop. The Mounted Rangers is one of them irregular military outfits that's got up by civilians to raid and bushwhack and murder, just like the one I was in. I rather suspicioned it was on the Southern side, but I warn't sure, so I didn't say nothing, and just kept the conversation to small talk before I thanked her and got up to leave a few minutes later.

Just as I was saying my good byes, the back door was flung open, and a young man come in. He stopped short when he saw me and gives me a wild-eyed, hateful stare. "Who're you?"

"He's a Pony Express rider," his mother says, quick like. "This is Lance Barlow. Lance, this is my son, Gregory."

"Howdy," says I, sticking out my hand. But it's like trying to be friendly to a strange bull. He ignores me and rakes one hand through his long, black hair, kind of distracted like and says: "Ma, I won't be here for supper. I . . . I got things to do tonight. Important things." He glances toward me like he doesn't want to say what he's about while I'm there. So I say — "Nice to meet you." — and slide out the back door. As

71

I'm climbing up on Hammer, I see a lathered horse tied to a tree near the back door. Probably Greg's. I ride off thinking if I never run into him again, it'll be a couple days too soon. He don't look no more like Jane Holland's brother than a wolf looks like a cocker spaniel. But some families are like that.

By the time I was back at my station in Marysville an hour later, I'd plumb forgot about Greg Holland. But Jane had left a nice taste, sort of like the strudel her mother made. But mostly I had other things on my mind. Tomorrow was April 3rd, the day the Pony Express was due to start, and I was nervous and excited all at once.

I didn't sleep too well that night, which is kind of disgusting since I was going to need my strength. But Ephraim Hanks come to me next morning after breakfast and says the station keeper, Nathan Rising, is in town talking to a reporter and just blowing about his own part in this great endeavor, and so on and on. Hanks says the reporter got word that a special train with just a locomotive, mail car, and caboose on the Hannibal & St. Joseph Railroad is bringing the mail across Missouri. It's all the letters that's been collected in the East that people want carried to California by the first pony run. They've cleared the tracks, and the train is high balling across the state, trying to set a speed record. This don't make no sense to me, since all they had to do is start a day or so earlier to get to St. Joe on time. But Hanks says it's for publicity, so everybody will be all fired up about the Pony Express even before it gets started. I reckon maybe they're timing the mail all the way from the East Coast.

Even though the rider won't hand off the mochila to me before sometime late tonight, or early tomorrow morning, I get dressed in my denim pants, buckskin shirt, then clean and load my Colt revolver. There's a small leather pouch on my gun belt where I store a few extra lead balls, a tin of caps, and my powder flask. It don't weigh but a few ounces. And I reckon, even with my boots and gun and clothes, I don't weigh more than one-forty.

A clatter of hoofs brings me straight up out of a doze in the stable where I'd just shut my eyes for a minute, it seemed like.

"Here he comes!" Hanks yells, holding a saddled pony that's jumping around.

There's a lantern on a nail close by that's throwing some light, but it's dark as sin outside. I reckon it's long after midnight. They ain't nobody around for this excepting me and Hanks which is fine by me. Then I see the skinny Nathan Rising walking toward us.

Just then a lathered pony busts into the light, sliding to a stop in a swirl of dust. Johnny Frye leaps off and flings the leather mochila at me. Without thinking, I sling the mochila over my saddle, and grab the reins from Hanks. Before I know it, I'm up on the pony, and he bolts away like he's shot from a cannon, and I grab the saddle horn to keep him from jumping out from under me. My heart's pounding, and it takes a few scary seconds before my feet find the stirrups and I get my balance. Without a touch of spur, this animal is ready to run, and Marysville is left behind in a flash. No moon's lighting the way, but it ain't hard to get the pony pointed west toward the Holland Ranch. When my eyes get used to the dark, there's nothing but me and the pony and the stars overhead, and the faint reflection of road underneath.

Like I said earlier, I ain't no expert when it comes to horseflesh, but this horse is really something. He stretches out those long muscles and settles into a rhythm that's smooth as the pistons of a steam engine. The wind is whipping his mane back, and my hat brim is bent up against my forehead from the speed. He ain't a large horse, but he's mighty powerful and has a gait that don't make it hard to stick on his back. It helps that the saddle's got a deep seat, and the motion is mighty like a rocking chair on this level road.

In no time at all, I see the lights of the Holland Ranch through the windbreak up ahead. The stock tender is on the job as I pull up and jump down. The mochila snags on the saddle horn, but I get it loose quick and slap it over the saddle of the horse he's holding.

"Good luck!" he hollers, but I ain't half listening, since I got my hands full with this fresh mustang. I head him up along the emigrant trail that follows the Little Blue River north, and I'm wondering if Jane Holland was awake to watch me pass by. It must be close on to three or four o'clock in the morning, so I don't reckon she is. But I wish I could've seen her anyway, and I try to picture her face for the next few miles while I'm riding with only half a mind on the job, and the horse is thundering along underneath me.

It's surprising how quick a body can get used to something like this. My run is a tad over a hundred miles, which is some longer than a lot of the other riders. I reckon it's because the country is open, with no mountains or Injuns hereabouts.

Two stations later, at Rock Creek, the dawn begun to creep up, and the soft light shows the wide Nebraska prairie rolling away on all sides. Directly the sun pops out, and the green and brown swells of land is all sparkling with millions of jewels where the sunlight hits the dew on the grass.

By the time I reach Liberty Farm, it's close on to noon, and I'm sweating under my buckskin shirt. But it ain't till I've handed off the mochila to Tom Ranahan, the next rider, and go inside for a little food that I begin to feel tired. After some ham and potatoes served up by Mrs. Tucker, the station keeper's wife, I shuck out of my clothes and drop into my bunk in a little hut built of cottonwood logs and a short ways from the house.

The first pony mail is on its way to California, and I brought it like a night wind over a hundred miles! My heart's still thumping with the adventure of it. Sleep don't come at first, because it feels like I'm still moving. But I finally drowse off and dream of swooping high and fast over the prairie like a hawk.

I was kind of tired and sore the next day — both from that long, hard ride and from the pounding I'd taken before that from the long ride on Hammer. So I just lounged around Liberty Farm, resting and eating and walking around, feeling good about things in general and enjoying the spring weather that was still fair. I hadn't figured on spending as much time on this end of the run as I did at my home station in Marysville, so I hadn't left none of my stuff here. I didn't even have a pipe. But I fixed that soon enough. Down behind the farmhouse a short ways was a little shed that was just piled full of dried corn cobs. They was used for fuel in the cookstove, because there warn't no wood to speak of, except along the stream bottoms, and most of that was used for putting up and repairing small buildings. Some of the farmsteads out this way used twisted prairie grass for fuel, but this place didn't have one of them hayburners. Anyway, I found me a good cob, cut it the right length, hollowed it out with my knife, and fit a good stem to it I found down by the river. I bought a little sack of tobacco from the station keeper, and I was in business.

The food was sort of dull, but filling. Mrs. Tucker, the station keeper's wife, mostly fixed what the company had supplied — ham, bacon, coffee, tripe, pancakes, and dried fruit pies, corn bread, and now and then I had some good sour pickles to perk up my mouth.

Since I had more than a week to kill before the eastbound

rider come in with the mail, I borrowed a horse from Silas Tucker and rode on over to the next station, Spring Ranch, and even farther west to the next one, 32-Mile Creek. There warn't much to see at these places. They was mostly tucked down in the hollows out of the wind and was pretty crude affairs, the one at 32-Mile Creek being built of sod. But the folks was nice and give me a big welcome, and always rustled me up something to eat, even if it warn't meal time. I didn't worry none about gaining no weight with all this eating and lazying around, since I could always eat as much as I wanted of anything and never got any heavier.

By the time the eastbound mail come through a few days later, I'd got bored and scoured the place so I pretty much knew every cow and pig at Liberty Farm, and was ready to be gone. Sam James was the rider who come streaking in with the mochila about 7:30 on the evening of April 12th. I'd been expecting him most of the day, and I was ready. The stock tender had a sorrel pony ready and saddled when James rode up after supper and jumped down. I grabbed the mochila from him and flung it over my saddle, swung aboard, give him a yell, and was off, swatting that pony's flanks with my hat.

The ride back to Marysville warn't quite as exciting as it had been coming up, even though most of it was in the dark, like before. This time I had a partial moon which helped some. The shadows along the river valley kept me from seeing the ground too well, but I just had to ride hard and trust to luck that the ponies wouldn't step in no holes or stumble. I tried to stay right on the emigrant road which was pounded down considerable, although there was ruts. When the rains come, I'd have to ride on the prairie up above to keep out of the slick mud.

Again, I didn't see nothing of Jane Holland, because it was away late in the night when I changed horses at the Holland Ranch swing station.

Chapter Seven

Two things happened during the next month. First off, I got to be a regular visitor to the Holland Ranch. Jane and I got to know one another better. She had a quick wit and a good laugh and didn't seem spiteful or stuck on herself like a few other young women I'd been acquainted with. By and by, I asked her to go to a dance with me, and she went. We had a whopping good time and stayed till the last fiddle sawed. From then on I took her to dances in town, to picnics, and was a guest at the Holland Ranch for supper a goodly number of times. She seemed to cotton to me. I don't know why. I ain't too bad looking, I'm told, but I sure warn't big and strong — just kind of lean and wiry. And she sure had more schooling than I did, though I'd traveled around a good deal and had lots of stories to tell. Maybe she just liked the idea of keeping company with a Pony Express rider. She introduced me to several of her friends — maybe six or eight of them. I hadn't known there was that many fellas and gals about my age in this area. But we got along famously. As near as I could make out, there warn't a bad one in the bunch — all friendly and likable. We had some good times together. It got so there was occasions when I almost regretted having to go off to carry the mail for fear of missing some social or other.

And, speaking of carrying the mail, that was the second thing that happened — my runs were about doubled, so I was riding to and from Liberty Farm twice a week, because of more mail being sent by the faster Pony Express. Four hundred twenty miles a week was considerable, but twenty-five dollars a week was good wages. The first excitement had kind of wore off, and the job had settled down to some hard riding, both day and night. But I suppose nothing stays exciting for too long — especially if you're doing it regular, over and over. It warn't long before I knew every swell and gully and straight stretch of that ride. It even got so I could let the horse have his head, at a full gallop, while I kind of hunched down in the saddle and dozed, which I did after I'd been up too long with Jane. But I tried this once too often. One morning, just in front of sunup, my pony stumbled and almost went down. I come awake, sudden, flying upside down over the pony's head. I landed flat on my back, mighty near slamming my liver and lungs loose. I was a minute or two getting my breath back and making sure no bones was broke before I could think about the pony. He hadn't gone down, but had run off a ways, and was some skittish when I come toward him on foot. If it hadn't been just light enough to see, and if he hadn't snagged his reins in a bush by the river, I might not have caught up with him this side of Big Sandy station. Anyway, I was lucky, and didn't tell nobody about it, but you can bet I stayed awake from then on, and got me enough sleep so it didn't happen again. Maybe I don't have much schooling, but nobody ever said I couldn't learn from my mistakes.

By the middle of May, the Pony Express was running reliable and regular from St. Joe to Sacramento and San Francisco. Anybody who could afford five dollars an ounce could get a letter across the country in ten days — a time I wouldn't have believed a couple months ago. And with the full bloom of the season come good rains to green things up. The mud slowed the ponies some, but not enough to worry about. This was made up for by the warmer weather and the wildflowers that streaked colors over miles of prairie that warn't cultivated. Most of the hard rains come when I was between runs, but I had to put up with the slop. I hadn't had no trouble riding when it was dry underfoot, but my heart stayed in my mouth when I felt the ponies' hoofs slip every few steps. I'd have preferred my slower, but sure-footed Hammer. There's adventure, and there's fear, and I reckoned this was some of the last. But, I'll have to say, it sure kept the boredom away.

All in all, things were going pretty well, and I hadn't no complaints. But I should've known not to get too comfortable. When things seem to be going best, that's the very time something bad generally hits you from the blind side where you can't see it coming.

Jane Holland warn't expecting me that night, but I was getting mighty stuck on that girl and just had to see her again before I headed out on my run the next day from Marysville. So I rode over the few miles to the Holland Farm after supper. It was one of them May evenings when the air is soft, and everything seems perfect. Even a full moon was lighting up the evening sky.

I should've stayed in my room and gone to bed early that night, but I warn't tired and the pull of the Holland house was strong.

Jane opened the kitchen door herself when I rapped.

"Lance?" she says, kind of hesitating.

"Sure," I says, knowing she could see my face plain in the lamplight.

"What're you doing here tonight?"

My heart kind of sinks 'cause I figure I've caught her with another fella.

"Well, nothin' was going on. Thought I'd drop by. . . ."

"Quick! Come in!" She grabs my arm and pulls me inside, taking a quick look behind me as she does.

"Where're your folks?" I ask.

"Daddy's playing poker in Marysville. Mama's in the sitting room."

She's nervous as a cat about something, but I can't figure

what. "Want to take a walk? There's a full moon out." There warn't no front porch or I would've preferred to set and swing. "Lance, don't get me wrong. I'm awful glad to see you, but you shouldn't have come here tonight."

"Why?"

"The Rangers have been all over this area the last couple of days."

"So?"

"They're looking for any Southern sympathizers. I've told you my family leans toward the Free-Soilers," she says. "But we don't take an active part in any of this business."

I still don't see why she's telling me all this. We're still standing in the kitchen, and she hasn't even asked me to sit down.

"You met my brother, Gregory," she says.

"Yeah, but only once, the first time I stopped here. Haven't seen him since." I don't add that I haven't been the poorer for it, either.

"Mama told you he's an officer in the Mounted Rangers. He's a very active Free-Soiler," she adds, kind of apologizing, but wringing her hands at the same time. "Maybe you better stay away from here until things calm down," she says, looking at me close to see what I'll say.

"If you're Free-Soilers, they won't bother you," says I.

"No, but they could find *you* here. Several of that bunch are in and out of here a lot, since Greg's one of them."

After we'd got to be good friends, I'd told her about my days riding with the Border Ruffians, and how I'd come to leave them. In fact, I'd even seen William Hartz just yesterday going into a hotel in Marysville. But I'd ducked around a corner to avoid meeting him. I didn't feel comfortable around the man, so I warn't looking to renew any old acquaintances, even though we'd parted on good terms.

80

"Greg's very radical when it comes to fighting for his cause," Jane says.

"A lot of people are," says I, trying to make light of it. "That's why I left that outfit. They were too radical for me. I don't want nothing more to do with either side. I just carry the mail now." I smile at her, and she eases up a bit. "Don't worry about me. I've been coming here to see you pretty regular for the past few weeks, and everything's been O K. I don't think anybody around here even knows about my being in the militia."

"Yes, they do," she says, looking forlorn. "I told Greg one day when he made some remark against you. I was just trying to show him what an exciting, adventurous life you've led. I wasn't thinking. I'm sorry. Greg knows you took part in raids on farms and helped steal a lot of guns from the riverboats."

"Greg doesn't want me seeing you?"

"No. He hates all Southerners, especially those who've fought against the Free-Soilers. It's a personal insult to him."

"Well, I'm riding out on a run tomorrow, and I had to see you before I left," I say, not leaving no room for argument. I help myself to a cup from a nearby cupboard and pour some coffee from a pot that's still steaming on the cook stove.

I set down at the table, and she joins me. I turn the talk to other things, and she tells me she's going to be off to a school in St. Louis this fall.

"I think I've had all the schooling I need," she says, "but my folks want me to learn French and study English literature and learn some more of the social graces." She makes a wry face. "I think Daddy just wants me out of the way of all the riffraff on the frontier. Not meaning you, of course. Daddy likes you," she adds, quick like, putting a hand on my arm.

"Sounds pretty dull," I say, thinking how I'm going to miss her.

"You don't know the half of it," she says. "I was around some of these snooty rich girls when I visited my cousin in St. Louis last year. They're so self-centered and conceited, it made me sick."

Just then her mother comes into the kitchen, and we all chit-chat for a while. Mrs. Holland is a plump, matronly type, but has a quick wit and a good head on her. You can tell she's from quality stock. She knows I'm always hungry, and, without asking, she fixes me a roast beef sandwich while we're talking.

I'd finished eating and was sipping a second cup of coffee when the back door flies open, and four men bust in. Before I can move, one of them has clapped a pistol to my head. The other three men spread out in the kitchen, covering us with carbines.

"Now we've got you, you son-of-a-bitch!" the man hisses in my ear. My heart's going like a racehorse, and I grit my teeth, just waiting for the bullet. I don't have no idea who these men are, but I feel sure I'm going to die.

"Check the rest of the house," one of the men says.

"There's nobody else home," says another voice behind me.

"Greg!" Jane screams as her brother walks into the room.

"Gregory, what are you doing?" His mother seems like the only one who's not scared — just plumb irritated at him misbehaving.

"This is military business, Ma," he says.

"You've got me confused with somebody else," I yell. "I'm not in the military."

"Oh, we've got the right one, all right," the man with the gun says. "You rode with the mounted militia. You and that bunch have burned out and killed many a poor farmer who was trying to keep the Union free."

"I've seen you at the Leavenworth levee, robbing river-boats, bold as brass," says another.

There ain't no use denying it, 'cause I was there, more than once, but I'd never killed nobody. But I was about to take the blame for it all.

"Take him out and hang him!" Greg says, cold and hard.

I go all numb. Like in a dream, I hear Jane and her mother crying and pleading with the raiders. Hands are pulling me out of the chair, and then we're outside in the moonlight.

"Did you get his gun?" Greg asks, ignoring his mother and sister.

"He ain't armed."

My arms are tied to my sides, and several more men who are outside half drag me to where there's two big oak trees in front of the house. At first, I expected to be shot. But now, I'm going to be hanged. I can't believe this is happening. One minute I'm sitting in a kitchen, drinking coffee and visiting with two ladies, and the next, I'm about to be hanged. I'm so stunned by the suddenness of it all, it's like some strange nightmare where I can't move nor talk. There's eight men around me, and they're all rough looking and armed. Jane is pleading and crying, and Mrs. Holland is threatening her son with all kinds of punishment, but he ain't paying no attention.

A heavy coil of rope is slung over a limb of the oak. I can't show no fear, but have to buck up and harden myself to this horrible end, 'cause I don't see any way out.

In those few moments, while I wait to die, some of the good things and bad things I've done in my short life come quick to mind. There was so much I still wanted to do, I hated to end it now, like this. What was on the other side of death's door? Would I go to heaven? Would I be punished?

Somebody touches my shoulder. "We're ready. It's time." He don't sound mean — just all business. He slips a hangman's noose over my head. This jars me out of my stupor, and a thought of William Hartz jumps into my head.

"Greg, there's something you should know," I say, calm like, trying to keep my voice from shaking.

"It ain't about my sister, is it? If you've done something to her, I won't wait for the rope. I'll choke you with my bare hands."

"Do you know William Hartz?" I ask.

"Everybody knows Mister Hartz," he kind of sneers. "What of it?"

I tell him about taking Sergeant Everard hostage and saving the Hartz family and their home.

"It's true, Greg," Jane chimes in, wiping her tears. "He told me all about that some time ago."

"Just a desperate lie to save his thievin' neck!" Greg spits on the ground. "Get on with it!"

"It's true!" Then I have a flash, and play my last card. "You can ask him!" I yell. "Just go and ask him! He's in Marysville this very minute at the hotel. I saw him there yesterday."

"Just check out his story," Jane pleads, a little calmer. "What can it hurt? It won't take long."

I'm wishing Mr. Holland was here. But I doubt even he could stop this crazy son and his Free-Soil raiders who're bent on having a hanging. Maybe the full moon has made them wilder, I'm thinking.

"Please, Greg! Do it for me," Jane says, her voice trembling. Her mother is crying, quiet like, but pipes up and says: "This boy deserves a chance. Even a criminal gets a trial. If you hang this boy without at least seeing if his story is true, his death will be on your head. Ride to Marysville. It won't take more than an hour," she adds when he hesitates. Then she throws in the clincher. "If you don't go find William

Hartz, you are no longer my son, and I never want to set eyes on you again!"

Thank God for mothers! This last plea by her finally tips the balance, and Greg says to his men: "Keep a good watch on him. I'll go check his story. Stand easy until I get back."

He mounts up and gallops off toward Marysville. The next hour was the longest of my life. The dark figures of the seven men with guns, and the two women stand around me. The bright moonlight dapples the ground here and there where it shoots through the overhead leaves of the oak. My knees are so weak and wobbly, I'm afraid they won't hold me up. The rope around my neck is looped loose over the limb, so, if I fall down, I won't hang myself, but I almost wish I was seated on Hammer. That way maybe I'd break my neck and die quick when he jumps out from under me. Leastways, then I wouldn't choke to death like I'm bound to do if they just hoist me up. I'd never actually seen a hanging, but others had told me that the eyes and tongue kind of bulge out and the man turned all black in the face. If I was due any punishment for my sins, I reckon that would surely take care of it.

I look around to try to distract my mind from this awful picture. "Jane. . . ."

She tries to come to me, but is pushed back by one of the men with his carbine. I hear her sobbing, soft like.

If William Hartz has left Marysville and gone back home, I'm a dead man. Even if he's still at the hotel in Marysville, will he come back here to identify me? Surely, he'll remember the episode of seven months ago, even if he don't recollect my name. A slight breeze begun to dry the sweat on my face.

Time drug on until it mighty near seemed eternity. The moon was nailed to the sky, and didn't move. I try to think of reason for hope. But I had just as much cause to despair.

Finally, my ears catch the far-off sound of galloping hoofs.

Was it one horse or two? I strain to hear the dull thudding on the soft turf. Nearer and nearer came the sound. There were two horsemen, sure enough.

Then the next thing I remember is a great feeling of relief as William Hartz is in the torchlight, ordering my arms unbound, and then shaking my hand and assuring me I was safe.

"This man is no criminal!" he booms. "Lance Barlow is a hero. At the peril of his own life, he saved me and my family from sure death at the hands of the Border Ruffians!"

He pulls Gregory Holland aside, and they have a whispered conversation. Then he comes back and says: "Glad to be able to do you a good turn. Stay well!" With that, he mounts up and rides off.

I'm taken back into the house and told I can go, but several of the men are grousing about being cheated. They was all charged up for a hanging and don't take this with good grace, so they get some satisfaction by emptying my pockets of a three-dollar gold piece I'm carrying, along with a Barlow knife and my leather billfold with three one-dollar bills. They leave me the fringed buckskin shirt I'm wearing and my boots, but take my mule, Hammer, and the saddle.

I'm put afoot, and Greg tells me to get going and never come back to the Holland house without I'm just passing through, carrying the mail.

Jane throws off her brother's restraining arm and follows me outside as I set out in the night. I kiss her and thank her, and she hangs to my neck a long minute or two, then I push off and head toward my lodgings, several miles away near Marysville.

That tramp in the moonlight give me plenty of time to think of how lucky I am still to be living — how lucky it was William Hartz was close by. But, then, everyone in his life has a certain portion of luck. I just hope mine ain't all used up in one night.

I owe my life to Jane and Mrs. Holland and also to William Hartz. I figure I'll probably never come any closer to dying than I done this night, and it give me a whole new way of looking at the execution of outlaws. Hanging is just too ghastly. They'd be a lot better off being shot by a firing squad.

I reckon Greg Holland ought to be disowned by his parents. But, knowing a mother's love and capacity for forgiving almost anything, it ain't likely.

I'd grown right fond of my mule, Hammer, and now he was gone, but at least I still had my Pony Express weapon, the Colt revolver, because I'd left it in my room.

But, most of all, I'd been impressed at how fast everything is passing, and vowed I'd make the most of whatever time I had left in this world.

Chapter Eight

I kept on riding my regular stretch of the Pony Express route from Marysville, Kansas, to Liberty Farm, Nebraska, even though the Free-Soil raiders had thrown a good scare into me. I was a wanted man by both sides now and never went out without I had my .36 caliber Colt revolver strapped on. And it hung by my head on the bedpost at night. I even went to a gunsmith in Seneca, Kansas, and bought me an extra cylinder which I kept loaded and capped in the side pocket of my buckskin shirt. In case of trouble, I could quick like change cylinders and have six more shots without taking time to reload — time I might not have in a tight spot. I would've carried a shotgun, but the company wouldn't allow no extra weight. And knowing how these killers skulked around like a pack of hungry wolves, looking to take me unawares, I might not have had a chance to use it anyway. I became as skittish as a jackrabbit, starting at every sound. And, like my furry rodent friends, speed and cunning would be the only things that would probably save me if they come at me again.

They knew where I was, 'cause there warn't no way I could vary from my mail route, since I had to go the shortest, quickest way. It wouldn't be no trouble for somebody from my old militia outfit or Greg Holland's Mounted Rangers to waylay me, day or night, along the lonely stretches of that hundred-mile trail. I didn't have no doubts that some of them hot heads would come after me again, in spite of William Hartz vouching for me. Hartz was a man who carried a power of weight where the Free-Soilers were concerned, but if I just disappeared some rainy night along the Little Blue River, he wouldn't be able to help me.

I stayed away from the Holland Ranch for a spell, though I saw Jane now and then and waved to her as I was changing horses. One day, just as I was slinging the mochila over the saddle of my fresh mount, she come out of the stable and slipped a little piece of paper into my hand. I reckon she knew nobody was watching, except the stable boy, or she wouldn't have done it. I don't let on to notice, but when I get down the trail a ways, I opened up the crumpled paper and read.

Meet me at Lone Oak 7:00 PM. Thursday.

It sent a thrill through me to read those words since I hadn't said nothing more than hello to her on the fly, so to speak, in more than two weeks. She still wanted to see me in spite of the danger. Lone Oak was a place on the back side of the Holland Ranch where we'd ridden for picnics. It was a pretty spot along a creek that run into the Little Blue. She knew I'd be back in Marysville by Thursday. When I come to think of it again, I wondered if I should go to meet her there. She warn't too careful about keeping secrets, so somebody else might be there, waiting for me, too. But then, I reckoned that near hanging in her front yard has probably made her a mite more cautious, especially where her brother's concerned.

The next thing I thought of was how to get there. I'd have to borrow a horse, or rent one at the livery in Marysville. I hadn't told Nathan Rising, the station keeper, or Ephraim Hanks, the stock tender, how I'd lost my mule. Hanks had asked me where Hammer was, and all I said was: "Lost him." He didn't ask for no explanations. For all he knew, I might've lost him in a poker game. After I got over being scared, I got mad, thinking how that bunch had stole a ninety-dollar mule from me. But I reckon that was still a cheap price to pay for my life. And I even grinned when I thought of him jarring somebody else's backbone with that trot, like he'd done mine.

But, when I get back to Marysville on Wednesday, three days later, I persuade Ephraim Hanks to lend me his own horse to go meet Jane the next evening. I ain't due to catch the return mail till Friday morning, so I have plenty of time to rest up.

The next evening he's at the stable after supper, and I confide to him where I'm going and what I'm doing. In fact, just on a hunch, I tell him about what happened at the Holland place and how I'm still mighty nervous.

"Thought you were acting pretty edgy the past few weeks," Hanks says. "Figured something was wrong." He looks at me kind of worried. "You be mighty careful."

"Don't worry. I'll take good care of your horse."

"I'm talking about *you*. I know some of the boys who ride for both sides. And they aren't the kind you'd want to invite home for supper. They wouldn't know a good cause if one smacked 'em in the face. This is just a good opportunity for them to raise hell, robbing and burning and beating people up. Just plain mean. They seem to be especially fond of lynching folks they figure are the enemy. If they didn't have the protection of the guns they ride with, most of 'em would be in jail. Scum of the earth!" He shoots a stream of tobacco juice into the dusty straw to show what he thinks of the whole bunch, and wipes his mouth with the back of his hand.

"I'll watch my step," I assure him, taking the reins of his horse and mounting up. The afternoon sun's pretty high in the sky, but I'll still have to get a move on if I'm going to make it to Lone Oak by seven o'clock.

When I get near the Holland Ranch, I give the house a wide berth, and come around to the back side of the property by the long route. When I get close, I dismount and walk up and look over the last low rise. Sure enough, there's Jane, pacing along the creek bank. Her horse is tied to the big oak by a long line and is grazing on the new green grass.

I get my horse and lead him on down. She sees me coming and runs up and throws her arms around my neck. I can't get over how good it is to hug her again.

"Oh, Lance, I've missed being with you!" she says, pulling back, holding onto my arms and giving me a searching look.

"I ain't been having the best time myself," says I.

We hold hands and saunter along the creek. The wildflowers are speckling the sloping banks where the low rays of spring sun are still hitting. I take a deep breath of the soft, fresh air, and relax. It's a magic time and place that makes a man feel like all the cares he ever had was just a bad dream.

We don't say nothing for a spell, only just stroll along, enjoying the quiet and each other's company. Finally I ask: "Is your brother still riding with those Mounted Rangers?"

"Yes," she nods, "but we haven't seen much of him since that night. I think he's ashamed to show his face around our folks. Ooh, Papa was furious when he found out what happened. He just ranted and stormed around and said he should have horsewhipped that kid when he was younger and maybe he would have grown up to be law abiding and respectful of other people's rights."

"Really?"

"Yeah. Mama finally got him calmed down, but it's a good thing Greg wasn't there when Papa got home late that night."

"It's a shame about all this fighting," says I, "but I'm scared it's only the beginning."

"That's what Papa thinks, too. He believes this slavery and states' rights business should have been settled ten years ago. I overheard him and some men talking the other night. They all think it's too late to prevent a war now."

I recollect Blather Murphy saying that a civil war would shut down the Pony Express. I warn't about to get mixed up in no more fighting, but I'd likely be out of a job again if the country come to blows.

"You're from Missouri," Jane is saying, looking sideways at me. "And you rode with the militia for a few months. Would you fight for the South if war breaks out?"

We hadn't never talked about this before, and it kind of takes me by surprise. It ain't so much the question, but her tone of voice that sounds a mite accusing.

"I don't want no part of any fighting . . . for either side," I tell her firmly.

"But you *must* lean toward loyalty to your home state that is pro-slavery," she insists.

"I joined the militia mostly for excitement and also because I wanted to help get rid of a lot of pushy Northerners who come down here, trying to force their way o' thinking on people," I say, hoping I can make her understand.

"Then you believe in slavery," she says, like it just naturally follows, if a fella tries to defend his Southern home place.

"No. I don't hold with slave owning," I say, struggling to find the right words. "It's just something I grew up with, and never thought much about till I was about thirteen and ran away from home. Just figured it was a normal state of affairs."

"Then your family *did* own slaves," she says, with kind of an edge to her voice.

I don't know what she's getting at, but I stop walking and make her face me direct. "No. My pap was a drunk. He didn't own much o' nothing. Couldn't even hold a job." I don't add that he beat me till I run off. "Well, I lived with my Aunt Martha off and on. She owned a nigger she inherited, but. . . ."

"Did you ever own one?" she cuts in.

"No. Of course not."

"Then, what about *this?*" She pulled a folded paper out of the side pocket of her riding skirt and shoved it toward me, her eyes gleaming with tears. Soon as I unfolded and saw what it was, I knew why she was acting so strange. It was one of them handbills I'd had printed up in St. Joe offering a two-hundred-dollar reward for Shad as a runaway slave. And right there at the bottom of the poster was the words: **Contact Lance Barlow, Patee House, St. Joseph, Missouri.** I'd plumb forgot about those handbills. My tongue kind of clove to the roof of my mouth for a few seconds, and I reckon she took this for a sign I was guilty of being a lying slave owner.

"Well . . . ?" she says, sort of cold like when I didn't answer right away.

"He warn't . . . he ain't my slave. I mean, he ain't *nobody's* slave. He's a free man . . . ," I stammer, making me sound like even more of a liar.

"That's not what this says."

I take a deep breath and back up. "Let me explain what this handbill is all about."

She don't say nothing while I tell her about Shadrack and me, and how he disappeared, and how I had these flyers printed and spread around, as a last hope it might make him turn up.

"Me and Shad've been friends since I was just a kid," I finish up. I can tell by the look on her face that she's wanting to believe me, but she just can't bring herself to do it. I reckon I should've told her all about this when we first met, but didn't reckon it mattered, so I never mentioned it. Besides, since she and her family were such strong Abolitionists, she might not have cottoned to me. Now it was too late, and I was damned by my own words in black print. She won't believe nothing I say from here on.

"Where . . . where'd you get this?"

"Never you mind where I got it," she says, taking the hand-bill and stuffing it back into her skirt pocket. Her lip is trembling, and her eyes are just brimming with tears.

I don't say nothing for a minute, only just set down on the grassy bank and stare off at the little stream where it's rippling over some rocks, a dull ache in my stomach. I couldn't believe how happy I was a few minutes ago, and now everything has gone to smash. This must have been why she wanted to meet me here — to ask me some questions to see if she could trap me in a lie. And she'd done it, slick as grease. Only she didn't have the straight of it. But I reckon some people who've got their minds made up beforehand won't never be persuaded otherwise, no matter what.

"I sure wish I knew where Shad was now," I say, chucking some little stones into the creek, and not looking at her. "I reckon he's probably dead."

"No, he's alive, all right," she says.

"What?" My heart gives a bound. "He's alive?"

"I should say he is. But he's with some *other* slave holder now," she says, tossing her head. "He's not where you can get your hands on him again."

"Where is he? How do you know it's him?" I ask, jumping up and grabbing her by the arms. I can feel my heart pounding.

She pulls back, looking scared, like she thought I was going to do something wild.

"He . . . he's down at the Culbertson Ranch."

"Where's that?"

"About twenty miles southeast of here," she says, answering fast, like she's afraid not to.

"Who's Culbertson?"

"A pro-slaver. He keeps a few blacks to work his ranch,

but he mostly buys and sells them. That's how he makes his money, I hear."

"What makes you think it's really Shad?"

"If you'll quit squeezing my arms, I'll tell you."

I open my grip and step back. "Sorry."

She looks at me like she don't really know me and begins rubbing her arms as she paces around. The last shafts of sunlight are making her dark blonde hair glow like a golden halo around her head — a beautiful sight, but it's Shad I'm mostly interested in.

She seems a little calmer when she says: "Papa brought that handbill back with him after he'd been to St. Joe on business. He showed it to me and Mama and said something like . . . 'This is the kind of trash that's being circulated . . . one human being offering a reward for the capture of another. This is what Greg is fighting against. I guess we can't blame him if he gets a little radical. . . .' "

"What about Shad?" I bust in.

"I'm getting to that. I read the description you wrote, and was trying to imagine what this runaway looked like. It was the very next afternoon that I was over in Seneca with a girl friend, and we saw Mister Culbertson buying supplies at the mercantile. He had a black man driving his wagon who fit the description on the handbill, right down to the burn scar on his right arm."

I started to say it could've been happenstance, when she adds: "And to clinch it, old man Culbertson called him Shadrack."

Now I'm convinced. Whatever else Jane Holland was, she had keen eyes, and she didn't take to lying. That was *my* weakness. I was excited, and my mind was already racing ahead, trying to think of a way I could get him loose from this man. Then I haul up and say: "Why wasn't Shad trying to get away? Maybe he was just working for Culbertson."

"Not with shackles on his ankles," she says.

"Jane, we've got to figure a way to rescue him!"

"Why? So you can have him back as your personal slave, and not have to pay the two-hundred-dollar reward for his return?" she says, scornful like.

"No, dammit!" I'm getting fed up by now. "Because he's a free man, and he's my friend."

She looks at me, steady, her hands on her hips. Finally she says: "I don't believe you. Whatever you plan to do, leave me out of it. I just wish you had been honest with me from the beginning." She tries to brush a tear from her cheek without me seeing. "I think it would be a good idea if we didn't see each other for a while." She goes over and unties her horse and begins looping up his long tether.

I stand there like a dummy, not knowing what to do or say. Then she mounts up, gives me kind of a sad look, and spurs away, galloping up and over the rise and is gone.

I just stand there in a trance for some time, until the sun goes down and the pale blue sky turns to a soft pink. My mind's in a whirl, and my insides are torn by lots of different feelings. In the space of less than an hour, I'd found Shad again, but I'd lost the friendship and love of a beautiful girl. If I hadn't made up that handbill, I'd likely never have known what happened to Shad. On the other hand, because I lied in print, I'd lost Jane. Sometimes the world didn't make no sense at all.

Chapter Nine

If Shadrack had taught me anything, it was to look at the bright side of things, no matter what. Tough as it was, I had to put the thought of Jane Holland out of my mind for now. I needed something to fill my head during those long hours when I was pounding over my mail route. And that something was to puzzle out a way to rescue Shad from Culbertson.

The first thing that had to be done was to locate the Culbertson Ranch and take a gander at this slave owner so I'd know him at a glance. Then I had to find out a lot of other things — like how many niggers were on the place; if there was enough to have an overseer besides the owner; if they was locked up at night; if Shad was a field hand or a house slave; and the general lay of the land. I sure could've used some help, but Jane had made it pretty clear that I couldn't expect none from her direction.

I stretched out on my bunk at Liberty Farm the next evening after supper, smoking a pipe and searching my brain to come up with somebody I could trust to help me. Mr. Holland was out of the question. He had influence, and was strong anti-slavery, but I didn't know him well enough to ask him to raid another man's ranch. And no telling what Jane might have told him about me. There was just an older couple running the Liberty Farm station, so they wouldn't be no help. Nathan Rising, the Marysville station keeper, was too standoffish and was busy trying to get into politics. Ephraim Hanks, the stock handler, might help, but he warn't taking sides on the slavery question. What about Blather Murphy at Log Chain station? He would be all for it, except he was 'way too fat and would talk the rescue to death before we ever got started. Then I thought of Bill Cody, and wished he was here. I'll just bet he'd be game for an adventure like this. He'd have the nerve and the stamina. But he was off riding ponies out of the Julesburg station a few hundred miles West.

When it comes right down to it, I was pretty much on my own. I'd just have to plan careful and go it alone, and trust to Providence.

With that thought, I rolled over and went to sleep. It warn't close to being dark yet, but the eastbound rider would likely be in before midnight, and I'd have to be ready. With the mail picking up all the time, we didn't have much time between runs.

The next night, back in Marysville, I handed off the mochila to Dan Ivers who tore out toward St. Joe to finish the eastbound run. We were always coming and going and didn't see much of each other even though he shared the small frame house that was the Marysville station. He struck me as pretty much of a loner. He was some older, and, the few times I'd exchanged small talk with him, he sort of gave off the air that this job was just something he had lowered himself to do whilst he was waiting for bigger fish to snatch his bait.

I had to make another run to Liberty Farm and back before I had about a day and a half break in the schedule. Of course, we never really knew whether a rider coming East was going to be delayed by some problem out West. But I knew when the mail was due to start from St. Joe. And, riding the second leg, I could plan when the lead-off rider would arrive at Marysville.

I'd thought and thought, but couldn't come up with no plan but to ride right up to the Culbertson Ranch and make up some tale about why I'm there. I'd had considerable practice at lying, and figured to say just the first that come into my head. But Jane had told me the Culbertson place was about twenty miles southeast and I needed a mount.

I cornered Ephraim Hanks while he was running a curry-comb over one of the sleek ponies in the stable. Watching him a minute or two, I could see he really enjoyed his work and loved the fast mustangs he was grooming. I hesitated to ask him again to borrow his horse, but I finally screwed up the courage and done it. He was accommodating, but curious, so I felt obliged to tell him where I was going.

"The Culbertson Ranch?" He stops his currying and squints at me. "What in the world do you want with *him?*"

"Well . . . I'd rather not say just now."

He give me a sharp look and says: "If you're not already involved with him in some way, then stay clear. He's a sharp dealer. And ruthless." He goes back to his grooming.

I'm feeling uneasy, but don't want to say no more than necessary. Hanks is too nice a fella to get involved in slave stealing. The thought of going to the law occurred to me, but there ain't no way I could prove that Shad was a free man, 'cause I'm sure his paper has been stolen or destroyed. Aunt Martha's dead, and it'd take no end of legal trouble to get a copy of her will that give Shad his freedom. And Kansas ain't what I'd call a law-abiding territory. At least not one that I wanted to depend on. I'd right off chucked the idea of going to the law; it was just too chancy.

"How long will you need him?" Hanks asks, referring to his horse.

"Maybe a day. No more."

He don't say nothing for a second. Then: "You're welcome to borrow him." But he don't sound too happy.

"Thanks," I say before he can change his mind. I'm already grabbing the saddle and getting ready to go.

Ten minutes later I'm riding southeast, following the general directions Hanks has given me. I figured to arrive there an hour or so before dusk, and I hit it pretty close, not having no trouble locating the place, on account of the good directions.

The house is nothing special — just a one-story, white-washed affair about a half mile off the road, set back in a grove of cottonwoods and oaks like most farm houses in this plains country.

When I rode up, easy like, four or five hounds come running from somewhere, barking fit to raise the dead. It was all I could do to hold Hanks's roan gelding who was for getting out of there. Whilst the horse is jumping and walling his eyes at the dogs all around, a man in his shirtsleeves comes out onto the porch. I can barely hear his voice over all the barking, but, whatever he says, the dogs shut up pretty quick and go to wagging their tails and slinking off satisfied they done their job.

"What do you want?" the man says, none too friendly.

I slide out of the saddle. "Easy boy." I go to stroking my horse's neck to calm him down. The man on the porch is wiping his mouth with a napkin and don't look too pleased about me busting in on his supper.

"Sir, I'm lost," I say, trying to sound sincere. "I was heading towards Marysville, but I reckon I must have took a wrong turn somewhere, because I figure I should have been there by now. Where am I?"

He looks me over a second or two, and I can see he don't consider me no threat. I'm wearing my gun inside my buckskin shirt, out of sight.

"This is the Culbertson Ranch. I'm the owner. You sure did take a wrong turn. Go back up this road about four miles," he says, pointing. "There's a clump of trees near a little stream. Take the right fork in the road there, going west.

100

Marysville's about another twenty-three miles. Should be a sign there at the fork."

"There warn't no sign when I come by there," I say, putting my hat back on. "Reckon the wind might have knocked it down or something."

While I'm talking, I'm eyeballing Culbertson pretty close. He's at least six foot four and walks kind of stooped, like he's banged his head on too many doorways. He's bareheaded, and the breeze is blowing his straight, blond hair around. But it's his face that gets my attention. There ain't no hint of whiskers on it at all. His round, rosy cheeks have big dimples, and his tiny mouth is kind of drawn up like he's been eating too many green persimmons. Except for the little, beady, blue eyes, his face looks a lot like one of them cherub angels you see statues of in church. I ain't never seen a face like that on a grown man. It's one I won't forget.

"Might I water my horse before I go?" I ask, indicating the stock tank and windmill off to one side of the house a ways.

"Help yourself."

I lead my horse to the tank. There's a few head of black Angus standing around and grazing. The windmill is turning slow, but quiet, like it's well greased, pumping water into the big tank. While the horse is drinking, I cup my hands and catch a good, cold drink from the gushing pipe. All the while, I'm looking quick to see what I can see. There ain't no niggers in sight, but there's three log outbuildings about fifty yards behind the house. Whilst I'm looking, a nigger woman comes out of one of them and pitches a pan of water onto the ground and goes back inside. There's a privy and a woodshed and, farther down in back, a fair-sized barn. A split-rail fence zigzags around a big garden plot. The land slopes down in back a long way toward a line of trees that

I expect borders a creek I can't see from here.

That's about all I can gather because, when I turn around, there's Culbertson who's come around the side of the house and is watching me. So, with one last glance at the place, I gather up the reins and mount up. I ride off slow, giving him a friendly wave as I head back out to the road. It's only then I notice he's wearing a gun belt. Kind of unusual for a man to sit down to supper in his own house, wearing his gun, I'm thinking. Unless he's expecting trouble. But, maybe with the situation in Kansas Territory like it is, he has good reason to be wary.

There were big padlocks hanging in the hasps on the doors of them slave cabins, so I figured they were locked up at night. But the place didn't look big enough to have no overseer, so I reckoned Culbertson was the man in direct charge. I wondered if he had a wife or kids. I didn't see no evidence of them, but they could have been inside at the supper table. Culbertson looked to be anywhere from thirty-five to forty-five years old. But it was hard to tell with that peaches and cream face. I could feel them beady, blue eyes on my back as I rode out, but I never looked back.

I arrived back in Marysville about nine that night after an easy ride. By that time I'd formed up a plan to spring Shad. It warn't much of a scheme, but then I warn't much of a schemer. It was this: I'd have to figure some way to get Culbertson away from home some time after dark, and then I'd bust into them slave cabins with a crowbar. If Shad warn't in one of them, I'd go for the house. I'd have my gun if some of the family was home. Then we'd ride like the very devil was after us. But ride to where? I hadn't figured that far. Would Hanks's horse carry double? To hell with that. I wouldn't use Hanks's horse. As long as I was into this, I'd go whole hog and borrow two of the Express ponies that were fast and had plenty of stamina. I might lose my job over it if I was caught, but the chance was worth it to rescue an old friend from illegal slavery.

Then I got to thinking about all this again the next day whilst I was galloping up the trail, sitting on the mochila stuffed with mail. I didn't have no assurance that Shad was really at the Culbertson Ranch. I hadn't seen him there. Jane's word that she saw him driving Culbertson's wagon in Seneca with his ankles shackled was my only reason to think Culbertson had him in slavery. And I had to trust Jane's word that this was really Shad and not some other black man who looked like him. But, since she said the slaver had called him Shadrack, I had to figure that the chances were strong that this was him. It was a long shot, all right, but I wanted to believe Shad was still alive, and I'd have dared anything to get him loose. I know he would have done the same for me.

When I returned Hanks's horse to the Marysville Pony Express stable, he warn't there, for which I was grateful. That way I didn't have to answer no questions, and it give me a chance to take a good, close look at the company ponies in the corral. Hanks took care of them like they were his own animals. And he selected them to work on a regular, rotating schedule, making sure each one had enough rest between runs. I knew which two would be the freshest the following Tuesday night when I'd have a day and a half layover at my home station. I'd ridden all of them, and I picked two of my favorites — a deep-chested, little mustang, and a mare pinto that had the smoothest gait of all. There were extra saddles in the tack shed. There shouldn't be no trouble taking them because I knew Hanks's routine. He was a man with dependable habits.

I was mighty nervous, I can tell you. By the time I rode back into Marysville Tuesday afternoon and handed off the mail to Ivers, I couldn't hardly tell you my own name, what with thinking about what I was going to do that night. I didn't want no supper, but just took a walk off by myself so I wouldn't run into nobody I had to talk to. I come back to my room when it got good and dark and cleaned and loaded my Colt, put on my buckskin shirt, then slipped the extra loaded cylinder into the side pocket.

I lay down on my bunk and waited. I didn't have to worry about staying awake, I was so wrought up. When it got quiet, I waited another half hour or more before I got up and crept outside to the porch and slipped on my boots. The station keeper was spending the night in town, as usual, so nobody was around, except Hanks, who was asleep in an upstairs room.

The horses all knew me, so it warn't no trouble to catch the two I'd picked out. Working only by moonlight, it took a little longer than I expected to snub them to the center post of the corral, one at a time, and get them saddled. I dasn't light a lamp for fear Hanks would wake up and see it. Streaks of ragged clouds was blowing in from the west, making the moonlight kind of fitful, but I finally got the job done, then put a long lead rope on one of the ponies and mounted the other and rode out as slow and easy as I could, so as not to make no noise. I'd filched a crowbar and a hatchet from the tool shed and had them slung from the saddle horn in a potato sack.

I didn't ride hard getting down to the Culbertson place, wanting to save the animals and to kill some more time. I didn't have to avoid no towns since it was all open country, and it warn't likely I'd meet anybody on the road this time of night. I wanted to time it so's to get there about three in the morning when everybody should be dead asleep.

It didn't look like I'd get no moonlight or starlight, since it was clouding up fast. When I was about halfway there, I suddenly remembered the dogs. They probably slept around outside the house and under the porch. If they commenced to howling, my plan was shot. I reckon that's why Culbertson kept them — they were better than armed guards. If I hadn't been in such a sweat to get away with the Express ponies, I might have remembered to snatch a few hunks of salt pork or dried beef to distract them. As it was, I just hoped they were sound sleepers.

Maybe because I was mighty nervous about this whole operation, it didn't seem like no time until I was coming up to Culbertson's place. I slowed down and walked the horses off the road and circled away down behind the house and outbuildings. I come up behind the barn, keeping it betwixt me and the house. Thank God the wind was puffing up and blowing right into my face. That would keep my scent away from the hounds. Now, if I could just stay quiet enough. . . .

I tied the ponies to some bushes a good fifty yards behind the barn, in case there was any stock in there. Then I crept up toward the house, my eyes and ears wide open. My eyes warn't able to take in much of anything on account of the dark, but my ears were catching mighty near every sound, from the wind sighing through the windbreak of trees around the house to what sounded like a loose board or shutter banging somewhere. Once I froze in my tracks when I heard a snuffle and felt something big move close by. My heart give a skip or three until a familiar smell come to me, and I knew I'd almost walked into one of them big, black Angus.

It took a couple minutes for my knees to quit shaking and my breathing to calm down. Then I moved on, holding my sack with the crowbar and hatchet so's not to let them clank together. I finally come up behind them nigger cabins, and durned if one of 'em wasn't showing a light through the single window in back. It was kind of dim, like a lamp that's turned low. Maybe somebody sitting up with a sick child or somebody couldn't sleep. Otherwise, they wouldn't be burning no coal oil at three o'clock in the morning, unless maybe someone had to let a slave out to do the milking.

But when I set down in the grass and got to studying on it a minute, I think maybe this is a good thing. The window was high up and small with some kind of grating, so there warn't no chance anybody could get through it. As long as I had a choice of three log cabins, I decided to go for the one with the light first. But how to get in without making enough noise to rouse up the dogs?

Whilst I was setting, there come a flash of lightning that makes me jump. A couple seconds later, thunder went to booming and grumbling down the western sky. I figured it was still a good ways off, but I could smell the rain on the steady breeze that was blowing. It was almighty scary and lonesome, setting there by myself, knowing if I was caught at this, I could very well be shot or hanged. I swallowed hard, recollecting how it felt to stand under that oak tree in the Hollands' yard with a noose around my neck. I could still turn around, get the ponies and ride on back to Marysville. It warn't too late. I could be home before daylight, and nobody would be the wiser.

But I quick shoved that idea out of my head. I warn't going to think about what *could* happen. I'd concentrate on what I had to do, and make sure I could get away if I had to.

The lightning flashed again, and the thunder boomed quicker, closer. I had to get to it. Gripping the cloth sack with the hatchet and crowbar, I snuck around the cabin, not knowing what I'd do if the padlock was on the door.

But a flicker of lightning shows that the padlock is just hanging loose, and the heavy plank door is even standing open a crack. Has somebody forgot to lock it? Did the slaves slide out and escape? I take a deep breath and ease the door open toward me a few inches. I still can't see nothing but a lamp on a table. The low-burning flame ain't hardly giving off no light through the sooty glass chimney. I pull the door open a little farther, and a sudden gust of wind yanks it out of my hand and slams it back against the wall with a bang. Curse the luck! Without thinking, I step back and my breath stops in my throat because I'm staring at a buxom, black woman sitting up in the bunk, and the tall white form of Culbertson stumbling to his feet. They's both stark naked. Ain't nobody else in the room.

"What the hell . . . ?" he rumbles, looking right at me, but he's fogged by sleep or the whiskey that's setting on the floor or it's too dark outside for him to see me clear.

All this hits me in about two heartbeats, and then I jump sideways and run for the next cabin. The padlock's secure on this one, but I slip the crowbar down under the hasp and yank with all my weight. The screws pull halfway out of the logs. One more jerk and it's loose. I fling the door open.

"Shad! Shad! Are you in here? It's Lance!" I yell as loud as I can.

It scares somebody 'cause there's a scrambling in the dark, and I hear voices.

"Shadrack! Come on!" I bellow.

Drat the luck! He ain't here. Just then the hounds set up a ruckus of barking. With them coming from one side and Culbertson from the other, I know I ain't got time to try the third cabin.

Of a sudden, a sizzling crack of lightning hits nearby. And there's Shad, standing in the doorway, all lit up in the blue-white glare. I give a yell of surprise and fear and fall back off the rock doorstep. Then all sound and sight is swallowed up by the booming blackness. I'm kind of stunned for a second by the thunder that's shaking the ground. Then I feel a hand grabbing my arm, and Shad says: "I's here, Lance. Run!"

That clears my head, and I find my tongue again.

"That way! The horses!"

I point, forgetting he can't see my arm. He's still got hold of me, so I just take off running. But I'm still blinded by that flash of lightning and only take about a half dozen steps before I smack right into somebody, and we all go down in a tangle of arms and legs.

You know how it is in a dream sometimes when you're being chased, or you're wading through a swamp and you can't seem to make your limbs move. That's the way it was. I was struggling with all my might, but I couldn't seem to get shed of Culbertson. Somewhere, in the back of my head, I could hear the dogs howling and yapping and getting closer.

A flash of lightning lit up everything just as Shad was yanking me away from Culbertson. The tall man was naked, but in that second or two of light I saw he had a whiskey bottle by the neck and was trying to get his arm free to swing it at me.

Three things happened all at once — Shad pulled me free of Culbertson, the hounds reached us, and the storm broke. But it warn't no regular rainstorm. It's one of them crop-flattening, window-busting, summer hailstorms, and it just pounded us like fury with big hunks of ice that's bouncing everywhere. Culbertson lets out a howl louder than all the dogs. I reckon the hail's stinging and cutting his bare hide like a blast of freezing gravel.

I was in such a panic to get away that I didn't really pay no attention to it, even though it was hurting my head and face. But the hail took care of the dogs, too. They went yipping away like somebody was whipping them.

"Let's go!" I yell.

Shad and I busted past Culbertson who flung the bottle after us. It whanged off my head without breaking and sloshed whiskey down my neck. There was a sharp pain over my ear, but I kept going. It seemed like a powerful long way to where I'd tied the ponies. But when we finally got there, a flash of lightning showed me the ponies has somehow pulled loose and gone!

My heart falls flat down amongst my bowels and gizzard. I couldn't say nothing, and I couldn't move for maybe ten seconds.

"Lance! What's wrong? Where d'horses?" Shad yells in my ear over the booming of thunder and clatter of big hailstones.

"They *was* right here," I finally gasp.

"Dey must've busted loose and headed for shelter," he says, loud, so I can hear him.

I'm hoping they didn't run for the barn when I yell back: "The creek. Down there in the trees by the creek."

We take off running again. I didn't want to look back, but I had a picture of Culbertson skinnin' along after us, naked as a jaybird. I'm hoping he didn't have no gun in that cabin.

I'm also praying I guessed right about the horses. When we finally get into the trees, we're panting hard, and my knees are weak.

Just then another eerie lightning wavers across the sky, showing the ice still pelting down, but the trees are sheltering us from most of it.

"Dere dey are, Lance!" Shad yells and points. I have just time enough for a quick look before we're in blackness again.

Then comes a *CRACK!* But this time it ain't the storm, I realize, when another bang shows a flash of gunfire from the direction of the house.

"Somebody shooting at us! Get down!" I have my pistol, but I don't want to shoot back unless I really have to. Besides, I don't figure I could hit nothing in the dark at this distance with a hand gun. We duck and run toward the ponies that'd been spooked by the storm. They're mighty skittish, and it takes some doing to catch them. But Shad's good at this, and the animals is hindered by the reins that's dragging on the ground and snagging in the brush.

We're just leaping up into the saddles when I hear Shad kind of gasp as he leans forward over the neck of his pony.

"You O K?"

"Yeah. Let's go!"

I kick my pony and guide him out of the trees, heading east and north, angling away from the Culbertson place toward the road, maybe a mile away. The hail has eased up and now it's mostly just rain slashing at our faces.

I glance back a time or two to make sure Shad's behind me. He ain't had the practice of riding these fast Pony Express mounts. He's kind of bouncing around and seems to be having a tough time sticking to his pony's back when our animals really stretch out and begin to run. But he's game and hangs on. These ponies are used to running ten miles or more at top speed. After we'd gone about that far, I feel safe enough to ease back to a canter, and then to a walk to let them blow a little, and to check on Shad.

There's a lump on the side of my head where the whiskey bottle clipped me, but the skin ain't even broke. I've had bigger knots from a bee sting.

Shad is still behind me, so I pull up and wait for him. He's bent over, and my stomach kind of balls up when I see he's hurt.

"What's wrong? Are you hit?"

"It ain't nothin'," he says, but he sort of grits it out between his teeth. He's favoring his left side.

"You're shot," I say, trying to keep my voice steady. There ain't no light, so I can't stop and examine him, and with the rain still falling I can't light no matches. "Where'd it get you?"

"Top o' my left arm," he says. "How far we goin', Lance?"

I'd headed toward Marysville without giving it a thought. "Marysville Pony Express station. About another nine miles. Think you can make it?"

"Yeah," he says. "Just don't go too fast."

I ride up alongside. He ain't got no shirt on, and the rain is keeping the blood washed off. I think maybe I could make up some kind of bandage to tie around his arm, but there ain't no cloth to use. "Is it bleedin' much?"

"Hard to tell. I don't think so."

"Can you move it?"

"Yeah, but it's pretty sore."

"Hang on until we get there. We got a good ten-mile start on Culbertson, and nobody's going to track us on a night like this." The lightning and thunder's moved on east, and a steady, chill rain has settled in. "Can you ride that far?"

"I'll make it. Jest don't lose me in de dark."

"Here. Let's do it this way." I take the long rope off my saddle horn that I'd led the extra pony with earlier and fasten it to his pony's bridle. "You just think about hangin' on. I'll lead your horse."

By the time it's coming on to gray dawn, me and Shad're safe and dry in the stable at Marysville. I'd fetched some dry clothes from the house. They were just some old work pants and a shirt that belonged to Nathan Rising, but Shad's too big to wear any of my stuff. A bottle of carbolic and a clean cotton shirt of mine ripped up for a bandage took care of the flesh wound in the upper arm.

"Durned lucky shot," I say, tying the bandage snug on his arm. "Bullet went clean through. Didn't hit no bone nor blood vessels. Couple inches to the left, it would have missed you."

"Lance, I tol' you befo . . . you's de best friend I evah had."

"Shad, you don't know how glad I am to see you. I'd given you up for dead. Figured the river had got you sure."

"Lance, de last few months has been some o' de wust o' my life," he says, lounging back in the clean straw I'd forked into one of the stalls.

"I want to hear all about it," I say, turning down the wick of the lamp as it gets lighter outside.

"And I want to hear all about it, too," says Ephraim Hanks, stepping into the stable and glaring at the two of us.

Chapter Ten

In all the excitement, I'd 'most forgot about Ephraim Hanks.

"Better bring those two ponies in here and give them a good rubdown," he says, sounding like he's trying to hold his temper. "And when you get done, give them some oats."

"Yes, sir," I say, feeling kind of shameful at deceiving this good man.

"Did you cool 'em down easy?"

"Yes, sir. Just walked 'em the last few miles."

"Good. Then you haven't forgot everything I taught you. Of course, your irresponsible actions mean I'll have to rest these animals an extra day."

He doesn't say nothing more until I've led our two ponies in from the corral and put them in the stalls. He just leans against a post with his arms folded and watches, grim faced.

While I'm rubbing those sleek ponies with a rough towel, I begin talking, easy and calm, so's not to rile Hanks any worse. "I know I should have told you about all this," I say, "and I'm sorry. But I couldn't see no other way to do it."

"To do what?" he asks, eyeing Shad who's sitting in a pile of straw with a horse blanket pulled around his shoulders.

So then I commence to telling Hanks the whole story.

When I get through, he says: "If you'd confided in me, I could've helped you." He's sort of softening up. "But, as it is, you've endangered the Pony Express by taking company stock without permission. And there's a chance you'll bring the law down on us by bringing this man here."

"I doubt Culbertson got a good look at me. And, even if he did, he don't know I'm a pony rider," I say. "Besides, it was raining so hard last night, he couldn't track us."

113

"Don't be too sure about that," Hanks says, running his fingers through his hair and looking thoughtful. "What about you?" he says to Shad. "What's your story?"

"I's a free man, suh."

"You don't have to call me sir. The name's Ephraim Hanks."

"Yassuh, Mister Hanks. Lance and me been knowin' each other since he was just a youngster. His Aunt Martha was my mistress till she passed. . . ."

"Set him free in her will," I chip in.

"I helped Lance when he run off from his pappy who was beatin' him. . . ."

"He was a drunk," I add.

"Anyways, we didn't see nothin' of each other for quite a spell after that, and then we met up again a few months back."

I jump in and tell the tale of Shad saving my life at the Hartz Farm the night of the raid, and how we'd hid out in the cabin, and then how I'd lost track of him again.

"Well, suh," Shad takes up the story, "de mornin' I went over to de Johnstone Farm to tell him I'm quittin', he invites me inside for a cup o' coffee. It was a cold, wet day, you see, and I reckoned he was gonna try to talk me into stayin' on. Dis wasn't his regular way. Fact is, I'd never been inside his house befo' . . . anyways, he's actin' unusual friendly, and I'm gettin' nervous to draw my pay and go, so Lance and me can catch de ferry over to St. Joe. Den two men come in with guns. Johnstone acts like he's expectin' dem, and dey take de five hundred dollars I got in my pocket and my paper dat says I'm free. One of dem laughs when he reads dat paper and just ups and pops it into de stove. It 'most broke my heart when I see dat paper burn up, 'cause I know right den dat I's bein' sold back into slavery." He shakes his head, mournful like. "Dey put a blindfold on me and shackles on

114

my hands and feet and lock me in a room. Sometime dat night, dey chained me in de back of a wagon, covered me with a blanket, and we rode all night. I didn't have no idea where I was goin' or where I was when dey took off de blind and gave me a drink o' water and a little bite to eat."

He's staring off outside, thinking about the misery of being a captive again, I reckon. Then he says: "I heard some men talkin', and I know Johnstone's sellin' me to dat Mister Culbertson. I knew I must be 'most fifty miles from St. Joe, but I don't know what direction. But I must still be west o' the Missouri River, 'cause we ain't crossed no ferry." He takes a deep breath and kind of winces as he moves his wounded arm.

"So you've been a slave at Culbertson's all these months?" I prompt him.

"Yeah. He know I be tryin' to run off if I gets a chance, so he keeps de shackles on my legs all de time I's workin' so I can't run nowheres. He keeps me locked up at night wif two or three other field hands in dat cabin. He don't treat me bad, but de food ain't what I'm used to, and I get mighty lean."

"Yeah. What'd he feed you, anyway?" I ask. "You sure are skinny."

"Well, he give us lots of chicken soup, and some rough corn bread. But I think he made de soup by puttin' boots on a rooster and runnin' him through some hot water."

Hanks and me bust out laughing.

"But I work real hard and try to please him," Shad goes on, "because I's afraid he's thinkin' on sellin' me off downriver to one o' dem big plantations where things is really hard, and I might never have a chance to get away. I hear talk amongst de other niggers, and I see 'em comin' and goin', so I know he's sellin' and tradin'."

"I figured them cattle was mostly for show," I say. "Jane told me Culbertson's got a reputation as a slave trader."

"Some o' dem big bucks he had locked up told me dey was free men like me. Dey'd been snatched off riverboats where dey was workin' as deckhands," Shad says. "Mister Culbertson don't care about no legal papers. I reckon he just makes up his own."

"That would be no problem for a man like him," Hanks agrees. He looks at me as I finish rubbing down the second pony. "If Culbertson got a look at you, he'll surely recognize you from the other day when you rode up there in broad daylight."

"I reckon so. But he don't know I'm a pony rider."

Hanks looks at me like I ain't got no sense at all. "You don't think he won't ask around and give a description of you? It's not like we're in a big city. Out here there aren't that many people, and we're pretty scattered. There're plenty of folks who've seen you riding the mails since April. If he goes to looking, Culbertson won't have any trouble finding out who you are and where you are." He shakes his head and goes to picking his teeth with a piece of straw. "You didn't just steal a man he considers his slave. You insulted Culbertson by going right to his ranch to do it. And you even caught Culbertson with one of his black wenches. You think he's going to just let that slide? Not by a durn sight. I know what he's like. That's why I warned you to stay away from him."

"I had to get Shad loose," I say, kind of lame.

"There were better ways of doing it," he snaps back.

I scoop a bucket of oats and pour them into the feed box, wondering what Hanks is getting at. He don't seem all that irritated with me no more — only like he's thinking on something.

"We've got to figure out where Shadrack can hide until he

can get out of the territory," Hanks says, pressing his lips together and rubbing his mustache with the back of his hand.

I hadn't thought past just getting Shad free. Like most other things, I figured just to trust to luck and do whatever come handiest. "Shad's wound probably ought to have a doctor see to it. Don't want it to mortify, or nothin'," I say.

Hanks shakes his head. "No doctor anywhere around here. We'll just have to take care of it the best we can. I've had considerable experience with cuts and wounds on horses and such, so I think I can do it all right."

I was hoping for a real doctor, but at least Hanks seems to be dealing himself in on our side. I have a feeling he'll be a powerful help.

Hanks looks from Shad to me. "I reckon we need to get some hot breakfast into both of you. Then we can decide what to do next. Mister Rising won't be out here from town today, so we've got a little time. I'll figure something later to tell him about where his old clothes disappeared to. And there aren't any mail riders due in here until early tomorrow morning."

We all go into the house, and me and Hanks dig into the company supplies in the pantry, and he sets to cooking up a big breakfast. He even collects a few fresh eggs from the chicken house out back to go with the bacon and fried potatoes with onions and biscuits and jam.

While he's filling the kitchen with all them aromas, I go into my room and peel out of the wet buckskin shirt and soggy jeans that were beginning to itch something awful. Sliding into some dry clothes sure did make the morning feel a lot better.

Shad digs into the grub like he ain't seen food in a week. By the time we're finishing up with some hot coffee, the sunshine is just flooding in the windows of the kitchen. The hail and rain has moved off to the east, and a glorious summer day is blooming up over the plains. It makes me feel like I can do anything. Except for being a little tired from no sleep and the night's adventures, I'm feeling great. And I know Shad is, too, in spite of his arm wound.

Hanks waits until we're done eating and are just sipping our coffee before he starts in to talk. But I reckon he's been thinking the whole time, because his words are slow and deliberate. "I have a farm about forty miles southwest of here where Shad can rest and recuperate," he says. "Unless he has a safer place he knows about." He turns to Shad. "Do you have any people, or any place you want to go?"

"No, suh. My wife and child are in Cape Girardeau, but they's still slaves. I reckon I'll go back there later on." He looks at me. "Lance's the onliest friend I got around here."

"You got me, now," Hanks offers, and my chest just swells up with pride at hearing him say it. I had him figured for not taking sides on the slavery argument, but I reckon when it comes to helping one man who's been oppressed, he ain't short on compassion.

"Not safe for you to be traveling alone just now," Hanks goes on. "Not in this territory or in Missouri without any proper papers to show you're free."

"I reckon a Colt would do him more good than that paper done," I say.

Hanks nods. "Just so. That's why it's necessary that he be some place fairly close, where he'll be safe, until he's well enough to travel on his own."

Hanks has told me he's a farmer, but I didn't know that much about his background. "Who lives on this farm?" I ask.

"Nobody right now. There's just a two-room cabin on the land, but my brother is planting a wheat crop on it while I'm doing this job. Tom's a strong anti-slavery man. I'll tell him about Shad, so he can keep an eye on things there. The cabin is stocked with enough food. And there's a rifle there, if he should need it."

While he was talking, planning things out, I'd begun to get an idea. "You know, Shad's good with animals, especially horses. Sort of has a feel for 'em. When all his problems started, he was just fixin' to apply for a job with the Pony Express as a stock tender."

"If you're thinking maybe he could work here, it's out of the question," Hanks says. "I could use the help, but too many people would see him. Too dangerous. He needs to be away from here, out of sight."

"I warn't thinking of the company hiring him to work here. I was thinking of transferring out to the Western end of the pony run, myself, maybe to Utah. Then me and Shad could travel together. If the company still needs good stock tenders out there, both of us could be far away from here."

This would solve two problems at once, I'm thinking, and get both of us out of danger. It would be a perfect solution, except for leaving Jane Holland. The thought of that is kind of like grating down on a hunk of sand in a bite of apple strudel. She thinks I'm a lying slave stealer, anyhow. And she told me she was going off to school in the fall. But those things don't make it no easier to give her up. The recollection of her kisses and her quick wit and her smile and her generous ways has got to be put behind me.

"Not a bad notion," Hanks says, bringing me back to myself. He gets up and pours each of us more coffee from the big pot on the stove. Shad stirs a big dollop of honey from a clay jar into his cup. "Mister Lewis in St. Joe would have to approve any transfer, and any hiring."

"Shouldn't be no problem. There's plenty of fellas would like to replace me here, I'm sure," I say.

"They'd have to find a place for you on the other end," Hanks says. "And also a place for a stock tender."

"The riders tell me the company has trouble keeping riders out there," I say. "When they find out it ain't all that much fun and adventure, a goodly number of 'em quit."

"Some get scared off by Indians, too," Hanks adds. "I been reading in the newspaper about the Paiutes raising hell somewhere in the Utah desert."

"Yeah. And sometimes the riders get sick or hurt. So there should be lots of places where I could fit in. Shad, too. I got experience and a good record."

"Are you sure that's what you want to do?" Hanks asks, raising his eyebrows.

I nod. "Things were getting pretty hot for me around here even before this. I figure this is the best solution, all around, if I want to keep working for the company. What about it, Shad? You still game to get a job as a stock tender?"

"I shore am. Dis here arm'll be purty much healed up in a couple weeks, and I'll be able to do a good job with dem horses. Wild Injuns can't be no wuss den bein' a slave."

"Shad, don't forget you're a free man," Hanks says. "You don't have to go along with any of the suggestions we make. You can decide for yourself what you want to do."

"I knows dat, Mister Hanks. I been a free man for a few years now, so I's used to takin' care o' myself. I can get along wif 'most anybody, even one o' dem cross-grained station keepers."

"Well, maybe you'll get a good one," Hanks laughs. "You're about due for a run of better luck." Hanks stands up and stretches. "It's settled, then. Shad, you better sleep in the stable so you'll be out of sight and safe, and where I can keep an eye on you, and out of Nathan Rising's way. No use getting him involved in this. The fewer people who know about all this, the better. I'll bring your food out there." Then he turns to me. "You'd better catch some sleep today. You've got the run to Liberty Farm early in the morning. When you get back . . . no, that won't work . . . not enough time. I tell you what . . . write me up a request for a transfer, and I'll ride over to St. Joe and give it to Lewis. Then he can authorize your transfer in writing, and I'll bring it back here to you. It'll take me a good three to four days to make the round trip."

"Who's going to tend the stock and have the ponies ready for the relay while you're gone?" I ask.

"I can do it," Shad pipes up.

"No. Too dangerous," Hanks says. "It'd be just your luck somebody'd see you, and the word would get back to Culbertson. Besides, I'd have to tell Nathan Rising who you are, and why you're taking my place for a couple of days. No, I don't think it's a good idea, especially with only one good arm."

"Who, then?" I ask.

"I don't know. If you had enough time off between runs, you could ride over to St. Joe and do it yourself. But it's a good hundred miles each way. I could probably get Nathan Rising to fill in as stock tender, but that wouldn't do for two reasons . . . first and foremost, he wouldn't lower himself to that kind of work. And second, we'd have to find some place besides the stable to hide Shadrack if Rising had to go messing around out there. Too bad the telegraph isn't completed this far. We wouldn't have to leave here at all."

"The telegraph will put the Pony Express out of business soon enough," I say, echoing what Blather Murphy had predicted earlier.

"I'll get my brother, Tom, to come up from the farm for a couple o' days and fill in here," Hanks says, brightening up.

"Better yet, why not get Tom to ride to St. Joe with the request for transfer?" I say.

"Good idea. I'll write up the request, and you can sign it. We won't say anything at all about Shad."

"I'll just put down my reason that I hear they's having trouble filling some of the vacancies out there, and I have a hankering to see some wilder country, or some such reason. I'll make up something that sounds reasonable." Here I go, stretching the truth again. It seems mighty strange that I'm forever getting into situations where I have to tell something besides the rock-solid truth. My conscience goes to giving me fits about that sometimes, especially when I'm worn down and tired, or late at night when I can't sleep. I wonder why it is that humans can't deal with one another straight up and honest? But maybe if we did, there'd be more wars and heartache than there is already. Humans are strange creatures. Maybe if I warn't one of them myself, I'd understand them a lot better.

Anyway, it was finally agreed that Hanks would get his brother, Tom, to ride over to St. Joe to request my transfer to somewhere in the Western division of the Pony Express route. I insisted on paying Hanks and his brother something for all their trouble. I made sure it warn't so much money that Hanks would suspicion I stole it. I just took forty dollars in cash out of my remaining reward money Hartz had give me that night. Since it warn't a great amount, I figure Hanks would think I'd saved it out of my rider's wages. But I wanted Hanks to know how grateful I was.

After breakfast, Hanks goes off to work at the stable, and I give Shad a quick rundown on what I'd been doing since we'd lost track of each other. His eyes go wide when I tell him about how the Mounted Rangers mighty near hanged me.

"Lawdy, Lance, dat was worse den bein' a slave. Leastways, nobody tried to kill me."

We fixed Shad up a little place in the tack room that was inside the stable. Since there warn't no loft in this little stable,

122

we cleaned out an empty stall, and piled it with fresh straw for him to sleep in, or hide in, if he needed to. Hanks would see to it that he got food and water and that nobody would see the fugitive until the two of us got ready to move out.

And, for once, our plans went off without a hitch. Maybe it was because I warn't doing all the planning myself. Most of my plans seem to stumble and fall when I begun to carrying them out. But this time, everything went fine. I kind of held my breath for the next few days whilst Hanks's brother, that I'd never met, rode on a mission for me. He was back on the evening of the fourth day with the written approval of Mr. Lewis, my division superintendent, but I didn't get the good news until the next afternoon when I rode in with the mail from Liberty Farm.

As soon as Dan Ivers had pounded away with the mochila, Hanks reaches inside his shirt and hands me an envelope, without saying nothing. I can't read his face to see if it's good news, but only tore open the envelope. Mr. Lewis had wrote:

May 22, 1860
Dear Mr. Barlow,

Request for transfer approved. You will report to Howard Egan, Division Supt. at Deep Creek Station, Utah Territory, as soon as is practicable after your replacement arrives at Marysville within a week. It would be advisable if you would ride your route to Liberty Farm at least once with the new man. Mr. Egan will place you at one of several possible home stations in his division. Thank you for a job well done and good luck with your new assignment.

**Best,
A. Lewis**

I give a whoop and jumped for Hanks to give him a big hug, which he looks like he could've done without.

Shad comes out of the tack room, and I read the message out loud to him. He grins and says: "Lance, it appears our luck's fixin' to change."

How right he was! But if I'd known *how* it was going to change, I believe I'd have chucked the whole idea and just hunkered down to take my chances with the devil I already knew.

Chapter Eleven

I reckon everyone has a little good luck fall on him now and again that's as welcome as a sprinkle of gold dust. Without a little good luck, our own struggling wouldn't amount to much. I reckon my Aunt Martha would have called it Divine Providence, but whatever it is, it begun falling on me and Shad starting with my finding out he was alive, then his rescue, then Hanks coming in to help us, and then my transfer being approved, then Culbertson not finding us before we got gone from Marysville.

Like I figured, there were lots of fellas just straining to ride the Pony Express, because my replacement was waiting at Marysville when I got back three days later. His name was Henry Wallace, a lean fella a couple years older and a couple inches taller than me, and a natural-born horseman, if I ever saw one.

He followed along behind at a lot slower pace on my next mail run to Liberty Farm. This was necessary because the hosteler wouldn't have but one fresh horse ready and waiting at each way station.

"You got a new rider comin' along shortly!" I yelled at every stock tender while I was slinging the mochila over the saddle of my fresh mount. "He's learnin' the route. Going to be replacing me."

"Where *you* going?" was the question at every stop.

"Out West!" Then I was in the saddle and thundering away.

When Henry caught up with me at Liberty Farm the next day, I give him a quick course in the details of Express riding, while we had a little time before the eastbound mail comes in.

"You got four pockets on that mochila," I say, "with the biggest two in back. All of them's fastened with small padlocks. The master at each home station has a key to the way pocket which is the left front one. When you get to a home station, the master will unlock the way pocket. He'll add any letters he has that need to be sent on, and he'll take out any that are to be dropped off at way stations in between for delivery."

Wallace nods, all eagerness.

"There's also a card in this way pocket that the station keeper uses to record the time of arrival and departure. He'll tell you how much time you have to make up if the Express is running behind. Ephraim Hanks will do this at Marysville most o' the time because the station master ain't there a lot."

By the time both me and Henry Wallace wind up back at Marysville — me by the fast ponies, and him by one slow one — I had a feeling this leg of the Express was being left in good hands. Mr. Albert Lewis knew how to hire good men.

Since Hanks's judgment of horseflesh was a lot better than mine, his last favor to me and Shad was to buy us two horses from the local livery. When I paid him for these animals, my stash was pretty lean, especially since Shad didn't have a penny left. He'd been saving his five hundred dollars, but he might as well have spent it, because Johnstone and Culbertson stole it from him anyway, so he didn't get no good out of it. I had less than a hundred dollars in greenbacks, but I'd make sure it saw us through.

I was in a sweat to get going, because every hour and every day we delayed was giving Culbertson just that much longer to find us. I'd been going everywhere with my eyes and ears wide open and my hand close to my gun. I warn't about to be surprised again. But Providence, or luck, was still with us. Shad's arm had been getting good care from Hanks for more than a week now, and was healing well, even though still pretty stiff and sore.

I knew we'd have to ride at night until we got away off from here. Just so's to be traveling along a familiar route, I figured to follow the Pony Express trail to Liberty Farm as usual, then on up that same trail to Fort Kearney. This route was all pounded down and rutted by hundreds of horses, oxen, and wagons of the emigrant trains that had rolled out early in the season. So there warn't no way anybody could track us. The only problem with this route was that we'd see more people and stand a better chance of being recognized.

There was only a sliver of moon the night we got our stuff together and packed the saddlebags. Shad didn't have nothing to carry but some cold fried chicken and biscuits and some tins of peaches Hanks give us.

Just after ten o'clock, when it was good and dark, we saddled up, said our good byes to Ephraim Hanks, and rode away from the Marysville Pony Express stable. I didn't really feel like I was leaving, because I'd ridden out this way so many times with the mail. It was just like another run to Liberty Farm, except we were traveling a lot slower. At this pace, we'd be the better part of two nights reaching it.

When we passed the Holland Ranch just after midnight, the house was dark except for one light in an upstairs window. I wondered if that was Jane's room. Was she up there reading, or maybe writing a letter, or maybe she had fallen asleep with the light on. I really wanted to see her once more, and I had a sudden urge to stop and knock on the door. But the hour was late, and I was afraid of waking her father or mother or the stock tender who roomed downstairs.

So the horses plodded on past the big, dark house and stables, and we were soon up and over a rise and down along the Little Blue River, heading north. We urged the horses to a lope for about fifteen minutes or so, then walked them for another thirty. This way, we covered a good bit of ground before daylight begun to creep up over the land. If I'd been running the relay ponies flat out, I'd've been close to Liberty Farm by now, I'm thinking, when we finally pull off the trail into a clump of trees growing by a tiny stream that feeds the Little Blue River.

We hobble the horses down in a swale in the prairie, and then have a bite of cold chicken to eat. We finally have to build a smoky fire to fight off the swarms of mosquitoes. We mighty near have to sit in the smoke to keep them from eating us alive. We sit and talk a while and have a pipe before covering all our exposed skin and drowsing off to sleep.

Sometime that afternoon I was wakened by voices. For a few seconds, I couldn't remember where I was. Then I hear a whip crack and the sound of wagons rumbling, and I come awake quick and look through the bushes. It's just an emigrant train passing along the valley of the Little Blue a couple hundred yards away.

I rouse up Shad who's still sleeping sound, and we eat a little more and drink water from the canteens. When we finish up, the sun's still high in the sky and darkness is still about three hours away. But we're anxious to get going and don't want to wait till night. Shad and I talk it over and decide to chance it.

So we saddle up and start out. It ain't long before we catch up with the wagon train that's just pulling off the trail to go into camp for the night. We wave and ride on by without stopping. I'm thinking that, at the pace they're moving, they won't reach California or Oregon until the seasons begin to change again. It wouldn't be a bad way to spend the summer, but there are probably a few of them that's starting out with high hopes who'll leave their bones along some lonely stretches of trail. Then, again, I'd found out that life's a gamble, no matter where you are.

We pick up the pace to an easy canter, trying to cover as much ground as possible while we still got some daylight. Finally the sun slides on down the western sky as we ride up out of the shallow river valley, and we're treated to one of them long, lingering sunsets of reds and golds. It almost takes my breath to watch, but directly it just slithers away like gold dust through a drunk's fingers.

We ride on into the darkness as the stars begin to wink on overhead so we don't feel lonesome. The familiar trail flows up and down over the gentle heave of prairie, and I only talk now and then, mostly just to hear Shad's voice and know he's close by. When I was carrying the mail over this route at night, I'd come to know it well, but I was either thinking about Jane Holland, or I was so concerned with watching where I was guiding my galloping pony that I never took the time really to look at the big vault of black velvet sky. It's all spangled with stars that look like ice chips or diamonds or something. I try not to think too much about how far away they are, 'cause it just makes me feel tinier than I am.

By and by I get sleepy, even though I'd just slept most of the day. This generally happened to me an hour or so before sunup. I'm drowsing in the saddle when Shad says: "Let's run 'em a little. We all need to wake up."

So we gallop the ponies for a few minutes and then dismount and lead them for a while, just to stretch our legs and let the horses blow a little.

We passed on by the few Pony Express relay stations because there ain't no need to bother them. We don't stop when morning comes, but only ride on until we finally spot the buildings of Liberty Farm. I'd figured to spend the day here, but a rider was occupying my bunk, waiting for Henry Wallace to bring the mochila from Marysville, so me and Shad paid our respects to the old couple who ran the station. They looked at Shad kind of curious, but didn't ask no questions. We go off into the grove of cottonwoods and bed down, after I'd bought some grain for our horses and put them into the corral.

That evening we start out again, after eating supper in the farm house. We ain't got much food left, but I know we can stretch it out until we reach Fort Kearney. Another night and part of the next morning and we spot the flag snapping in the breeze over Fort Kearney. I leave Shad out of sight down along the Platte River and go into the sutler's store to lay in some supplies. The prices are higher than I'm used to, but most of the stuff is sold to wagon trains and has to be hauled in here from a long ways off, so that's why it costs more.

There's a wagon train camped on the flat just outside the fort with lots of people milling around, so nobody pays me no mind. I stock up with sacks of rice and slabs of smoked bacon and dried apricots, some tobacco, salt, a little frying pan, coffee pot, and tin plates, flour and some other stuff I reckon won't be too heavy to carry, and won't spoil along the way.

I get one sack of corn for the animals, but grain is higher than a cat's back, and too bulky to carry, so from here on they'll have to get along on the prairie grass that's really taking hold.

Shad and me start out again that evening, since we're both anxious to get to Utah. But this time we travel only long enough to get good and tired, sometime after midnight. Then we stop and camp. From here on, I reckon there ain't no need to travel at night, since we're far enough from Marysville.

In the six days it took us to reach Julesburg, the scenery hardly ever changed. I didn't have to refer to the map I carried because the trail followed the broad, flat Platte River valley, and every day was just like the one before. Even the weather never varied — warm and dry with a wind out of the south or west, and a few high clouds drifting along. Several times we had to detour a mile or more off the trail to find enough good grass for the horses, because all the wagon trains coming through here had stripped the valley bare of anything edible for a mighty wide path all along this river. But we had the shallow river for a cool bath every day. We had to settle the silt and sand out of it for our drinking water, but it warn't too bad after that.

We found lots of junk that'd been pitched out — mostly furniture that would have been nice in a house somewhere back East but warn't no account out here, where every mile those extra pounds had to be hauled burned up the draft animals and wore out the wagons. Since there warn't much in the way of firewood along here, we busted up a dresser or a desk a time or two and cooked over it, although I never felt right about doing it because it felt like I was burning up part of somebody's dreams. But some evenings we couldn't hardly find a stick of dry wood along the meandering Platte. The spring floods had scoured away most of the growth, and the rest had been picked clean by the emigrants for fuel.

Now and then we'd stop at a Pony Express station to say howdy and pass a sociable hour with the station keeper and stock tender. We even stayed the night under roof of a log station at Gothenburg, Nebraska. It seemed kind of smothery after sleeping outdoors.

All in all, we had a pleasant trip and finally come to where the Platte split. We took the south fork and come to Julesburg, just into the corner of the Colorado Territory, but, of course, there warn't no boundary markers or nothing. But here the trail turned back north into Nebraska to the North Platte

River. The land was mostly treeless and desolate as we climbed up the long, gradual tilt toward the Rocky Mountains.

"Lance, blamed if dis ain't de biggest, emptiest blasted country I evah seen!" Shad busted out one afternoon when our horses were plodding along and we were wearing our bandannas over our noses and mouths to protect them from the fine grit the wind was whipping across miles and miles of open space.

"You're right about that. Back when I worked with that freighting outfit, I figured we were gonna fall off the edge of the world before we ever come to Santa Fé."

We passed Chimney Rock, a sandstone spire, poking up high out of a broad cone of red dirt and shale on the plains, and visible for miles. Then we passed Scott's Bluff and Horse Creek and Cold Springs and finally come to Fort Laramie, the military post that was like a little island in the rolling sea of short grass. Its neat white buildings made me think somebody had set a little village down in the middle of nowhere. Besides the blue-coated soldiers, there was a hodgepodge of Injuns, trappers, traders, half-breeds, and settlers, and lots of other folks milling around. Shad and me camped just outside the big quadrangle and treated ourselves to some smoked oysters and stocked up on supplies. We'd taken care of our horses, and they were still in good shape, so we camped here almost two days to rest them — and us. Shad had pretty much got the full use of his arm back now. It bothered him only a little.

Early one morning we splashed our horses across the shallow river and rode on up along the North Platte, passing stations every few miles — Nine-Mile House and Cottonwood, which we bypassed. The next station was Horse Shoe, the home station of Division Superintendent Joseph A. "Captain Jack" Slade. He had a reputation of being a mighty affable fella — when he was sober. But he went on drunken rages and, it was said, had killed several men when John Barleycorn had him by the neck. I didn't want no part of this man, so Shad and me bypassed this station, too. Bill Cody, the skinny youngster I'd made friends with in St. Joe, was riding the mail out this way somewhere, but we didn't see nothing of him.

We spent the next several days following the faint trail, mostly with the help of my map and pocket compass and a few landmarks. We rode past stations with names like Elkhorn and Bed Tick and Red Buttes. Then we come down the headwaters of the Sweetwater to places like Devil's Gate, Warm Springs, Big Timber, Ham's Fork, and then into Utah Territory to Quaking Aspen, Echo Cañon, Mountain Dale, and finally into the basin cupped by mountains where the Mormons had stopped and were building Salt Lake City. It warn't much of a city so far, but they were working like beavers, putting up buildings, including a huge temple, digging irrigation ditches, planting crops, and the like.

The place was bustling with activity, but we didn't linger but one night, bought a few supplies, engaged the services of a farrier, and pushed on. I got the feeling that a Gentile and a nigger warn't the most welcome folks here, unless they had money.

The trail got fainter, and I had to use my map and compass a lot more as we bent on south and west around the lower end of the Great Salt Lake, and then skirted the bottom edge of the Great Salt Lake Desert. This was one of the most fearsome sights I'd ever seen — just miles and miles and miles of nothing but white sand and salt that we couldn't hardly look at in the sunlight without hurting our eyes. Not even a blade of grass.

Now we begun stopping at every Pony Express station to rest ourselves, but mostly our horses, and to get water, because the early June heat was just sucking us drier than a buffalo chip. My lips were cracking, and the skin of my face felt like it couldn't hardly stretch over my skullbone, even though I'd kept my hat on all the time during the day.

The way stations were sometimes just dugouts in a hillside, or adobe, or rock huts. I was thankful we'd had our horses newly shod in Salt Lake because this rocky desert was really rough on our animals' feet.

"Hullo, the station!" I yelled as we rode up to a rock hut on a rise of ground my map showed as Point Lookout. Low, rolling hills, covered in sage and desert scrub, swept up about a mile away on either side. It was early afternoon, and I didn't see nobody. Then I see a rifle barrel slide back out of one of the loopholes, and I know we're being watched.

"Friends!" I shout. "Just want some water!"

The wooden door swings open, and a man steps out holding a rifle at his belt as we ride up and dismount, stiff and sore.

"Lance Barlow and Shadrack, just on the way to Deep Creek to meet with Superintendent Howard Egan," I say, thrusting out my hand. "I'm a pony rider transferrin' out from Kansas."

"Bill Deweese, station keeper," he says, gripping my hand. He shakes hands with Shad, too, which surprises me some, since most white strangers don't make a habit of that. "Come on in and get some grub."

"Thanks, but we ain't hungry," I say, knowing he probably ain't got none to spare, as we step into the dim interior of the little rock house. Deweese is short and stocky and has a thick beard.

"Where's your stock tender?"

"Rode up to Salt Lake for a few days." I guess I look a little curious, because he goes on. "Haven't you heard? The

Paiutes and Gosiutes are pickin' off any pony rider they can catch or ambush between here and away over toward Carson City. Killed off several men and burnt a station just northwest of here. Several other stations have been attacked. Forced the Express to stop running more than a week ago. Alexander Majors said he couldn't risk his employees' lives any further."

"What?" I'm so shocked by this news that my mouth just drops open.

"I wondered why we ain't seen no pony riders for a while, Lance," Shad says.

"Stopped, you say? I didn't think nothing could stop the Express."

"Yes, sir. Stopped 'em cold. That's why I was so careful when you rode up. A man don't make but one slip-up in this country. He don't get a second chance. I got the horses in a rock corral just behind here."

I kind of slump down at the little wooden table while he hands me a dipper of spring water from a barrel in the corner.

As I drink, I'm thinking that this has been a long, dry ride for nothing. Now me and Shad are on our own in the middle of a God-forsaken desert, nearly broke, and with nowhere to go.

Chapter Twelve

People who don't expect nothing good to happen, generally ain't disappointed when it don't. Thing is, most folks can't help getting their hopes up. Maybe we should all be more like horses who just take things as they come without no expectations.

I reckon that's why this news of the Express kind of knocked the props out from under me for a time. It was almost an hour before I begun to perk up. And that was after Deweese had made us some coffee, and we'd carried our cups outside to sit in the shade of the hut to drink it.

We were sitting on a couple of big rocks, letting the warm breeze fan us. It was too hot for any kind of moving around, but it warn't all that miserable in the shade. I reckon the desert air was so dry we were drying off as quick as we were sweating. Every place has its good points and its bad points; back home the mosquitoes would have been feasting on our sweaty hides.

We chatted about the weather and horses and other things, not bringing up the subject of the end of the Pony Express. Deweese did most of the talking, like lots of men who spend a good deal of time alone.

After nearly an hour of this, and a second cup of coffee with sugar, I begun to get my strength back and feel better. Guess I didn't know how tired I was.

Finally I say: "What're the chances of getting the Express running again?"

Deweese kind of shrugs and looks off toward the low desert hills. "Who knows? I been stuck here since one o' the riders come through, changed horses, and passed the word there weren't going to be any more mail runs for now."

He picks up his rifle and steps around the corner of the rock house and takes a good look to the south and west. "I guess the Paiutes are the ones who'll decide if or when the mail starts running again."

No doubt this station was built on this small hill for defense. Except at night, nobody could sneak up on this rock hut or corral without being seen. Loopholes for rifles were built into the walls on all sides, but the roof was just boards, and, if any Injuns really put their minds to it, they could set it afire.

I was thinking if maybe we could get on over to Deep Creek station and talk to Superintendent Howard Egan, maybe we could get a handle on what the situation really was.

"How many miles to Deep Creek?" I ask.

"A far piece from here by the regular trail . . . just over ninety miles."

"Then we'd best be moving," I say, getting up and stretching my tired muscles. "We got a few hours of daylight left."

"That's mighty foolhardy, if you ask me," Deweese says, "crossing that desert by yourselves. You'd be better off waiting for an emigrant train. Safety in numbers." He looks at me and Shad. "That pistol the only weapon you got?"

"Yeah. But I've got an extra loaded cylinder," I say, patting the side pocket of my buckskin jacket. "We can't wait here for weeks. I've got to get to Deep Creek."

"No need to hurry, since you don't have a job right now. You're welcome to stay here."

The thought of running into some riled-up Paiutes on the open desert with no place to hide was only a little worse than the thought of holing up at this tiny rock station for days or weeks.

"Appreciate your hospitality, but we need to get going," I say.

"Tell you what," he says, eyeing me and Shad, "just stay the night here, and start out about four in the mornin', just before daylight while it's still cool." He walks over and runs a hand over the dusty neck of my mount. "Your horses look like they could use some rest. I'll cook us up a good meal tonight. Besides that," he says with a twinkle in his eye, "I need a little company."

So that's the way it come about that we stayed the night at Point Lookout station. It turned out to be one of the most enjoyable evenings I'd ever spent. Bill Deweese didn't favor nothing when it come to looks, but he had two hidden talents — he could cook, and he could tell stories. He didn't talk much about himself. The only thing I learned about him was that he was from somewhere in upstate New York and had come West as a young man to seek his fortune. The fact that he hadn't struck it rich didn't seem to bother him none at all.

He whipped up a stew of tripe and dried beef and onions and potatoes that would've made him a favorite at the court of an old-time French king. By the time we'd stuffed ourselves with that and corn bread and dried apple pie, I figured he must have worked as a chef before he took this lonesome job.

After supper, he eased into telling some stories that probably warn't truly all that funny, but he had a way of telling them that had my stomach sore from laughing. And even Shad, who was usually happy, but not really jovial, was grinning from ear to ear and chuckling.

Then Deweese commenced to spinning some tales that mighty near made my hair stand on end, about murders and bloody dead men walking at night for revenge and such. He swore they was all fact, that he knew the men who'd seen these things happen, but, thinking about it later, I figured he'd just conjured up a lot of stories out of some old Western legends, trying to scare a couple of tenderfoots. Maybe he figured Shad for an uneducated, superstitious nigger and me for a young and gullible kid. I reckon he was just having some fun at our expense, figuring he'd pump us full of them stories about ghosts and fairies and scare the daylights out of us. And he just about did. But it was first-rate entertainment, because I don't know nobody who don't like to be scared 'most to death by a good story.

Anyway, it didn't seem like no time until we were yawning and knocking the dottle out of our pipes and getting ready to turn in. Deweese insisted that Shad and me take the two bunks that was built, one atop the other, against the back wall.

"I'll stretch out here on the floor. I'll be fine," he says, turning the lamp down and shrugging out of his galluses and pulling off his boots.

"What about standing guard?" I ask.

"No need. Too dangerous to sleep outside. I'll just have to take a chance with the horses. Wish this building was big enough to hold 'em. When my hosteler's here, we take turns at sentry duty, but tonight we'll just fort up in here." He slips the bar across the heavy, wooden door and checks the gun ports in the walls. The only window is glassless and high up in the wall. "Your horses are in with mine. The stone corral is the best we can do. It's a bright, moonlit night. If there are any Paiutes around, I don't think they will try to slip up this bare hill and take a chance of getting drilled for the sake of a few horses."

I warn't so sure about that, but didn't say nothing, since I figured he knew more about this area than I did. Being smaller, I climbed into the top bunk and gave Shad the lower one. Deweese spread a tattered old buffalo robe on the wooden floor, said good night, and blew out the lamp.

I reckon those scary stories of his didn't keep me awake or make me dream, because the next thing I know Deweese is rousting me out, and it's still dark outside. And cold. I had shivered up into a ball under that single blanket from the night air that was flowing in the nearby window.

Deweese sent us off, fortified with warmed-over coffee and corn bread, slathered with blackstrap molasses. Couldn't ask for a better breakfast on a cold morning.

It was pitch dark when we guided our horses down the hillside away from Point Lookout, but Deweese had pointed the way. He'd looked at my map the night before and made a few corrections and noted some distances with a pencil. "North around these low mountains, then bear left. . . ." I had memorized the route all the way to Deep Creek.

When the sun come up sometime later, the wind begun to stir, and by noon I couldn't remember ever being cold. We plodded along, hats pulled low, and squinting against the glare, just sipping water from our canteens. We didn't talk much, but kept a good watch for any Injuns, though I don't know what we would have done if we'd seen some.

Eight miles out we rode through a pass in the low desert mountains, and the trail curved around south to Simpson Springs, a few miles farther. Distances out here in these open spaces was a lot different than back home. Something that seemed to be "just right over there" turned out to be a two-hour ride away.

Simpson Springs was built out of rocks that're scattered all around there and was a good, solid station, with a small spring flowing close by. But the place was deserted. We stopped and rested ourselves and our horses for about an hour, filled our canteens, let the animals drink, and washed ourselves in the clean spring water. It seemed strange not seeing any

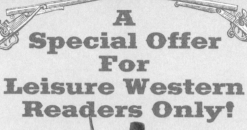

GET YOUR 4
FREE* BOOKS NOW—
A VALUE BETWEEN
$16 AND $20

Mail the Free* Book Certificate Today!

FREE* BOOKS
CERTIFICATE!

YES! I want to subscribe to the Leisure Western Book Club. Please send me my 4 FREE* BOOKS. Then, each month, I'll receive the four newest Leisure Western Selections to preview FREE* for 10 days. If I decide to keep them, I will pay the Special Member's Only discounted price of just $3.36 each, a total of $13.44 ($14.50 US in Canada). This saves me between $3 and $6 off the bookstore price. There are no shipping, handling or other charges.* There is no minimum number of books I must buy and I may cancel the program at any time. In any case, the 4 FREE* BOOKS are mine to keep—at a value of between $17 and $20!

*In Canada, add $5.00 Canadian shipping and handling per order for first shipment. For all subsequent shipments to Canada the cost of membership in the Book Club is $14.50 US, which includes $7.50 shipping and handling per month. All payments must be made in US currency.

Name _____

Address _____

City_____ State_____ Country_____

Zip_____ Telephone_____

Tear here and mail your FREE* book card today!

If under 18, parent or guardian must sign. Terms, prices and conditions subject to change. Subscription subject to acceptance. Leisure Books reserves the right to reject any order or cancel any subscription.

Get Four Books Totally F R E E* — A Value between $16 and $20

Tear here and mail your FREE* book card today!

PLEASE RUSH
MY FOUR FREE*
BOOKS TO ME
RIGHT AWAY!

LeisureWestern Book Club
P.O. Box 6613
Edison, NJ 08818-6613

AFFIX
STAMP
HERE

people around. It was almost like they'd just stepped out for a few minutes and would be right back, because nothing inside was disturbed.

"Maybe the Injuns *didn't* get 'em, after all," I say to Shad. "Looks like maybe they just skedaddled."

"Shore enough," he nods, looking around. "De place ain't burned or looted or nothin'."

Finally we tighten up our cinches, climb aboard, and move on. Eight miles or so brings us to another deserted station marked on my map as Riverbed. There are two buildings and a well that has some water in it. There's a wooden stable, and a decent-sized wooden station with a rock chimney up one side of it. Again, everything looks to be in good shape, except there ain't no people or animals anywhere around. This station is built in a low spot, and there are the usual desert mountains a little ways due south. The land all around is dotted with lots of desert shrubs like sage and mesquite and tufts of coarse grass. But the thing that gives the place its name is a dry, sandy riverbed that winds right past, going north and south. I reckon maybe the runoff from flash floods collects and flows north into Salt Lake.

The only reason I even give this place a second look is because Deweese told us a story about it last night. He said Division Superintendent Howard Egan hadn't been able to keep a station keeper here because three different ones had already been scared off by "desert fairies." Claim they saw white shapes at night, drifting around in the desert near the buildings, and heard eerie noises. I couldn't put no stock in what Deweese said, because he filled us with a lot of bunkum, and this place sure looked harmless enough in the daylight.

Shad is mounted up and ready to go as soon as we'd taken a quick gander at the place. "You about ready?" he asks when I'm still walking around, looking and listening.

"In a minute." I feel foolish telling him I'm trying to find some sign of the fairies that Deweese told us about. I don't know why this station would be any more prone to the supernatural than any of the other isolated places we've seen. I figure, in spite of the oath against drinking that every Russell, Majors, and Waddell employee has to sign, maybe these station keepers had been nipping at the sauce too heavy to ward off the loneliness and fear of Injuns, and maybe conjured up the Irish wee folk.

Finally I swing up into the saddle. Just then I hear a kind of moaning sound, and, if I didn't know better, I'd swear it was the low, wailing hum of a spinning wheel, rising and falling. In spite of the heat, a chill goes up my back, and I turn my head this way and that to see if I can tell where it's coming from. But I can't. I look quick at Shad to see if he hears it, but he don't give no sign of it. Then, directly, the sound fades, and I'm left wondering if maybe it was the wind I heard whining around the corners of the buildings. I tell myself it can't be a spinning wheel away out here, and it can't be fairies, so it's got to be something natural. But this thought don't comfort me none as we ride off southwest toward the next station at Dugway, ten miles away.

I didn't know it then, but it would be a good while before I would be thinking about fairies or strange noises again.

Blackrock was next, thirteen miles farther where an outcropping of volcanic rock gave the place its name. Here, too, was only a crude hut with no people. We rode on. Ten miles we went, with the faint trail bending southwest around to firm ground where the salt-mud desert could be traversed.

By the time we'd ridden and walked another ten miles to Fish Springs station, we were plumb wore down and ready to quit for the day. We'd traveled a total of about fifty-seven miles since early morning. Here we found three men who welcomed us, and we stopped for the night in a well-fortified rock station.

"How do you reckon these fish got in here, Shad?" I ask that evening after supper as we're looking at some of the small perch-like fish swimming in the pool formed by the springs. "We ain't close to no rivers or creeks. You reckon maybe they swum underground from wherever this spring started?"

"Lance, de Lawd can make enough loaves and fishes to feed de multitudes, so it sho' wouldn't be no trouble for Him to make a few little perch and put 'em in dis spring."

I just nod, wishing I had the easy faith in miracles that Shad always seemed to have.

The station keeper and two stock tenders here are as leery of the Injuns as Deweese had been. Since they were pretty much isolated, too, we didn't find out no more about the interrupted Pony Express than we already knew.

The next morning we started out early, rested and refreshed. By my figuring we had less than forty miles to go to Deep Creek.

Bid Boyd ran the next station, a one-room log hut near some low desert hills that were all beginning to look alike.

"Cañon Station was burned down, and two men killed and scalped there last week," Boyd told us. "Lemme see your map."

I pulled it out, and Boyd unfolded it on the table. "Right here is . . . *was* . . . Cañon Station. It's in Deep Creek Cañon, a nine-mile-long gorge you have to pass through. You might want to wait and try it at night for safety."

"Thanks, but we'll be moving," I say. "We've been too long on the road from Kansas."

"Suit yourself," he shrugs, and folds up my map.

We hadn't seen no Injuns, and I was getting mighty weary of hearing about them. Fact is, Boyd's warning went right into my head and out the other side without stopping. Shad didn't make no comment, so I reckon he felt the same as me.

We watered the horses and moved on. I was getting toughened up to the trail, especially to this hard, barren desert trail.

Willow Springs was the next station eight miles farther, followed by Six-Mile as the trail went northwest. I couldn't figure how the Injuns could live in such a place, or even wanted to, unless they'd been driven here by some other, stronger tribes. Deweese had told us the Paiutes and Gosiutes was a pretty poor lot, as Injuns go. They just hunted, still mostly with arrows, and gathered up whatever they could find to eat — piñon nuts being one of the main courses. Any tribe that eats pine-tree nuts as one of the biggest parts of their fare has got to be dirt poor. Besides, piñon pines didn't grow just everywhere. They were mostly a little higher on the mountain slopes. I don't know what they find in a desert like this, unless it's little rodents and mesquite beans. Compared to that, I reckon the white man's cattle and grain and stuff looks mighty inviting.

These thoughts were going through my head as we come closer to Deep Creek Cañon. As we advanced toward it, the land improved. The crusty salt gradually disappeared, and green grass tempted our horses to stop and graze. We had to keep pulling their heads up to urge them on. Gopher or prairie dog holes and snipes, willows, and wild roses told of some life in the area, and probably some water nearby, sort of like the slough we had passed near Willow Springs a few miles back.

Then the cleft in the mountains commenced, and, when we got a ways into it, the walls of the gorge rose up, steep, on both sides. The way begun to curve around so as to shut off the view a short distance to the front and to the rear.

Just naturally I begun to get a little edgy. If ever there was an ideal place for an ambush, this was it. The cañon walls warn't straight up in most places, but kind of folded back in waves, with sparse grass and sage and loose dirt and shale, looking like it would be a mighty hard climb for a man, and impossible for any animal but a lizard or a mountain goat.

I caught myself talking in kind of a loud whisper to Shad, like I was afraid somebody might hear me. In the rockier stretches, there was an echo and the hoofbeats of our horses sounded hollow and louder.

I reckon that was what give us the warning. We had stopped and were having a drink from our canteens while we were still mounted when we hear a sort of rumbling, clattering noise up ahead of us.

"What's that?" I say.

Shad's eyes are big as we look at each other. "Horses. No . . . cattle," he says, turning his head to catch the echoes off the cañon walls.

We slung our canteens and kicked our horses into a run. I didn't know where to go, but just pointed at a defile in the irregular cañon wall. I wanted to get out of the way and get a look at whoever was coming through the cañon before they saw us.

We were riding hard, but, before we could get out of sight, a herd of about fifty head come around the bend, driven by several mounted Injuns. They spotted us at the same time and about half of them broke off, unslinging their bows and rifles.

For a second I regretted being so brash and ignoring all the warnings we'd got. But then, I didn't have no more time for regrets, because they were on us.

Chapter Thirteen

Sometimes, in moments of terrible danger, fear just goes away, and you see everything really clear. This'd happened to me a time or two before, like at the Hartz Ranch the night of the raid, and it happened to me now. Things that were moving fast seemed to slow down, and I couldn't hear no sound at all.

Four Injuns were riding toward us, two of them with carbines and two with bows. I could see they was going to head us off before we could reach the defile, and I didn't want to be cornered there anyhow. I reined up and pulled my Colt. Shad pulled up alongside me.

The cattle warn't running, but they were moving along at a pretty good clip, just about filling the cañon, side to side. I saw all this at once, and knew in a flash what we'd do.

"Shad! Ride right at 'em! Through the herd!"

I fired at the closest Injun who was drawing back an arrow. He jerked sideways, and the bow flew out of his hand. A lucky shot. But I'm already firing again and yelling. The Injuns look confused that we're charging right at them, and they slow up and try to get their carbines to their shoulders, while their horses are still running. But we're leaning over our horses' necks and closing the gap fast.

The leaders of the herd begun to shy away from the gunfire and the yelling, forcing those behind to slow and turn. This crowds the three other Injuns who start trying to hold the herd from turning back on them.

We lean down and spur our mounts right toward the herd, with me firing, but my shots are going wild. One of the Injuns with a carbine gets a shot off, but everybody's moving too fast to hit anything. Before he can reload, me and Shad are in amongst the milling cattle and making mighty poor targets. Even though the big animals are slowing us down because we're going against the flow, they're also protecting us from the Injuns, who quit shooting, just as I figured they would, for fear of hitting the cows. I grab my saddle horn and hang as far as I can off the side of my horse when we finally bust out the back side of the bunched-up cattle and past the three Injuns who're more concerned with holding the herd from stampeding.

I can feel my horse beginning to tire, and Shad is crowding me. I straighten up in the saddle and fire a couple of quick shots over my shoulder without aiming. Just as I turn back around, a bullet tears off my saddle horn, just missing my left hand.

I spur hard, still yelling like mad, and my horse responds with a burst of speed. Another forty yards and we're galloping around a bend in the cañon and beyond sight of the Injuns and the herd. Our horses ain't the fast, half-wild mustangs the Express riders use, but they've got good stamina. We ease back some, but keep galloping, then finally have to slow to a trot. Even before this burst of speed, our mounts had already carried us about twenty miles today. I can feel my horse's sides heaving, so we can't push them too hard.

We finally slow to a walk and dismount to lead our animals. My knees are wobbly, and I can't hardly put one foot in front of the other. I keep looking back, knowing we probably ain't safe yet, but also knowing our horses can't run no farther without a breather.

"Dey ain't comin' aftah us, Lance," Shad says. "Dey got all dey can do to keep dem cattle bunched up after we spooked 'em good."

As usual Shad was right, because there warn't no pursuit,

although if we'd run into those Injuns when they didn't have nothing better to do, we would've probably been food for the buzzards before sundown. I take a deep breath and look up at a couple of black vultures swooping in lazy circles above the cañon walls, and give thanks we're still safe. I could just picture my fresh scalp, all dripping blood, hanging from some Injun's belt. The thought makes my head hurt, and I ease my hat back and wipe the sleeve of my buckskin shirt across my face.

My fear and my heartbeat begin to ease off some, and I remember to slip the pin out of my Colt, remove the empty cylinder, and replace it with the loaded one from my pocket. "Wonder if those Injuns owned those cattle?" I ask, locking the pistol back together.

Shad gives a snort. "Dem Injuns look just like poor niggers who don't own nothin'. Dey was brands on dem cows, and I never heard of no wild Injuns usin' no brandin' irons."

"They could have bought those cattle from some rancher," I say, trying to figure if maybe we'd just tangled with some peaceable Gosiutes that Deweese said roamed around this area.

"Dey bought dose cows like bears buy honey from bees," Shad replies, scornful like.

I nodded, thinking I should have figured that out myself. I'd never heard of any wild Injun using white man's money to buy his stock. Shad sees things like they really are, and it don't take him all day to get a handle on things, like it does me sometimes.

As I thought back over what had just happened, I recalled hitting the Injun who had a bow with my first shot. I don't believe it was direct to the body, because he sort of spun sideways. But I couldn't be sure. Several views of that close brush with death was fixed in my head like tintypes, and I could see them plain. I shook my head to get rid of them, but I knew they'd probably give me bad dreams in nights to come.

"Should've got a gun for you before we set out on this trip," I say. "Looks like you're going to have need of it."

Deep Creek station was about another fourteen miles, but we got there in the early afternoon without seeing nobody else. The adobe station, house and outbuildings, was a mighty welcome sight. There was even plenty of grass and water near the buildings where we saw a bunch of mules grazing among four wagons. There were some men milling around, too, but I didn't see no women and so didn't know if this was an emigrant train.

A man come out of the station door as we rode up and introduced himself as Harrison Sevier, station master. He was a man clean shaven, who looked to be in his thirties and very fit. He greeted us like long-lost kin, and I found out later he was a Latter-Day Saint, having been recruited in Salt Lake. Except for not having no coffee, tea, hot chocolate, liquor, or tobacco around the place, he was a mighty decent and kindly man.

As soon as we told him who we were and what we'd run into a few miles back, he said: "Paiutes. You were lucky. They've been raiding ranches, and emigrant trains, and anybody else who gets in their way. I suppose we'll be hearing about somebody losing that herd. Come on, let me introduce you to Mister Egan."

He led us across the wide, dusty yard and rapped on the door of the adobe house.

"He ain't there," a man yelled from a nearby wagon. He's over at the stables."

We crossed over to the third adobe building. Just as we got there, a man stepped out into the sunshine, talking to someone over his shoulder. "Take the rough edges off, but don't break their spirits. It won't matter if they're a little wild, but they have to be able to run."

He stopped short when he saw us, and Sevier said: "Mister Egan, this is Lance Barlow and his friend, Shadrack."

"Hello." He gripped my hand, and then Shad's.

I'd been told this man had charge of the Pony Express from Salt Lake City to Roberts Creek, one of the wildest, most desolate stretches of the run. He was one of five superintendents on the entire line. He was a man of medium height, about mid forties, balding in front, and wore a full, shaggy, brown beard and mustache. He had kindly eyes, and, after he'd said a few words, I caught some trace of a dialect that was fascinating to listen to. In a minute it came to me that he was a native Irishman.

I handed him my letter of transfer from Mr. Lewis, and he gave it a quick read.

"I didn't know Lewis could give up men that easily, but his loss is our gain, heh?" He gives us a searching look.

"Yes, sir." I don't give no indication why I transferred.

"This your servant?" he asks, looking at Shad.

"No, sir. Shadrack is a free man who is a friend of mine. He's looking for work as a stock tender. And he's mighty good with animals," I add.

"By the saints, Sevier, I believe we've struck paydirt. Two in one whack. Well, we've got plenty of work for the both of you."

"They had a brush with about a half dozen Indians who were driving a stolen herd of cattle through the cañon about fifteen miles east of here," Sevier tells him.

Egan takes in this information without no comment, then says: "You boys take care of your horses, and come on over to the house. I want to talk with you."

We did as we was told, and I got a long drink of fresh water and washed my face before we reported to Mr. Egan. I liked the look of this man. I'd heard good things about him, but I like to size up a man for myself. Egan seemed to be a man who deserved his reputation as strong, steady, and considerate to the people who worked under him. He'd been a rider, delivering goods and mail, even before the Pony Express was formed, so he never asked anyone to do a job he hadn't already done himself.

"Have a chair, boys," he says when he shows us into what passed for a setting room out here. We set in a couple of wooden armchairs, and he does likewise.

"Now, then, give me the details of your meeting with the Indians."

I commenced to tell him what happened, and Shad chips in a time or two when I'd forget something.

When I finished, Egan nods and says: "Now you can see what we're up against out here. That's why we've had to shut down for now."

He doesn't say nothing more for a second, and I jump in with: "Sir, when do you think the Express will start up again?"

"First of all, you needn't call me sir. Just Howard or Mister Egan will do."

"Yes, Mister Egan."

"To answer your question, I don't know. As quickly as possible. But, in the meantime, until we feel it's safe enough to get the riders back on a regular schedule, the mail will still go through."

I waited, figuring he'll tell us how.

"I got a wagon train of well-armed volunteers you see out there to accompany me here from Salt Lake City with all the accumulated mochilas that have stacked up there for more than a week. I was in a hurry, and we took a short cut to get here. Just stopped at a couple of the deserted stations for water."

So that's why Deweese and the other stations keepers we'd seen didn't know nothing about this, thinks I.

He waved his hands as if to dismiss all the petty details. "My counterpart, Bolivar Roberts at Carson City, is busy improvising a way to keep the mails running through this crisis. The mail may not be on a regular schedule, and the mochilas may be a few days late, but they'll get through!" He says this last pretty loud, slapping his hand on his knee, and raising some dust from his britches. "Here, look at this." He reaches over and snags a newspaper off the table and hands it to me, pointing at an announcement set off in a black box. "This is a copy of a Sacramento paper with a plea to the people of California from Bill Finney, our company man in San Francisco. It was brought in by Nick Wilson from Carson City in the last mochila that was able to get through."

I take the paper, hold it to the light coming in the window, and read it out loud for Shad's benefit. " 'Will the people of California help the Pony in its difficulty? We have conferred some benefits, have asked but little, and perhaps the people will assist. Can anything be done in your city towards paying expenses to furnish arms and provisions for twenty-five men to go through with me to Salt Lake to take and bring on the Express?

" 'I will be responsible for the return of the arms, will have transportation of my own, and can get men here. What is wanted is one thousand dollars for the pay of the men, five hundred dollars for provisions, and twenty-five Sharps rifles and as many Dragoon pistols. I will guarantee to keep the Pony alive a while longer.' "

I put the paper down and Egan says: "Since that was published, the people in Sacramento have raised and donated fifteen hundred dollars and most of the arms requested. Roberts is raising a party made up mostly of the regular Pony Express riders to bring the mail east from Carson City. Then, we'll take the accumulated mochilas west to meet them. The volunteers you see outside will ride escort. I don't think the Paiutes will try to jump us with that many guns."

"What're the Injuns so riled up about?" I ask.

He takes a deep breath, like he's real tired, and says: "Well, like a lot of wars, it's not any one big thing. It started over in the western part of the territory near the California border. Like most tribes, they resented the white man coming into what they considered their land. When the intruders started settling in numbers, they really got alarmed. Then, one raid resulted in a bigger retaliation by the whites, and it just went back and forth from there, with lots of misunderstandings, and just got bigger and bigger until pitched battles were being fought, mostly in the Pyramid Lake area. Then the Paiutes started trying to waylay the lone riders. One man who runs a trading post west of here is married to a Paiute woman, and he said the Indians were also curious about what was in the mail pouches that the white man was carrying on the swift ponies."

"Why are they hitting the emigrant trains?" I ask. "Most of them are just passing through to the West Coast. They're not settling here."

"All white men are threats to them, just as the whites don't take time to sort out which Indians are really the enemy. Plus, the wagons are an easy target and a source of food and animals. That may be where that herd came from you saw today. One of the Paiutes' grievances was that the miners and settlers were cutting down all the piñon trees whose nuts are a major source of food for the Indians."

I shake my head at the folly of it all, and think about the

whites living back East who're getting ready to fight each other. It didn't have to be white man against red man. But all I say is: "You think it will calm down soon?"

"I hope so. One or two of the Paiute leaders, young Winnemucca being the major example, are doing everything they can to make peace, but they've got a lot of hot-headed braves to control, and the whites have a lot of radicals who are keeping each other's fear stirred up with whiskey and speeches. Some of them won't be satisfied until all the red men are run back into the desert and the tribes scattered. There have been more than a hundred men killed on both sides already."

"No wonder several of the stations we passed between here and Salt Lake were deserted."

Egan nodded. "There's a few of them west of here like that, too. We'll take a large enough force to repair any damage and then leave five men at each station while this trouble continues. We'll also restock them with horses."

"That'll cost a good bit of money."

"You're right about that. The company has suffered some heavy financial losses already, and this has just made it worse." He stood up. "I'm glad you boys got here when you did. Our party was getting ready to head west in the morning to rendezvous with Bolivar Roberts and his bunch. You can ride with us. In the meantime, I'll decide where you'll be stationed. I can use Shadrack nearly any place. Good hostelers are hard to come by. We've had a number of men quit since all this trouble started. Can't say as I blame them, though, after what's happened to some of those poor men in the isolated stations." He rubbed a big hand over his balding head. "Ah, well . . . and to think I left Ireland mostly because of the troubles there." Then he grins at us. "At least, there's plenty to eat here."

Chapter Fourteen

By the time a span of mules is being hitched to each of the four wagons early next morning, I'd discovered something else about Superintendent Howard Egan besides the fact that he was from Ireland and was a brave and kindly man. He was dirty. It wasn't that he was just dirty about his person — which he was — but he also kept a mighty filthy station, with offal and rubbish thrown on the ground near the front door of his house. Now, I ain't one to be too picky, seeing as how I warn't real spit and polish myself. But you'd think a man, even if he don't wash or change his clothes regular, would at least take care of his horses and mules, especially out here where these animals were his livelihood. But no. Since there was a goodly number of men at the station just now, and me and Shad were latecomers, we volunteered to sleep in the stables. This warn't no hardship for us since we'd done it lots of times before. But the swarms of flies in there drove us out before we'd hardly got settled good. They were nearly driving the animals wild, too. It was a calm, starry night, and we threw our blankets down in a grassy spot about forty yards from the nearest wagon, and slept tolerably well.

I found out next morning that Harrison Sevier, the station keeper, did his best to keep the place clean of flies, and had his hostelers hard at it all the time shoveling out the stables, but there was something about this place that just attracted these pests. It was either Egan's garbage, or the presence of water in the nearby creek and sloughs, or maybe there was just plenty of live flesh for them to feast on. Anyway, Sevier was fighting a losing battle, because there warn't no screens for the windows, and a man could wear out his arm and a dozen fly swatters a day here and not get the job done. It would be about as hopeless as trying to dip the water out of the Missouri River.

Before we started out, Mr. Egan picked two of his volunteers and sent them back over the hard trail we'd just traveled to Camp Floyd, just a little ways south of Salt Lake City. They were to notify the commandant, Colonel St. George Cooke, about the stolen herd of cattle we'd run into. The Army was there to try to protect the emigrant wagon trains, but with only two or three hundred men they were stretched mighty thin.

The rest of us, fourteen in number, started West with the mail, just as the sun was poking up over the mountains behind us. It was a far cry from the way I'd gotten used to carrying the mail. The mules, hauling those four lumbering wagons, made slow time, what with the drivers not wanting to push them hard in the heat, and the soft sand and salt dragging at the wheels. It looked like we were going to have a mighty slow and dull journey. I tried not to show how bored I was as me and Shad rode along beside the wagons, because I trusted Egan's judgment. He probably knew this was the only sure way to get the mail through. But it reminded me of that old story Aunt Martha once told me about a race between the turtle and the rabbit — only she had some fancier names for them that meant the same thing. Anyway, I was interested in the story until I found out how dumb the rabbit was. He was naturally a lot faster, and he'd run and get a long way ahead, and then stop and rest and just dawdle around, figuring he had plenty of time, because the turtle could never catch him. Well, you might know, the rabbit got careless and did this once too often, and the turtle, who was just plugging along, passed him and won the race. I reckon Aunt Martha could never tell a story just for the fun of it. It always had to have what she called a "moral." Anyway, I reckon that was Egan's idea, too. Slow, but steady, will get there safe. That warn't what the Pony Express was started for, but I reckon it would have to do for now, because letting the Injuns pick off the lone riders wouldn't get the mail delivered at all.

Yet what started out as a long, tiresome ride changed for the better before that first day was even over. We were nooning on a flat stretch of desert, with nothing but glaring stretches of alkali all around, broken only by clumps of bunch grass. Egan made it a rule never to stop or to camp near hills or gullies or any place that could hide Injuns.

I was standing in the shade of one of the wagons, gnawing on a piece of leather that went by the name of dried beef, when a voice behind me said: "By golly, Lance, I didn't know you were on this trip."

I turned around, and there was Bill Cody, big as life! We gripped hands, grinning at each other like a couple of 'possums. In the three months since I'd last seen him in St. Joe, he'd filled out just a tad, and looked to be fit and healthy. He was still lean and wiry, but brown as mahogany and, judging from his grip, strong, too. He was still growing, of course, and I figured he was gong to be a good-sized man some day.

"Where were you?" I asked.

"Driving that lead wagon," he said.

I shook my head. "Reckon I was about half asleep this morning. And we were riding off to the side to keep out of the dust. Guess I never took a look in the wagons."

Then I remembered Shad who was standing next to me. "Bill, I want you to meet somebody." I introduced the two of them, and they seemed to take to each other right off.

By the time Howard Egan yelled for everybody to get ready to move out, me and Bill had already got to catching up each other on what we'd been doing since we last met. But the rest of the telling would have to wait for camp that night. Through Bill, me and Shad made the acquaintance of about half dozen of the other men on the wagons, pony riders Cody knew and had worked with.

The ride the rest of the afternoon didn't seem as dull, even though the terrain didn't change much. It just got drier and hotter, but we pulled our hat brims down and squinted into the glare and now and then sipped from our canteens and watched the sage-covered hills slide past, really slow. Since we'd come into the Utah Territory, I'd noticed that most of the low desert mountain ranges all ran roughly northwest to southeast. I reckon, from an eagle's eye view of this land, it would look like the rippled ridges of sand that are formed by receding water. Maybe that was the way this land was formed — by some gigantic flood. As our horses plodded along, I ventured this idea to Shad. I should have known what he was going to say. "Lance, that ain't no surprise to me. This just be what's left after de great flood de Lawd sent on de land when Noah and his kin and all de animals was in de ark."

I was getting a bit tired of Shad forever explaining things with Bible stories, so I says: "If that's what happened, then why don't the woods and hills in Missouri look like this, too?"

"Dey's rushes and green plants and rocks under water in lakes and ponds, Lance," he says. "It's just dat dis happens to be sand and salt and rocks out here. Besides, de great flood didn't last all dat long."

I saw I warn't going to get nowhere with this, so I just let it drop.

But after I'd got the idea of the lay of the land fixed in my head, I could see it wouldn't be no big problem to find my way, even on the darkest night. The only trouble was most of these long, low ridges looked pretty much alike. A man would have to live in this country a good while to be able to tell them apart.

That evening the wagons were pulled into a half circle, and we camped on a wide flat. Egan posted guards, and we all scrounged up as much dry brush and sticks as we could find for campfires. It was enough for cooking, but not near enough for keeping warm, we discovered, after the sun went down. But that didn't chill our interest in socializing with Billy Cody over some hot coffee. Me and Shad packed our pipes and lit up while we chatted.

"Can I share a cup o' that coffee?" Cody asked, kind of hesitating, after a few minutes.

"Why sure," I said, pouring him a tin cup full and handing it over. "Sorry I don't have no honey or sugar to put in it. Didn't you bring no coffee in them wagons?"

"No," he says, glancing around. "Mister Egan's a Mormon and don't believe in it, so he wouldn't let us pack any."

"I don't reckon he'd approve of these pipes, either," says I.

"Not likely," Cody says. "A goodly number of the fellas who work for the Express out this way belong to the Church of Jesus Christ of Latter-Day Saints," he says, giving them their official handle, which is a mouthful. "I'm not a Mormon and don't share their beliefs, but since there are more of them, their ways are what everybody goes by."

"Seems like they'd let a man alone, if he was of a different persuasion," says I, taking a draw on my pipe. "As I recollect, they were run out of a lot of places back East 'cause most folks there didn't agree with *them*. They ought to know what it's like."

"I reckon they do. That's why they came out here to this wilderness so they could do everything their own way."

"I hear their own way includes having several wives each."

Cody nods. "That's true. But a man can have only as many as he can support."

"Seems to me there'd be a lot of squabbling and fussing at each other with such an arrangement as that," I say.

"I reckon dey be like children," Shad chips in. "One child be more trouble den five or six, 'cause a bunch o' children can kinda entertain each other."

"You got a point there," Cody says, sipping his coffee. "But I don't really know, since I've never had a chance to spend any time in a home where polygamy is practiced."

"That's got to be tough on the women," I say.

"Probably not," Cody says. "There's several of them to split up the work . . . washing and cooking and sewing and taking care of the young 'uns, so it don't put too big a load on any one wife."

"But with more wives, there'd be more children, so there'd be more work," says I.

"I hadn't thought of that," he admits. "But I think the whole idea is to have big families to help on the farms and to raise more people in the Mormon religion."

"Seem like each one o' dem wives'd feel mostly like a house nigger," Shad says, sort of serious and thoughtful after listening to this discussion. I reckon he would know, having been on the wrong side of slavery a goodly portion of his life.

I use the head of a shingle nail I carry to tamp down the glowing ember in my pipe bowl and spit to one side as the smoke bites my tongue. "I reckon that business of having more than one wife was what really riled up the Gentiles and the government," I say.

"Jealousy," Cody says, and we all laugh.

"You're right," I say. "I reckon a lot o' men think it'd be a great thing to have a houseful o' wives. And they're mad because their religions don't allow that."

"It'd be like somebody starting a religion that teaches you can drink all the whiskey you can hold, or steal anything you want. Just figure out something that you want to do, and then start a religion that justifies it."

We all chuckle while we're turning this over in our heads. But then Cody says: "I shouldn't have said that, 'cause the Mormons are good people, probably better than most, and they're hard workers. Sober and industrious, Egan calls 'em. And those who really believe and practice what it teaches, deny themselves any kind of stimulant or tobacco, so they're probably healthier, too."

"And a lot of poor Mormons probably don't have but one wife, like most other men," I say.

Cody nods. "And some of them aren't married at all, although, as a general thing, they get hitched pretty young." He drains his cup and holds it out. "How about a refill? I don't care if it keeps me awake all night. I haven't had a decent cup of coffee in a couple weeks since I came to help out on this division."

"Do you reckon you'll be going back to ride in western Nebraska as soon as the Pony starts running again?" I ask.

"Probably so. That's nearer to my home. I just came out as a volunteer with some of the other fellas when things shut down. Thought maybe I could help get the mail through Indian territory."

"I've heard some o' the men calling this area Paiute hell," I say.

"From the weather, and the looks of the country, you could probably leave the Paiute part off and be right on the mark."

Shad nods, puffing on his pipe. "Dis be about as close to de real thing as I ever want to be," he agrees.

We rambled on, talking until everyone but the sentries was bedded down in the wagons or around the dying campfires.

161

I told Cody the story of me and Shad and all the adventures and close shaves I'd had since we'd parted company in St. Joe. Cody allowed he hadn't had no adventures to match that, but then allowed that he didn't want none like that, either.

Finally we run out of stuff to say, except good night, and Cody starts toward his wagon. But then he stops and comes back and says to me in a low voice: "By the way, I know that was you who slipped those two double eagles under my door back at the Patee House in St. Joe."

I suddenly feel like a kid caught lying in school.

"I just wanted to say thank you. That kept me and my family going until I got my first pay. Don't know what I'd have done without it. I want to pay you back." He reaches into his pocket.

"It warn't a loan," I say. "Forget it. Maybe you can help me out some day."

"You sure?"

"I'm sure."

"There ain't many people who'd do that for a stranger," he says. "I won't forget it." He grips my hand and then disappears into the dark.

Cody and Shad and me were all pretty tired the next day, but we didn't care. I dozed in the saddle a few times when the heat kind of baked me into a stupor.

We stopped at Jacobsville and Dry Well to drop off some mail, but that was all, since there warn't nobody out this way to send any mail to, except for some newspapers to the station keepers. Most of the mail was letters and official documents going through to California.

We camped that night near the Smith Creek station, and the three of us had another good visit, but this time we called it a night a little earlier.

The next day we sighted several Injuns on horseback. But they were a good ways off, watching us from the top of a hill about a mile away. If they were looking for trouble or some easy prey, I guess they were disappointed, because they just disappeared, and we didn't see no more of them.

In the early afternoon we passed the Cold Springs station. It was a good-sized building of several rooms, built of native fieldstone. The corral was even included as a roofless room, attached to the rest of the building. It was in the middle of a sage-covered desert. We stopped just long enough to water the animals and ourselves, fill our canteens and water casks, while Howard Egan had a meeting with the station keeper and the three hostelers.

Then we moved on and, late in the afternoon, reached Sand Springs station. It was located in a shallow valley between two low desert mountain ranges. Except for the seeping springs that come from God knows where, it was about as bleak and dry a place as I'd ever seen. The late afternoon sun was slanting down across the alkali flats, but most of the valley was just drifting sand dunes, with hardly any scrub plants to hold them in place. Shad and I looked at each other, then at the barren land surrounding this rock station.

"How could a man live in a wilderness like this?" I ask.

"Dat spring be de onliest way," he replied, taking my question literally. His black face was dusted almost white from alkali blowing on a steady southwest wind. "Dis sho' don't look like de Promised Land."

We both grinned and lightened up the mood.

The wagon train halted here for the night. With sunset, the wind dropped down, and the night come on very clear and pleasant. We went to sleep on our blankets on the soft sand, staring up at the sparkling night sky. In spite of the people around me, I felt like I was clear to the end of the

163

earth, beyond all civilization.

The next morning, the mules were not hitched up, and no preparations were made to move on. Howard Egan had arranged to meet up here with the Bolivar Roberts party coming from the West.

And, sure enough, three wagons and some outriders come in, like clockwork, just before noon. It couldn't have worked out better. The rest of the day we spent just resting and socializing, and a lot of the riders getting acquainted with the riders from other divisions. There warn't no cattle at this station, but a mule that'd gone lame was slaughtered and the meat roasted over several campfires. I hadn't never ate mule meat, but Shad had. He said it was more toothsome than beef, and, sure enough, it was, but it was good to taste fresh meat again after a long time on jerky, dried fruit, and bread.

Shad seemed a bit backward when it come to meeting lots of them white riders and volunteers, but, except for a curious look or two, they accepted him without no comment. There was some mixed bloods amongst them riders, but I didn't see no other black men.

Egan swapped the mail with Bolivar Roberts, the other superintendent from Carson City, and the next morning both parties headed back the way they had come. I warn't looking forward to the long, dry trip back, but Cody and me swapped off now and again, with him riding my horse, and me taking a turn at driving the span of mules pulling his wagon. This give me a chance to get acquainted with two of the other men who was riding in the wagon. Then, sometimes, me and Cody just set on the wagon seat, talking and him driving while my horse followed along, tied to the tailgate. This made the return trip go a lot faster. Cody warn't no more than fifteen or sixteen years old, but he'd grown up on the Nebraska and Kansas plains and, like me, had to get out and hustle early to make some money to live. He had a little better upbringing and schooling than me, what with parents that cared about him and all. But we were enough alike that I felt a sort of kinship with him, almost like he was my younger brother, or a first cousin, maybe, but without none of the arguing and fussing that sometimes goes with being relations.

Shad didn't feel left out or nothing because of my being friends with Cody. Shad was about old enough to be Cody's father. And, besides, me and Shad were comfortable with each other, in our own way. It was just something I couldn't explain to nobody, not if my life depended on it.

When we got back to Deep Creek station, we'd been gone the better part of a week. I'd plumb lost track of the days, but when I got to counting up, I figured it must be about the twenty-first of June, which was the longest day of the year for daylight. But Harrison Sevier, the station keeper, who kept up with this sort of thing, set me straight. "It's only June fifteenth," he tells me when he and I begun discussing it. He points to a calendar hanging on the wall that has big, bold letters across the top of it that says USE THE BEST — MEXICAN MUSTANG LINIMENT — LYON MFG. CO. NEW YORK. I wonder why they call it *Mexican* Mustang if it's made in New York. I reckon some things just don't have no logical explanation.

The wagons stopped here overnight. Even though this was Howard Egan's home when he warn't in Salt Lake City, he planned to push on and return to Salt Lake, I reckon for another load of mail that's probably been stacking up there from the East.

"Barlow," he says to me, "when I come back from Salt Lake City, I will have more horses and men, as well as the mail. On my way back, I plan to restock each station along the way with fresh horses, and at least five men and all the supplies they'll need. Bolivar Roberts will be doing the same thing from his end. We'll bring tools and some wood to leave with the men to make repairs on the stations that have been raided and damaged."

I wait for him to say what all this has to do with me.

"I've decided to assign you to the Simpson Springs station, east of here, between Riverbed and Point Lookout."

"Yes, sir, I know where it is," I say. "But it was empty when we come past there."

"It is now," he says, "but I'm appointing a man named Cyrus Brown as station keeper. That will be your home station. You'll ride between Simpson Springs and Willow Springs, a distance of roughly sixty miles."

"What about Shad?"

"Oh, yes. Since the two of you are friends, I'll put him at Simpson Springs, too, as a stock tender."

"Thank you, Mister Egan. That would be great." I know my face is all over smiles. If he hadn't offered, I would've tried to persuade him to station us at the same place. But, then, if I'd known who this Cyrus Brown was, I might've requested that my home station be at Willow Springs.

Chapter Fifteen

Shad and me rode on up the back trail with the wagon train, said our good byes to Bill Cody, and dropped off at the deserted Simpson Springs station while the train went on toward Salt Lake City. There was still some supplies stored there, and we figured to make do until Egan come back through with more stuff in a week or so. Mr. Egan left us a Sharps and some ammunition, so we could defend ourselves and the station if we happened to be attacked.

After being around people for about ten days, it seemed almighty silent when that last wagon rolled away out of earshot. But me and Shad got busy cleaning up the place as best we could. This station hadn't been attacked, only abandoned, so it was just a matter of washing the utensils and bedding, digging around to see if any mice had got into the stored grain sacks, and such things as that. There warn't no animals except our own two horses to care for. It was kind of like being on a deserted island. I told Shad about the story of Robinson Crusoe that I'd got acquainted with when I was going to school. My schooling had ended before we got through the book, but I told Shad what I knew of the tale, and he seemed right fascinated with how a man could get along on an island like that all by himself. When I come to the part where the black man that Crusoe named Friday shows up, he really got interested, and wanted to know all the details. Well, I'd forgot a good many of them, so I invented a few. There warn't no copy of the book handy, so I had to conjure up the remainder of the story myself. Disappointing Shad warn't my style, and I hadn't had no practice lying lately, so, when we sat around the stove after supper of an evening, I just took a deep breath and turned myself loose, making up the durndest things I could think of. The next day, I snuck around and jotted down some notes with a pencil and paper I found, just to make sure I didn't forget what I'd told him, in case he asked me to repeat it some time. I didn't figure there was nothing wrong with this, because I was doing it only for entertainment and to kill time. It didn't hurt nobody, and Shad enjoyed it. He was a mighty kindly and thoughtful man, but he warn't long on imagination, so he really liked hearing somebody else spin yarns.

But three days later, before Howard Egan had a chance to return, a force of about forty men rode up to our station in a swirl of dust. Bill Cody was with them, along with several of the volunteers who'd been on the wagons.

"We're tired of waiting around, and just being on the defense against the Indians," Cody says to me and Shad. "While the company is shut down, a bunch of the boys decided we'd go after them. Mister Egan is having a hard time buying good, fast horses in the Salt Lake Valley, so we got up an expedition on our own to go after some of the stock that's been stolen."

I look over the men who're sitting their horses there in the sun. Every man is armed with a rifle and at least one pistol, and they're a hard-looking bunch. Bill Deweese, station master at Point Lookout where we'd spent the night, is with them, too.

"Stock tenders, ranchers, and pony riders, mostly, with a couple of stage drivers," Cody says, seeing me giving the men the once over. "Why don't you and Shad ride along with us? Shouldn't be gone more than a few days."

I look at Shad, and he gives me a nod. "We'll go," I say. "Give me a few minutes to pack some grub into our saddlebags."

Less than twenty minutes later, we're packed and saddled.

"I hope Mister Egan knows about this," I say, swinging into the saddle. "I'd hate for him to come back and find us gone."

"Don't worry. We told him what we were doing, and he approved."

"Hang on a second. I'll leave him a note, just in case."

I jump down and run back inside and write him a note saying where we're gone, and put it under the edge of the coffee pot on the big table where he'll see it. A minute later I'm back outside, and we're riding off, leaving the Simpson Springs station as deserted as we'd found it.

"Bill Hickok, one of the wagon drivers, is heading up this party," Cody tells me as we ride out. "Some of the boys who can track found the marks of a herd of shod horses heading north toward the mountains east of Salt Lake. We just took a detour down this way to see if you and any of the other boys at the stations wanted to join us."

"You had to come right by Camp Floyd," I say. "Why didn't you get the soldiers to help?"

"These stolen horses belong to the company, not to the Army," he says. "Besides, there weren't but a handful of soldiers left there. Most of the others are out trying to protect the emigrant trains, or running down that herd of cattle you and Shad saw."

I nod. "Just as well we're doing this ourselves. Thanks for coming to get us. You think we'll have a chance of catching up with them?"

"Hell, yes," Hickok replies, who had ridden up in time to hear my question. He was tall and much too heavy to be an Express rider, and he wore his hair long as did Cody. "They've left a trail a blind man could follow, so I don't reckon they're in fear of any pursuit. They probably think all the white men are cringing in their fortified way stations, waiting to be attacked."

"There's not much way they could hide the trail of that many horses in this desert," I point out, but not being sassy or nothing so I don't rile this long-haired leader. "But it might be a different story if they get into the mountains."

"We'll see," he says, tight lipped and determined looking, as he rides on ahead.

By the next afternoon our party entered the red-rock gorges and verdant ravines of the mountains east of the Salt Lake Valley. Here our trackers discovered where another band of Indians had joined the first, and the trail turned northward. It was late in the day, and Hickok decided to camp. We were in a beautiful little valley with plenty of green grass for the horses and a clear stream running down the middle. The leaders held a conference that night that didn't include us. Cody told me later he overheard some of what was said, and that Hickok and the others were a mite nervous we'd find more Injuns than we'd lost. But they figured a well-armed party of forty experienced frontiersmen could handle whatever came. And, as Hickok had indicated, surprise was on our side.

The trackers had said we warn't more than twenty-four hours behind, but it took us another two days to catch up. Knowing we were getting close, we kept a sharp lookout and went forward more cautious than before.

"Do you reckon these are all Paitues?" I asked Cody as we rode side by side.

He shrugged. "Don't know. Could be there're some Gosiutes, Shoshones, or Bannocks."

"Those tribes don't usually join forces, do they?" I asked.

"Not as a rule. But the white man is posing a bigger threat than any of them realized. I guess they can see their lands are being taken, so maybe they've stopped fighting each other for a while. All I know is, I've never seen the tracks of that many Paiutes at one time, although I hear tell they fought in large

170

bands over near Pyramid Lake."

"And, make no mistake," one of the men nearby said, "the Paiutes are fierce fighters. They may be poor and ragged as a rule, but they're warriors. Thank God, not all of 'em have modern weapons. A lot of them still use a bow with flint-tipped arrows. And they're mighty proficient with 'em, too."

"Charley, quit tryin' to scare these boys with your wild tales," Hickok said, edging his horse closer. "You know you've never been in a fight with the Paiutes in your life."

"Maybe not," the man grumbled into his beard, "but I knew a man over near Carson City who did battle with 'em."

Late that afternoon, two of our outriders spotted a number of horses grazing in a valley about three miles ahead. They saw no Injuns, but the grazing horses was a fairly sure sign they were about.

Hickok and the leaders put their heads together and decided, on Hickok's advice, to wait until dark, while our scouts located their encampment. Then, well into the night, we'd hit them with a surprise attack, riding through their camp, just whooping and shooting, to stampede the horses and drive them off. It all sounded simple enough, but I heard some of the men say that the Injuns, judging from the tracks of their unshod ponies, outnumbered us at least three to one. If our surprise didn't work, we'd sure enough be up to our eyeballs in Paiute manure.

The scouts located the camp, and luck was with us. The Injuns warn't expecting nobody to follow them and hadn't posted no sentries. So our surprise worked. We took turns napping, and waited until only an hour or less before dawn, when they was all asleep. Then we bunched up, quiet like. My heart was pounding like I'd run ten miles. Then Hickok give the signal, and we charged down the valley, yelling and firing like there was twice as many of us. Well, we spooked all the horses and went thundering through their camp, trampling campfires and blankets and gear and scattering the Injuns every which way. We got not only our own horses, but all of theirs, too. We run them up and out of the valley and was gone a good long ways by the time it come up light enough to see good an hour later. By then, we were able to slow down and the horses were winded enough so we could handle them without no trouble. Four or five men had stayed behind for about ten minutes to take a few shots at the Injuns to give them something to think about whilst they were running around on foot, trying to get their bearings. Then these men rode on and caught up with us when we were a good dozen miles away and had brought the herd to a walk.

Shad sidles his horse up alongside mine and says: "Dose Injuns be like de Pharaoh when de angel o' death come callin'."

I grinned. "About as surprised, I reckon. But, if we killed any of 'em, it was probably some wild shots by accident, or the horses might have run down one or two."

Two more days of driving the herd brought us to Salt Lake City where a few of the best of the hundred or so Injun ponies were kept by the company, and the rest were sold for cash. Our own horses, marked with the X P on the hip, were turned over to Howard Egan. He was still looking for good, fast ponies because of the heavy toll that desert country took on the company stock. The whole idea was for the riders to outrun any Injuns they saw, not to fight them. And, to do this, they had to have better, faster, stronger horses.

Shad and I said good bye to Bill Cody and the rest of the men and rode on back south to our Simpson Springs station where we spent the next four days hashing over the adventure we'd just had, and working around to clean up and put the station in good order. During this time we didn't see hide nor feather of an Injun, which was fine by me.

Then Howard Egan come back through with the same four wagons and about thirty men who were driving along a herd of ponies. He told me he hadn't been able to hire as many men as he wanted on short notice, so he could leave us only one hosteler to help Shad. This was a young fella who was 'way too stocky to be a pony rider, but he seemed nice enough. He had a round, chubby face, but at least he looked to be made up of more muscle than fat. His name was Carter Barrington. It remained to be seen how good he was with animals, especially the six ponies the riders cut out of the herd and ran into our corral. They were kicking and biting each other and looked to be more than half wild. It was a wonder to me how they were able to drive them down from Salt Lake City.

But we didn't have but a brief time to size up Barrington, because then Egan was introducing our station keeper, Cyrus Brown. I distrusted Brown right off for two reasons. He didn't have a firm handshake, and he didn't look me in the eye when he spoke.

"Mister Brown is a first cousin of the Brown who is Postmaster General in Washington," Egan says, proud like, as if this fact were going to make Cyrus a bigger man in our eyes.

"Pleased to make your acquaintance," says I, lying in my teeth. But I try to be polite and introduce him to Shadrack. Brown don't hardly give him a second glance, and don't bother to shake his hand, which tells me a lot about the man.

First chance I get, I catch Egan by himself near the stone corral that's about sixty feet from the station and ask him about this Cyrus Brown..

"I was told to appoint him by my boss," Egan says, kind of apologetic. "He wouldn't be my first choice for a station in this part of the country. But his cousin, the Postmaster General, did this company a big favor back in May."

173

"How's that?" I ask, kind of gritting my teeth at another political appointee, and thinking of Nathan Rising, a do-nothing station master if I ever saw one.

"Postmaster Brown annulled the contract held by George Chorpenning to carry the mail from Salt Lake to Sacramento, and awarded that contract to the Central Overland California and Pike's Peak Express Company — the Pony Express — with payments of two hundred and sixty thousand a year. George Chorpenning was hauling the mail with coaches and mules, and I'm sure we'll do it much better and faster. But, still, the Postmaster General did the Pony Express a great favor. And, m'lad, whether you know it or not, favors in this world must be repaid. Appointing his cousin as station master here was certainly the least we could do to show our gratitude."

"Yes, sir," I say, not liking it one bit, but swallowing any more words because it ain't really any of my business, since I'm only a rider and not one of the higher-ups in the company. I'm grateful that Egan had even given me this much information. "Thanks, Mister Egan. We'll get along."

"Now, Lance," Egan continues, "on another subject, we're in a rush to get the mail runs back on some kind of regular schedule. The longer we're shut down, and have to haul the mail by slow wagons, the worse the chances the company has of securing the full mail contract which is worth almost three quarters of a million dollars a year. So, I'll push this train through as fast as possible to meet with Bolivar Roberts, and secure and supply the stations along the way. Then, the Pony will be off and running again. What I'm saying to you is, be ready to ride within the next few days."

"Yes, sir."

"And that means getting a hand on those horses we just left you. Only two of those six are horses your party recovered from the Paiutes. The other four were the best mounts I could buy in Salt Lake City. But they must be the spawn o' the divil himself, by the look of 'em." He was leaning on the top of the circular corral wall and, quick like, yanked his hand back as one of the mustangs took a nip at his fingers.

"Better than a bunch of broken-down plugs," I say, trying to grin, but my stomach's knotting up, thinking about having to finish breaking these wild animals that look to be spoiling for a fight.

"The rest of those recovered horses that were still fit for service I'm spreading around to the other stations," Egan says.

The wagon train hauled out in less than an hour toward the next station to the south, leaving me and Shad with the two new men. We did our best to show them everything about their new home and make them feel welcome. Barrington seemed willing to learn and was friendly. He claimed he'd had some experience dealing with horses on his father's ranch near Salt Lake. Cyrus Brown, on the other hand, said little, and only grunted when I showed him how the station was laid out, where all the supplies were stored, and where the well had been dug inside the corner of the middle of the three rooms so we'd have water in case of a siege — showing considerable foresight on the part of the people who'd built this place. But Brown never changed expression. He had the hang-dog look of a man who's been severely put upon. I couldn't tell if he was mad because he'd been stuck 'way out here instead of being given some plusher assignment, or if this was the way he reacted to everything.

Cy Brown was a rather short, middle-aged man who was sort of going to pudge in the middle. He had light brown hair, parted in the center, and a thick, brown mustache that drooped like it was real tired on both sides of his mouth. He was dressed in brown boots and brown corduroy trousers, a pale yellow shirt, and a brown leather vest. A layer of light brown dust covered him from head to toe, so that, if he stood real still and closed his eyes, you'd have had a hard time telling him from a sandstone statue.

We came back into the main room of the station where he'd tossed his tan felt hat and his leather grip when he first entered. "Let's get a couple of things straight," he says, pretty blunt, speaking up for the first time since I'd met him. "I'm in charge of this station, and anything I say goes. My orders and my instructions are to be carried out to the letter. Is that understood?"

Well, you can bet I was taken back, hearing this come out of this dusty, little man. I take another look at him. Maybe he's some kind of former military man, some colonel of volunteers to be spouting orders like this. After the surprise wears off, I have a hard time choking back a laugh. I'd heard this kind of snappish talk from bosses before, but this man warn't my boss. I would just live and ride out of here, but I didn't take orders from this barking bulldog.

"What're you referring to?" I ask, kind of cautious, looking over at Shad and Barrington, who're both gawking at Brown.

"Just what I said," he growls in a deep voice, taking in the other two with a black look.

"I don't notice anybody bucking your authority," says I. But then I add: "I'll sure do everything I can to work with you." I don't say it nasty, but maybe he'll get the hint that I ain't under his direction.

"Just so there's no misunderstanding about that," he says again. "O K, let's get busy and get this place cleaned up," he says, rubbing his hands together.

Shad and me look at each other, thinking the same thing, I reckon. We'd just spent most of a week cleaning up.

"You . . . what's your name again?"

"Shadrack."

"Okay, Shad, you get a shovel and scoop the manure out of that corral. It's a mess. Spread it around on the ground near the south side of the building. If this soil isn't completely barren, and the heat doesn't get 'em, maybe we can grow some fresh vegetables."

Then he turns on Barrington. "You're good and husky. Start moving all the food stuffs into that second room. And stack it so we can easily get at everything. Put the grain for the animals in the third room, nearest the corral, along with the tack and tools."

"Yes, sir."

"Now then, you . . . Barlow. Is there a tin bathtub in this place?"

"No, there's not. Just one round washtub, but it's too small for bathing."

"It'll have to do for now. Fill it with water from the spring and set it in the sun to warm. I want to wash some of this road dust off."

"There's a well inside . . . ," I begin, but he cuts me off.

"I said to draw the water from the spring. Our first project will be to rock up a bathing pool near the spring that will be constantly filled by the flow."

"There's no mortar here," I say.

"Look around you, man," he says, kind of sneering. "There's local clay everywhere to make it. Where do you think the mortar for these rock walls came from?"

I can feel my face going red, but just choke off the words I started to say about not being his personal lackey. I go off to fetch the wash tub. I set the tub outside and then commence to fill it with a bucket from the spring which means carrying it from about fifty yards away.

While Brown's out splashing off the dirt, I stood in the main room of the station and took a close look around. I'd paced it off earlier with my three-foot stride, and the whole building was just over fifty feet long, and thirty-five feet wide, divided into three rooms with canvas hanging in the doorways between each. Ceiling beams support a willow thatch roof that's covered over top with a sandy, loamy soil. The two small windows have glass in them, and there were rifle loopholes in the rock walls on all sides. The outside door was made out of the back end of a wagon box. The furniture in this main room was one large, rough, plank table in the middle, flanked by two log benches. There were also some three-legged stools. There was a smaller table near the fireplace where me and Shad had arranged a tin coffee pot, iron knives, forks, and the pewter spoons. On the several pegs driven into the walls around the room somebody had hung spare clothes, spurs, quirts, rifles, and revolvers. A shelf beside the door held a tin bucket, wash basin, and a tin can we used for a dipper. The whole floor was just smooth-packed clay, same as the floors in the other two rooms. I pulled the canvas door aside and took a look into the middle room where Carter Barrington was at work. There were two sets of bunks against two walls that would sleep four men. Underneath them were piled harness, saddles, sacks of wheat, oats, meal, potatoes, and onions. There was an iron stove set on some flat stones in the middle of the room. The place did double duty as a bedroom and storage room. I had to admit it looked pretty junky, but me and Shad could never hire out as housekeepers. We'd done the best we could, but I guess it warn't good enough to suit Brown. I reckoned I'd just have to stay clear of him as best I could until I got to riding again. But I felt sorry for Shad having to deal with him. I'd gotten Shad into this, and already I'd begun to regret it. If things got too bad, I figured I could get Egan to transfer him. Having been a slave, Shad could probably put up with men like Brown better than I could. I turned back from watching Barrington dragging sacks out from under the bunks. Before he was through, I figured Brown would have Barrington feeling like a slave, too.

I heard the horses whinnying and galloping around in the corral, and remembered Shad was out there trying to clean it. I figured I'd better get out there and give him a hand before he got kicked or stomped. At the very least, I needed to get our own two mounts out of there as well as Barrington's and Brown's before those wild mustangs did some damage to our saddle horses. Cleaning manure out of an outdoor corral warn't usual procedure, so I don't know why Brown had ordered it, unless he just wanted to fertilize a garden.

As I headed out the door with the manure fork in hand, Brown looks up at me. He has his shirt off and is drying himself with a towel he must have got out of his grip. He looks kind of like a squashed-down candle with that white roll around his middle.

"I want the bedding stripped off those bunks and hung outside to air out," he says. "We'll wash it later."

"Already did it last week," I answer over my shoulder, without stopping.

"I've changed my mind about that third room," he says to me. "Just store the feed in there . . . not the tack. I may want to use that room for an indoor stable if the Indians or the weather get too bad. There's already a ramp built into it."

"Tell Barrington," I say, almost out of earshot now. "He's in there working."

This man's going to be big trouble I can see already. But maybe he'll settle down. Some men are like that — they come into a strange group just snarling and snapping to establish their own place in the pack. What he says about the weather

179

is probably true, though. Egan had told me that Simpson Springs looked to be in a low desert between mountain ranges, but it was actually almost five thousand feet above sea level. This whole area was a high desert. No wonder it got cold at night, even in mid-summer. I could imagine what it would be like with the wind whipping across these open spaces in January. That fireplace and iron stove warn't inside there just for cooking.

Chapter Sixteen

Early next morning Brown saddled up and rode out before Shad had even finished fixing breakfast. The three of us didn't ask him no questions. I think we were glad to see him go and hoped he'd stay away all day or longer.

Barrington had sidled out to the corral and come back in just as Shad was dishing up some hot flapjacks and bacon.

"I watched him for a good long ways," he said. "He's headed straight for the Riverbed station."

"There ain't no hills between here and there, and I noticed you can just barely make out that station from here," I said. "It's about eight miles away, but, when there ain't too much dust in the air, it looks like a black dot right near the horizon."

"Why's he going down there?" Barrington wondered aloud for all of us.

"Maybe he wants to compare notes with the station keeper, or just be neighborly," I say.

"There's nobody there. Mister Egan told me on the way down here that the word is out about that place being haunted by desert fairies, and he couldn't find anybody to take it."

Then I remember Deweese telling us that very same tale, and the eerie wailing noise I'd heard there. But I keep this last to myself, lest Barrington take me for one who believes in ghosts. With Shad it was a different story. He'd been brought up to believe in witches and ghosts and spells and such. And, as moral and religious a Christian as he seemed to be, he hung onto this belief in the dark side, probably handed down from his African ancestors who didn't know no better.

After breakfast we just lolled around, enjoying our leisure and Brown's absence.

"I think I'll ride over to that hogback northwest of here and do a little hunting," I say around noon when the Sabbath hush had begun to hang heavy. There warn't nothing I could find to read. "Don't they call that Granite Mountain? I hear there's antelope over there."

"I wouldn't do that if I was you," Barrington says. "Mister Brown told me there'd be no hunting. I guess he doesn't want us that far away from the station, just in case of Indians. He said we'd do fine on the bacon and ham and dried beef the company supplies."

This raised my hackles some, because Brown ain't my boss. But I'd just let it slide for now. I may have to buck him later, but it won't be over something this slight. I try to calculate how long it'd take me to get over to that mountain range and back with a little time for some hunting. It'd be at least the rest of the day, so I give up the idea, since there ain't no telling when Brown will return.

Brown comes back late that afternoon around supper time. He come riding up and dismounted, giving his horse over to Barrington to care for. His horse ain't lathered, and don't act too fagged out, so Brown's taken it mighty easy with him, or else he ain't gone too far. I don't say nothing out loud, but figure he must've ridden on to the Dugway station which is the next one, about ten miles beyond Riverbed. If he warn't aiming for no place in particular, he might've gone out for a ride to see the lay of the land hereabouts. It's a sure bet he didn't visit no towns, because there ain't any. And I don't even know of any ranches within a day's ride of here. It's just the Express stations, desert, and mountains.

When he comes inside, he doesn't look real dusty or tired, so I'm guessing he must've gone no farther than Dugway, a round trip of not more than thirty-six miles.

Me and Shad had fixed up some supper, and Brown just washes up and sets himself down at the table like he's used to being waited on. He don't hardly say nothing while we eat, but just takes himself off to look over the station when he's done. I can hear him talking to Barrington in the next room, and it sounds like he's giving more orders. Sure enough, Barrington comes out and asks me and Shad to help him move one of the bunks into a corner of the main room where we'd just had supper. He says, under his breath to me, that Brown wants to drape a canvas around his bunk and make some private quarters.

"Actually, I'm kind of glad about that," I say to the hosteler. "That'll give *us* a little privacy, too."

The worried look fades off his face, and he grins. "Hey, you're right. I hadn't looked at it that way."

The three of us lift off one of the upper bunks, slip out the wooden pegs that're holding it, and carry it into the big main room.

"Right there against the wall," Brown directs us. "Not too close to the fireplace."

We don't have no spare canvas to hang from the ceiling beams to close off his berth, so we use some extra blankets. After we got things arranged to his liking, Brown just disappeared into his bunk with a book, and we didn't see no more of him that night.

Two days later, he made another ride down toward River-bed.

"Where're you off to?" I ask, kind of casual, as Barrington helps him saddle his horse.

"I'll be back directly," he says, without answering the question.

I notice he talks like a fella I used to know who was from

west Tennessee. But I guess that shouldn't be surprising, seeing as how his cousin, the Postmaster General, is a Tennessean, too. After he rode off, we watched him, but he faded into the distant, shimmering heat.

We were almighty curious about where Brown went every day or so, and tried to figure out ways to follow him. But the terrain was too open to tag along behind in daylight without being seen. Of course, that didn't stop us from guessing, especially when we were sitting around with nothing else to do. I warn't about to start no project of rocking up a bathing pool for his highness, as he'd ordered me to do the first day he arrived. And none of the three of us was rushing to start trying to break those four wild mustangs Egan had delivered. In fact, we just sort of looked at each other and said something like: "Well, maybe the two Express ponies that're in the corral with 'em will gentle 'em down some." And that was as far as it went for a while. After watching those mustangs, I figured it would be tough to ride them when the time came. They looked like they had been handled just enough to make them mean.

But finally that afternoon, when we got more bored than cautious, we roped one of the mustangs, then snubbed him up to the post in the center of the ring. It took a little doing, but we got him saddled and bridled. Two fifty-pound sacks of grain tied together and flung over the saddle took the place of a small rider while we led the horse around. He kicked and jumped some, but not too bad. By the time we'd done the same thing with two more of the mustangs, we were ready to call it quits for the day. I still warn't sure I could stick on the back of any one of them, but I'd have to try.

And I got my chance the very next morning. A rider come busting in just after breakfast from the direction of Salt Lake City. "Here yuh go!" he yelled, swinging down from his mount, and yanking off the mochila. "It's all yours to Willow Springs!"

Even though I was expecting to be back in the mail-carrying business any day, he caught me off guard.

Shad grabbed his winded pony, and Barrington ran for the corral to rope a fresh one for me.

"Come on in and have some breakfast," I say to the rider. He looks familiar, and then I remember I'd seen him with the volunteers on the wagons two weeks ago.

"Your name's Roy Brice, ain't it?" I say, sticking out my hand.

"Sure is. And you're Lance Barlow." He grins.

"Excuse me, but I got to get moving," I say. "Help yourself to whatever's there."

I slip into my buckskin shirt, grab my gun belt off the bunk, and strap it on. I check to see what else I might be forgetting. Then I remember my spurs hanging on the wall. It seems like a long time since I rode the mail. This is my first run in the West on Egan's division, and I'm mighty near as nervous as I was that first time out of Marysville.

A few minutes later I'm out the door, and Shad's holding a pony ready for me. Barrington's roped one of the mustangs instead of one of our two tamer horses, but I ain't got time to change now. Shad's holding him up near the bit, but is standing back as far as he can to avoid those hoofs.

Cy Brown is off to one side, leaning against the wall, arms folded across his chest, just watching and not saying nothing. I don't let on like I see him as I take the mochila and fling it over the saddle. Then I grab the reins from Shad, pull the pony's head around hard to the left, take a grip on the saddle horn, and, in one quick motion, I'm up.

"*Yeeehaaa!*" I yell and let him unwind, pointing him down the trail toward Riverbed. I reckon he's so glad to be out of that corral, that he don't mind the weight on his back, because he just bolts toward the open spaces. I was ready for it, so I'm able to keep my balance, give him his head, and hold on.

After five miles or so I pull him in a little because there ain't no remounts at the deserted Riverbed station, and he's got to run another ten miles to Dugway before he can stop. But this critter seems to have the strength and stamina for it. I'm glad now that Shad and I didn't bust ourselves trying to bust *him*. Even if we'd been successful, we might have broke his spirit, and I'd rather have a feisty horse any day — one that has the will to run.

We lope on by Riverbed, and I don't see nothing unusual. It looks just like it did the last time I saw it. I'm tempted to stop and see if I can find any sign that Cy Brown's been here. But the mail has to go through, and I can't be dawdling along the way.

Riverbed disappears behind us, and pretty soon we're at Dugway where a fresh horse is being saddled as I ride up.

I give the hosteler a holler, but only have time to stretch my legs before I'm up and gone in less than five minutes.

Then it's on to the swing stations of Black Rock, Fish Springs, and Boyd's with nothing but the glaring desert of alkali and sand, speckled with clumps of greasewood and sage in between. The trail winds around the flanks of the low, arid mountains.

Finally, along about two in the afternoon by the sun, I'm approaching Willow Springs, the end of my run of sixty miles. My horse is tired, and crossing about a hundred yards of marshy salt flats is no fun for him or me. From a distance it looks like a frozen lake, with the sun glistening off the millions of tiny salt crystals. But, when we start across, my horse sinks to his fetlocks at every step.

At last we make the far side and ride up to the adobe

building of the Willow Springs station. I jump down and pull off the mochila. I don't see my relief rider, but I guess they ain't expecting me so soon since the Express is just now trying to get back on some kind of schedule.

Peter Neece, the station keeper, comes out the door. He don't look happy.

"Where's my relay?" I ask, handing over my pony to the hosteler I recognize as a man named Bob Lynch.

"He ain't here. His horse came in without him an hour ago. There was an arrow stuck in the mochila."

Well, my stomach just fell down amongst my bowels when I heard this. I guess the Injuns warn't giving up, just because Alexander Majors thought it was time to get to riding the mail again.

I go inside, and Neece says: "That's not the only bad news. The only horse I got has come down with what may be a case of glanders. Since it's contagious, I had to separate him from the horse that just came in by himself, all done in."

I can only stare at him, not knowing what to say.

"You'll have to take his mochila back over the same route you came," he says. "Maybe we can at least keep the east-bound mail going. Too dangerous for you to ride on west. The only problem is, you'll have to ride the horse you just brought in."

"Then I'll have to rest him at least four hours," I say promptly. "I didn't spare him none these last ten miles, and he's pretty tuckered out. I don't want to kill a good horse who gave it all he had."

Neece nods and says: "Good. Set yourself down and have a rest."

"I'll start back about six this evening," I say, sinking down on a bench as Neece pours me a cup of coffee. Through the open door I see Lynch walking my mount around to cool him off. Then he'll rub him down and give him some water.

I drink my coffee and stretch out on a bunk for a while. But I'm too keyed up to sleep and, after about thirty minutes, get up.

Neece comes back in from outside and says: "Fancy a game of checkers?"

He's a big, clean-shaven, square-shouldered man with curly, blond hair who don't seem to let nothing rattle him. I ain't in no mood for games, but then I figure he's trying to settle me down some so I say: "O K."

He gets out the checkerboard, sets it on a small keg between us, and we commence. He whips me nearly every game, but my heart ain't really in it.

About four o'clock, Lynch comes running inside and slams the door. "Indians!" he yells.

"How many?" Neece asks, very cool.

"Seven."

"They appear to be looking for trouble?"

"Don't know. They're just riding up, big as you please." His voice sounds a little shaky.

"I better see what they want," Neece says, rising and hitching up his gun belt.

"Be careful," Lynch says, stepping back behind the door where he can see out the crack.

I follow Neece outside. The Injuns rode up and stopped. There warn't one of them that'd been overfed, I could see, and they looked dirty. But being dirty in this sort of country warn't something that could be avoided most of the time. I guessed they was Paiutes. Four of them had long guns, and the rest had bows and quivers slung across their backs.

"Food," the one up front says, making an eating motion.

Neece nods, steps back inside, and picks up a fifty-pound bag of flour that I can see is about half full.

When the leader saw Neece hold out the sack with about twenty-five pounds of flour, he shook his head. "One sack for each," he said, pointing at his friends, one at a time.

Neece's face kind of clouded up, and he held up the bag again. "This is it. Take it or leave it."

The Injun shook his head again, so Neece tossed the bag back inside, and said: "Get out. Beggars can't be choosers. If you don't want that, then I'm not giving you a damn' thing."

The two of us stepped back into the station pretty quick, because they looked like this made them mad. Sure enough, as they started to ride off, they saw an old, lame cow standing under a shed four or five rods from the station. I reckon they decided to take out their anger on something, so each of them shot an arrow into that poor, old cow.

When Neece saw that, he went into a rage. He yanked out two pistols and stepped out the front door and commenced firing. Two of the Injuns were hit and fell dead right off their horses. The others took off, two of them taking a couple of shots at the station as they went.

Neece ducked back inside, banged the door shut, and shot the bar into place. His face was red, and his eyes just a-glaring. "Boys," he says, "when that riderless horse came in with the arrow sticking in the mochila about noon, I rode out a ways to see if I could find the rider. No luck there, but I did spot about thirty Indians camped in a cañon northwest of here. I know these Paiutes. They'll be on us as soon as it gets dark. We'll have to fight."

"They can't get at us as long as we're holed up in here," Lynch says.

"Not unless they can set the roof on fire, or something like that," Neece says. "But you saw what they did to our cow. They could do the station some real damage by burning down our two wooden outbuildings, steal or kill our horses, or maybe poison our spring, if they think about it. Or they might just hold us hostage in here until we get so thirsty we have to come out for water."

"What do you think we should do?" I ask. "Maybe we could all mount up and head for the next station."

"No," Neece says, shaking his head. "Damned if I'm going to let them have this station."

I can see his jaw working as he grits his teeth. You might know I'd have the luck to get stuck here with a man who's got all the fight of a cornered badger. For some reason, I think of Jane Holland, and wonder if I'll ever see her again. Maybe it won't matter, because she don't want to see me.

Neece sets there, thinking for a minute, then he says: "Tell you what. We'll fight 'em outside. They won't be expecting that. We'll go out about a hundred yards and lie down in the brush. When they get close, we'll fire. Then we'll keep moving, so they won't know where to shoot. They won't have a fixed target."

"What if they come in daylight?" Lynch asks.

"They won't. They're cowards. You could see that by the way they attacked that defenseless cow instead of coming after us."

I warn't too sure about this idea, but figured Neece has had more practice at this sort of thing than I have.

"We'll load up all the old guns we've got around here," he continues. "We'll be ready for them when they come. There are three of us. We can stand off the whole bunch of them."

I warn't too good at arithmetic, but three against thirty didn't seem like good odds to me.

Well, I can tell you, I was mighty tense while the time dragged on toward dark. When dusk finally begun to pull the curtain down, we saw a big dust cloud over toward the mouth of the cañon that was about six miles away.

"Now, listen," Neece said as we were taking our places outside, "when you fire, jump to one side, so if they shoot at the muzzle flash, you won't be there."

We lay down about six feet apart in the sage, and I was really hugging the ground, my slim .36 caliber Colt in my hand, and a second .44 Colt Dragoon Neece had given me stuck in my belt. An hour ago I'd gone outside the station and fired all six rounds of my own weapon at some rocks just for practice. And I put in the spare cylinder and shot it up, too. This was mainly so I could load up both of them fresh to be sure there wouldn't be no misfires.

Pretty soon we could hear their horses' hoofs striking the ground. It sounded like thousands of them, and they just blended into a rumble. When they got close enough, I could hear their yips and yells that made chills go up my back.

The soil was sandy where we lay, with clumps of grease-wood holding little hillocks of soil in place, while the wind had scoured out hollows in between. By the time the Injuns got close, it was almost dark. Neece and Lynch fired and jumped away into the darkness as the horsemen come thundering, full tilt, toward the station. It took them by surprise, and their mounts started milling. Streaks of flame darted back as the Injuns fired toward the blaze of our guns.

I jumped several feet to one side. I hadn't never been in an all-out gun battle, and I was scared out of my wits. I leapt from hillock to hillock, half the time forgetting to shoot my loaded pistols.

The yelling and the constant blasting of guns kind of stuns me, and I ain't aware of much other than a general roar. I don't know how long this went on, or if anybody was hit, because I was concentrating more on surviving. The last time I jumped, I landed in a dry wash, the top of which was about level with my back when I was on my hands and knees. Peek-

191

ing over the lip of the wash, I saw what looked like Injuns on horseback. They warn't moving. Could they be humps of sand topped with clumps of greasewood? It was too dark to tell.

Sometime or other, the noise of the shooting gradually died down and stopped. I lay where I was, hugging the bottom of the wash, thinking I could still hear hoofbeats. But, after a bit, I figured out it was only my heart pounding in my ears. Everything got very quiet, and I stayed still for a long time.

Finally I decided to creep out and see if I could find my horse, staked with a picket pin near the station. If he was still there, I'd ride on back to my home station at Simpson Springs and report that both Neece and Lynch were killed, and that I was the only survivor of the Paiute attack.

I went crawling on around the adobe station on my elbows and knees, gripping both pistols. A light was shining from the small window in the back wall, and I figured the place must be full of Injuns. I had a knot in my throat, knowing Neece and Lynch were gone. So, before I crawled off to find my horse, I just sunk down flat on the ground to gather my strength and listen. Maybe I could hear what they was up to. It never dawned on me they wouldn't be speaking English.

After a bit, I heard a voice outside, near the front of the station. "Did you find anything of him?"

Another voice answered: "No, I guess he's gone."

It was Neece and Lynch. I let out a sigh that could've been heard clear to Simpson Springs. I didn't get up or yell out, but just lay there until I heard the door shut, because then I was almost too ashamed to go in. But I finally went around front, opened the door, and walked in.

"By damn!" Neece called out, jumping up. "There he is. How far did you chase them? I knew you'd stay with 'em and probably bring back a half dozen," he grinned.

I never said too much about what I'd been doing, but I

think Neece knew pretty well what happened. I caught him looking at me funny a time or two, and I knew all the blood had drained out of my face. But he was a big man about it and never said nothing.

I didn't ride back that night with the mail, because Neece insisted I stay the night and get some sleep. He said he wanted to be sure it was safe, thinking maybe there was still a few Injuns skulking around somewhere, although he doubted it.

In spite of a few scary dreams, I slept good that night on account of being so worn out. The next morning we found five dead Injuns, and I helped scoop a grave out of the sand big enough to bury them all. It didn't bother me none to do them dead Injuns this service, because I knew that no shot of mine had killed any of them. But the sight of them dead bodies would bother my dreams for some time to come. I was glad Shad warn't here, because dead folks seemed to give him the willies worse than it done me. The two cow-shooters Neece had cut down earlier in the day had been carried off by their friends while we were holed up, waiting for dark.

The return ride to Simpson Springs was fast, with me switching horses at every station except Riverbed. As I passed each swing station, I told what happened, but it warn't until I got back home that I gave the details of that fearsome adventure to Shad and Barrington.

Chapter Seventeen

I didn't have much use for Cy Brown, but, since he was the station keeper, I gave him a bare-bones report of what happened. He didn't say nothing at all, only just nodded, his eyes going kind of squinty, so I don't know what he was thinking. Then I just walked off and went about my business.

But the Pony Express didn't let up. They'd gotten one of our riders, but Neece and Lynch had gotten seven of them. All that killing made me sick whenever I thought about it. So I just had to push it aside and put my mind on working around the station and staying busy between runs, even if it meant running errands for Brown. I don't mind doing favors for nobody, even a man who ain't my boss or friend, but Brown was so prideful and pushy about it that it just made me want to buck him for spite.

Anyway, I managed to stay busy until the next rider come through, going East, a couple of days later. Barrington and Shad got him a horse roped and saddled in jig time, and he was off. Since the Express warn't on any regular schedule yet, the hostelers never knew when a rider was due in, so they couldn't have a horse saddled and ready.

About eleven that night Shad and Barrington sat at the big wooden table, playing cards, which didn't interest me none, and I was getting ready to turn in for the night. Cy Brown had taken off on one of his rides and hadn't come back yet. Shad said this was only the second time he'd been gone this late, but Barrington pointed out that Brown hadn't left until late afternoon. Brown always rode down toward Riverbed on the regular trail; he never rode the other direction. We still wondered some about this, but the Injun troubles had kind of pushed the actions of the strange station keeper out of our heads.

I was sitting on my bunk, pulling off my boots, when I heard the thudding of hoofs outside, and we all three reached for our guns as we headed for the door. But it was just Bob Haslam, the pony rider, bringing in the mochila from the East.

I was tired, and didn't much cotton to the idea of taking a hard sixty-mile ride just now. Except when I wanted to be with Jane Holland, this was the only time I wasn't raring to go, day or night, to carry the mail.

Me and Haslam exchanged greetings, while Shad and Barrington worked together to get a horse ready. "Where's your station keeper?" he asked me.

"Don't rightly know. He rode out somewhere this afternoon and ain't come back yet."

"You got a key for the way pocket?"

"No. You got some mail for somebody out this direction? There's no mail to pick up here."

"There's a letter in there for you," he says.

"For me?" A funny feeling grabs my stomach when he tells me this. All I can think of is some kind of legal summons from Culbertson for stealing his nigger. But that couldn't be, because Culbertson don't have no legal claim to a free black man. Maybe he's faked some documents, like a bill of sale.

"Who's it from?" I finally ask.

"Haven't seen it. The letter was locked in the mochila when I got it. I was just told to drop it off here," Haslam says, stirring up the dying fire under the coffee pot on the stove.

Well, I was just burning to find out what was in that mochila. Maybe it was a letter from Ephraim Hanks. Whoever it was from, I hoped it warn't bad news.

"Maybe I can use a knife on that lock," I say out loud.

"I wouldn't advise that," Haslam says, sipping a cup of

coffee. "You couldn't get it open with a knife, anyway. You'd have to slit the leather."

I knew he was right. I'd just have to wait. Messing with the mail was one sure way to get myself fired. Then I remembered that Pete Neece could open it for me when I got to the end of my run. This thought made me itchy to get going.

By then the horse was ready, and Shad says: "You be careful dis trip, Lance. Dose Injuns be mo' dangerous den de militia or dat slave holder back home."

"You bet I will," I assured him, taking the mochila and fitting it in place over the saddle. "See you in a couple of days," I say, mounting up and spurring my pony away toward Riverbed.

A half moon is showing in a cloudless sky tonight, and the eight-mile run down to Riverbed goes quick. Just as I'm passing by the deserted station, I hear a horse whinny. My heart begins to pound, because I figure there's Injuns hiding behind those buildings, waiting to ambush me. I guide my pony away from the station, and spur him. But he has already run eight miles, and there's no speed left in him. It's usually about here that I ease back on his pace so he'll last to Dugway. I look for some place to take cover, but there ain't nothing near except the buildings of the station. When I see I can't get no more out of my horse just now, I ease him to a stop and dismount. He's breathing hard, and I just walk him, keeping him between me and the station. If I can't make any speed, at least this will make me a lot harder target in the moonlight.

I ease my Colt in the holster, hoping I don't have to use it, but glad I've got it, just in case. I wish my horse was fresh so I could be making some dust toward the next swing station. But, if wishes were horses, beggars would ride, as the saying goes.

There ain't no shots and no hoofbeats in the next couple

of minutes while I'm walking, easy like. Looking over the back of my horse toward the wood buildings, I figure maybe it was a wild horse I heard. But wild horses generally run in herds. Then I hear a thump, and I stop to listen, holding my breath. The light breeze brings me some sort of snuffling sound and another thump, like a hoof kicking the boards of a stall. *There's a horse or two in that stable,* thinks I. I stop walking, taking a deep breath to calm my beating heart. It could be Injuns, or it could be robbers, or it could be some traveler just camping here for the night. Wild horses warn't likely to put themselves up in a stable, unless maybe they wandered in after some grain left in the feed boxes.

But whatever, or whoever, it was, I just had to find out. I made the excuse to myself that my horse needed rest, which was true enough, but not the real reason. No sooner said than done. I dug out my picket pin and the attached line. Then I led my horse another fifty yards off, and pounded in the pin with a rock, hoping he wouldn't try to yank it loose from the sandy soil.

I started back toward the station, creeping along through the sage and greasewood and clumps of grass. If anybody was watching, I'd be easy enough to see out there in the clear moonlight. I slip out my Colt as I near the stable and ease up to the wall and then around to the front. The double doors are swinging wide open, and the breeze bangs one of them back against the side of the building. I let out my breath, figuring that's what I heard. But that don't explain the whinny. The moonlight is making the interior even blacker, but I slide just inside, my gun ready, holding my breath and listening. My nose picks up the fresh smell of horses, and I hear their soft snuffling and shuffling.

If there's horses here, there's bound to be men, I'm thinking. The station house was only about a hundred feet away, and the front door was on the far side from me. I took a deep breath and decided as long as I'd come this far, I'd check there, too. It wouldn't take but a few more minutes, then I'd be on my way. But I knew, deep down, somebody was in that station. If Shad was here, he'd say it was foolish to go nosing around into something that didn't concern me. *You just be lookin' fo' trouble,* I could almost hear him saying. But it was like something was pulling at me. I had to know. There warn't no turning back now. I eased on out of the stable and started toward the station.

Whilst I'm crossing that open space, I hear a sound that nigh makes me wilt down in my tracks. It's a low, moaning wail, like I'd heard the first time me and Shad stopped here in daylight. My knees is so wobbly I have to drop down and crawl the last few feet into the shadow of the building. It's a keening sort of sound, rising and falling, mournful like. My eyes are wide as they can get, and I'm looking every which way, but still don't see nothing out of the ordinary.

I lick my dry lips and try to get some spit going so I can swallow. I finally buck up some, reasoning that if I can't see it, then it can't get me, whatever it is. But it has 'most scared me out of a year's growth. Shad would've been running for his horse by now, figuring the desert fairies were after him. But my knees were so weak I couldn't run now if my life depended on it.

After a couple minutes the wailing nearly dies away, and I get to my feet. There ain't no windows at the back side, so I slide around to the side, past the rock chimney, and then to the front.

I stop short, froze in my tracks. There's some low lamplight showing out the small window and around the cracks of the door. At last my shaking stops long enough for me to ease up to the window and look in. The bottom of the sill is nearly

198

as high as my chin, for safety reasons, I reckon. I slip my hat off and let it hang down my back and put one eye around the edge. I thought I'd got over most of my shock and fear, but what I seen just then nearly made me faint. It's Cyrus Brown and three Paiutes. They're standing by the table, talking. The only reason I could think of that Brown would be here was because he's trying to hash out some kind of peace settlement with them, so's to make himself an even bigger man than he already thinks he is. But, somehow, I didn't believe that was it. And the next few minutes proved my hunch right.

I pull back from the window, and, by pressing one ear against the board wall, I could just make out some of the words.

"No more rifles until you . . . ," Brown's voice says.

"We kill rider . . . braves die in fight. . . ."

"Our agreement was . . . food and . . . ," Brown says.

"You give us more guns, we stop ponies. . . ."

Most of what I could hear, I realized, was leaking out of the cracks around the door because the window was tight and the plank wall thick.

As near as I could make out, they were having some disagreement about guns and food and gold. The gist of the thing seemed to be that Brown warn't going to give what he promised because they hadn't delivered on their promise to shut down the Pony Express.

A chill went up my back, and my hair mighty near stood on end. It was words I'd never hoped or expected to hear from no white man, especially one who worked for Russell, Majors, and Waddell. Brown was the lowest kind of trash, selling out the lives of his fellow workers.

I listened another minute or two to make sure I warn't misunderstanding what was going on. Then I slipped away in the shadows as silent as death. I don't think I even took a breath until I got clear to the other side of the stables, then went to fumbling in my buckskin shirt for the spurs I'd taken off and wrapped in my bandanna.

I found my horse and led him a good long ways off before mounting up and galloping on down the trail toward Dugway. My mind was in a whirl. When I reported this, I'd be questioned close and had to be clear in my own mind that there warn't no mistake about what I'd just seen and heard. To me, it was as plain as a wart on your nose. But what to do about it? I had to report it, but who to? Shad would be told, of course. But should I just blab it to the next station keeper? No. I didn't know most of them that well. Even Pete Neece at Willow Springs was a man I'd only met lately. Could he be trusted, or not? He'd fought hard for the company. Surely he was loyal. Who else was in on this plot to betray the company? Brown couldn't do it all by himself. I had to be careful who I told. And why would Brown do such a thing?

I was most of the way to Willow Springs before it finally dawned on me. I'd plumb forgot how much politics had to do with the Pony Express. Or, more truly, with the *route* of the Pony Express. Brown was the first cousin of the Postmaster General who was a Tennessean. The Southerners in Congress wanted the Express to go by the longer route through Southern territory. If the central route, straight across from St. Joe to San Francisco, was not practical, then the Express mail would have to be re-routed to the south. And about all that could keep it from being practical year around was the weather, or hostile Injuns. The pony riders had already showed they could ride through deep snow drifts in the Sierras and burning deserts and hail storms. So the only thing left that could stop the Express was the Injuns. And Brown was bribing them to do just that.

Before I got to Willow Springs, I'd decided not to say nothing about this until I could talk to Shad. I figured Howard Egan, the division superintendent and a devout Mormon, would be the one I should report this to.

Another westbound rider I didn't know was waiting when I got to Willow Springs, sometime just after daylight. I dismounted and tossed him the mochila. Bob Lynch took my lathered pony.

Just as the rider was throwing the leather mochila across his horse, I yelled: "Hold it!" In all the excitement I'd almost forgot my own letter.

Neece unlocked the way pocket and found the letter addressed to me. I took a quick look at the creased envelope and the canceled stamps and the handwriting. There warn't no return address, so I still didn't know who sent it. But I just shoved it inside my buckskin shirt to wait until I was alone to open it.

The relay rider galloped away, and Neece offered me some breakfast. My stomach was so churned up, I felt about half sick. "No, thanks," I said. "Not hungry."

But when I smelt that bacon frying, I changed my mind and had a couple slices with bread and some coffee. After that, I took a walk around outside to settle myself and watch the sun come up. It promised to be another beautiful day, but pretty hot, dry, and windy.

There were two horses in the corral, so Neece had gotten some replacements. When I come back inside, he told me he'd hitched the dead cow to one of the horses to drag her about a quarter mile away for the buzzards to finish. He also had to shoot the horse that had glanders and bury him to keep the disease from spreading.

"Did you ever bury a horse, Barlow?" he asks, washing out his frying pan in a bucket. "Helluva lot of digging."

Then he goes on to tell me that the murdered pony rider had been found and buried where he fell by a search party from Deep Creek. "There warn't much left of him, I hear, after the varmints had been at the body."

I was feeling a mite poorly and didn't want to hear no particulars about that, so I excused myself and went off to lie down in a bunk in the other room.

I was really tired and didn't even open my letter right away. I just put my hand on it inside my shirt and closed my eyes. But curiosity wouldn't let me sleep. So I finally sat up, pulled out the letter, and slit it open with my Barlow knife. In a flash I see the name at the bottom of the thin, single sheet — **Jane** — and my heart skips a beat or two.

Dear Lance,

I don't know if I can ever forgive you for running off like that without even saying good bye. I'm sorry about that silly argument we had — Argument? As I recollect, it was mostly just one-sided accusations — **but I heard that you went and stole that slave of yours, or friend, or free man, or whatever he is. My, but didn't you put this place in an uproar! Mr. Culbertson went around describing you and Shadrack and even put a notice in the newspaper. When he finally discovered your identity, the two of you were already gone — transferred to the Western end of the Pony Express, they said. I should never have told you where your black man was, and none of this would have happened. You would still be here, and I would still be happy! But the deed is done and can't be undone, and you are hundreds of miles away, and I am so very lonely. I wish you would come back to**

see me before I have to leave for school in Sept., but that may not be possible after what I am about to tell you — as you know, my brother, Gregory, has no use for you. He came bragging to me yesterday that Mr. Culbertson is coming West over the Pony Express trail to find you and 'get his nigger back' as he put it, and to take revenge on you for stealing him. Lance, this Culbertson means to kill you, so <u>please, please</u> do all you can to avoid him. I pray this letter reaches you before Culbertson does. I wrote it as soon as I heard and sent it by the very next pony rider. Know that you are in my thoughts and prayers every day. Until I see you again, I remain,

Affectionately,
Jane

I look at the date on top of the letter. It was written eight days ago. My hands are all clammy, and I put the paper down to wipe them on my pants legs. My first thought is one of gratitude to Jane Holland for caring enough to send me this warning. Thank God she did, or I might be walking, unawares, into a bullet. From the way she wrote, Culbertson didn't mean to take me to court — he meant to leave me for the buzzards.

I read the letter again, slower this time to take in every word. I'm glad she ain't mad at me any more, but those happy feelings are all mixed up with cold fear of a man who's stalking me, probably somewhere along the trail right now, asking questions if he ain't already found out where I'm stationed. I look at the envelope. It's addressed to Lance Barlow, Pony Rider, Western Division, Pony Express.

This letter, with its vague address, caught up with me in only eight days. How long would it take Culbertson? I folded the letter back into the envelope and tucked it into my pocket. Shad and I had come West to get away from trouble in Kansas. But I reckon trouble ain't something you can run away from. It follows you like the wind.

Chapter Eighteen

I was all of a sweat to get back to Simpson Springs to talk to Shad. I'd been on my own for a few years now, but since we'd met up again, I'd come to depend on his advice. Yet, it was two days before a rider came in from the west so I could leave. On the way back in daylight, I swung wide around Riverbed station. If the wailing, moaning desert fairies were there, I didn't want to hear them.

It was about supper time when I handed off the mochila to Bob Haslam at Simpson Springs, and he took off at a gallop toward Salt Lake City.

Shad and Barrington warn't around close, but then I saw them off at a distance near the spring, doing something. I was hot and dusty and tired as I walked toward them. Brown was sitting on a rock, watching the other two laying rock with some homemade mortar. I guess nobody was even thinking about supper.

When I came up, I was disgusted to see they were hard at work building that stupid bathing pool Brown had ordered the day he arrived. It was all I could do not to say something about this being a waste of time and sweat, because I was the only one who knew that Brown wouldn't be around long enough to use it.

"Hello, Lance," Barrington says, looking up.

"Watch out, you're dropping that mortar into the water," Brown snaps, not even letting on that I'm there. He ain't never been too friendly to me — I guess because I didn't knuckle under to him right off — but I'm so jittery now about the way he's acting that maybe he somehow knows I was at Riverbed and saw him with the Paiutes. I have to get a grip on my nerves. There's no way he saw or heard me that night.

Shad staggers up, carrying two good-sized rocks. He drops them on the ground and nods at me, sweat tracing some grooves in the dust down his dark face under his hat.

"About time to eat," I say, pretty blunt.

"We have to get as much of this done as we can before this mortar sets up," Brown says, still without looking at me. He stands up, puts his hands on his hips, and takes a closer look at the work. *If he wants to get done faster, he could be helping*, I'm thinking. But why is this man having a bathing pool made? If his plan to stop the Express works, he'll be out of a job and gone. Seems like he's planning to fail, if he figures to be here a while. It don't make no sense. But, just to put a burr under his saddle, I say, all innocent: "Seems like it'd be easier to build a new corral right near the spring than to rock up a ditch for water all the way over here."

"This isn't for watering the stock," he says, sounding a mite irritated.

"I'll get supper started," I say, walking off to hide a grin. I don't know what I'll fix, but I ain't going to stand around there, and maybe get put to work. I know if Brown gives me an order, there will be a ruckus, and I don't want to start nothing now. Besides, I've got to keep my terrible secret and report it to the proper person. I don't have no interest in card playing, but the few times I've been drug into a poker game with my friends, my face gave away my hand every time. I know if I stay around Brown very long, he'll figure out I got something on him. So I got to go about my business and avoid him, and try to act like everything's the same.

By the time Shad and Barrington come dragging in, with Brown following along, the beans and sidemeat I'd cooked were getting cold. I'd made a stab at baking some biscuits, but they were pretty hard. However, the two stock tenders don't make no comment; they just set down and dig in. I guess they're so tired and hungry, they don't care. I join them while Brown takes his and puts it back on the stove to warm it up.

There ain't much talking while we eat. It's getting dark outside about the time I rise up to get the dried apricots I'd put to soak for dessert. So I stop to light a lamp and set it on the table. I try not to look at Brown, because my face will tell him that I know what a skunk he is. Actually, I shouldn't run down no honest polecat by comparing him to Brown.

I didn't have no chance to get Shad by himself that night. He and Barrington was so tired from all that hoisting and shaping and setting rock, they hit their bunks not too long after supper.

I guess Brown had got everything done with the Injuns he had to do, because he didn't go nowhere, except into his closed-off bunk with a book. But I noticed one other thing — he had a fancy bottle of Quaker Maid Whiskey with him. This told me two things — first off, it was a direct violation of company rules. Of course, this didn't mean nothing to a man who was out to destroy the whole Pony Express. The other thing is, this shows me a crack in his armor. A man who drinks whiskey straight from a bottle ain't what they call a "social drinker." He's either got a lot of pain to kill, or lots of stuff to forget. In Brown's case, I figure his conscience — if he ain't already killed it — is giving him fits.

But I've got the weapon that's going to do him in. The problem is, how to get the information to somebody in power before them Paiutes can do any more damage and stop the Express again.

It was the next morning after breakfast before I could get Shad alone. He was out near the corral with a bucket of water in each hand. I caught up with him just as he was setting them down to open the gate.

"Wait up, Shad," I said. "Come on around here to the far side away from the house where Brown can't see us. I've got something to tell you."

He looks at me kind of curious, and follows me to where the stone corral blocks us from the station.

I told him what I'd seen and heard at the Riverbed station the other night. His eyes just go wide, and he don't say nothing at first.

"But that ain't all of it," I say. "I got a letter from Jane Holland . . . you know, the girl at the Holland Ranch near Marysville."

"She be de one you's sweet on?" he grins.

"I reckon you could say that," says I, pulling out the letter. "But that ain't what I want to tell you. Listen to what she wrote."

I commence to reading the letter to him. When I finish, Shad is looking mighty solemn.

"What are we going to do, Shad?"

"Appears we's caught between de devil and one of his helpers," he says, kind of slow.

"Only thing I can think to do is quit this job and ride on over to Deep Creek and tell Howard Egan about Brown's plot with the Injuns. Then the two of us will have to go into hiding some place so Culbertson can't find us."

Shad looks thoughtful for a bit, then says: "Mistah Egan might not be at Deep Creek. Last we see of him, he be travelin' wif dem supply wagons, going from station to station, getting de Express running again. And don't he have a house in Salt Lake City, too? We could ride all over de territory and maybe not find him fo' weeks. By den, Culbertson'd be here and. . . ."

"I know . . . I'd be dead, and you'd be back in slavery."

Shad nods. "Sounds like Brown done got de Injuns all stirred up already, so maybe telling on him ain't going to help us none."

"We've got to force him to tell who's in on this plot to bribe those Injuns," I say. "Even if I can find Howard Egan, it'll be my word against Brown's. I ain't got no proof he's giving guns and food and gold to the Injuns to attack the Express."

"Dat's right. Egan most likely figure dose Injuns be attackin' just because dey don't like white settlers and pony riders coming into deir lands."

"The Paiutes are probably already riled up," I agree. "But the way I got it figured, Brown and his Southern friends are trying to make 'em even worse. You're right, though. There ain't no way I can prove it."

We both stopped talking. I was feeling mighty glum, I can tell you. We was in a box for sure, and I couldn't see no way out. I guess I'd been hoping Shad would have an idea of what to do.

"Shadrack!"

Brown's voice reached us from the direction of the station. Shad rolled his eyes and said: "I's got to go." Then he turned to me. "How long ago dat letter be written?"

I figured up right quick. "Twelve days now."

"Den we best be watchin' fo' Culbertson any time."

My stomach was in a knot. "Shad, we should run, but I sure don't want to quit this job. I hate to let him run us off. This is the best job I've ever had."

"Workin' wif dese fine horse be a pure joy to me, too."

"Shadrack!" Brown's voice was sounding irritated.

"Dis job been good to me in spite of *dat*," Shad says, jerking his head toward the sound.

"I don't know how you stand to take orders from that

man. You didn't hire on to be no rock layer."

"Lance, some folks *ride* de railroad and some fixes de tracks. I's been a track fixer all my life, so it don't bother me none, as long as he don't order me to do nothin' against de law. I's still gettin' my pay right along. And it's good to stay busy when I ain't foolin' wif de horses."

"Shad, I've still got that Forty-Four caliber Dragoon pistol Peter Neece gave me," I say. "I'll load it up and put it in your bunk. And I'll keep my gun with me all the time. All we can do is stay on guard and be ready for anything."

"Dat's right," he says. "We know he be comin', but he don't know we be expectin' him." Shad give me a grin and then headed off toward the station house to help Brown.

I took the water buckets he had set down and started giving the thirsty horses a drink. If we didn't have to keep these ponies in the corral most of the time, we wouldn't have to carry water and feed to them. But we couldn't afford to lose these horses to the Injuns. And now that I knew that Brown was in cahoots with the Paiutes, I figured he might arrange for these animals to be stolen.

Less than an hour later, pony rider Bob Haslam come in with the mail from the East. I warn't expecting him so soon, but the schedule was still pretty messed up. Barrington got busy saddling a horse for me. I sure didn't want to ride over to Willow Springs just now and leave Shad to face Culbertson alone, if the slaver should happen to come while I was gone. Trouble was, we didn't have no idea when he might show. But we both knew he *would* be here, and most likely it would be soon.

"Bob, there warn't nobody up your way askin' about me, or about Shadrack, that black hosteler, was there?"

He looked at me kind of funny, and says: "Like who?"

"A tall man with rosy cheeks and blond hair. No whiskers."

He shakes his head. "No. Nobody like that. In fact, no one's asked about you or him. And I ain't seen anyone of that description. Of course, there's lots of people up in Salt Lake City. He could be there, and I wouldn't have seen him. You on the run from somebody?"

"Thanks, Bob," I say without answering his question.

"Lance!" Barrington calls. "Your horse is ready."

I run out and swing into the saddle. I felt better knowing I'd left the loaded gun under Shad's blanket, like I told him. At least we'd be some prepared.

The July sun was getting mighty fierce, but I'd gradually gotten used to this kind of hide-tanning dry heat and kept my skin covered as much as I could — my hat pulled low, long sleeves buttoned at the cuffs. I had to shed my buckskin shirt because it was just too warm.

It took the better part of six hours to reach the end of my run at Willow Springs. I didn't push my ponies too hard.

I got there about mid-afternoon, handed off the mochila to my relay, and, before he headed out in the direction of Deep Creek, I thought to ask him if Howard Egan was at that station.

"He hasn't been there for more than a week. The boys tell me he's back in Salt Lake with the wagons. Taking care of company business there."

This warn't good news for me, because I'd made up my mind that he was the only one I was going to trust with my secret about Cyrus Brown, short of talking to Alexander Majors himself. And there warn't much telling where Majors was. I had heard that he'd moved his family upriver from St. Joe about a hundred miles to Nebraska City.

"Barlow," Neece says when the rider has taken off, "I'm going to need your help tonight."

"Doing what?"

"Those Paiutes aren't about to leave us alone since we shot several of 'em the other night. They're determined to run off our stock, even though we've only got a few head. Lynch and I have been guarding them each night, and I've come up with a way to do it without exposing ourselves. And it fools the Indians, too. Come on outside, and I'll show you."

The circular corral had been made by digging a trench and setting in cedar posts on end to a height of about six feet. The gate was eight feet wide, but it warn't a swinging gate. It was just an opening shut off by two long poles resting on notched posts on either side.

The corral was empty while the horses were out grazing nearby with Lynch guarding them. Neece took the bars down and then showed me how the end posts were set loose in their holes and could be lifted right out of the ground. "The best way to guard this corral at night is to remove one of these posts and have a man stand still in its place. In the dark, the guard looks just like part of the gate."

"Sounds like a good idea."

If I was going to be on night guard, I figured to get me some sleep first, so I went into the station, got a good drink of water, and stretched out on the bunk for a nap.

I'd been sleeping sound for about three hours when Neece called me for supper that evening. After we ate, we helped Lynch run the ponies into the corral for the night. Then Lynch came in and had his meal.

About the time it got good and dark, Neece and I went out and removed the posts on either side of the gate and laid them inside the enclosure. Then he took one side of the gate and I took the other, standing where the posts had been. We propped one of the crossbars in place with two forked sticks.

I figured it'd be a long night, standing still as a post in one spot. But I reckon, as crafty as those Injuns were about running off stock, it was the only way to be sure of catching them in the act. The first couple of hours went mighty slow because, if this scheme was going to work, we couldn't move around or talk. I was getting mighty stiff and tired of pretending to be a post, so I took my mind off it by thinking about other things, and naturally thoughts of Culbertson come to me. I tried to imagine what I would do when he showed up. How would he come? Would he bring other men with him to make sure I didn't get away? Would he come at night or in the daytime? Surely he would know by asking where my home station was. But he probably couldn't know when I'd be there, because even I didn't know that in advance. Maybe if he came to Simpson Springs while I was out on a run, he'd just capture Shad and leave. Was Culbertson a man of violence? Jane's letter sure made him sound like one. She was convinced he was out to kill me. While all this was going through my head, I was trying to form a plan of action for every possible situation. But there was just too many ways he could come at Shad and me to figure 'em all out. He could be sneaky, or he could come in with guns blazing. He had all the advantage of knowing what he was going to do, and I didn't.

Whilst these thoughts was running through my head, I started hearing the horses in the corral behind me. They'd begun to mill around and snort and act mighty uneasy, so I knew there was probably Injuns about. Either that or it was wolves that sometimes come down out of the mountains at night to hunt. I turned my head ever so slightly and saw the horses looking off south, so I figured there must be something out there. But, staring toward the sagebrush in that direction, my eyes couldn't pick up nothing in the dark.

Suddenly a gunshot blasted and something screamed right in front of my face. The next instant I'd done a flip backward and landed about a rod inside the corral.

When my heart started beating again, I hear Neece yelling: "Lance! You all right?"

"Yeah," I managed to gasp. My gun is in my hand, but I don't remember drawing it. I get to my hands and knees. "What was that?"

A second later Neece is at my side. "I just shot an Indian right in front of you," he says, helping me up. "One of them must have got up close to the corral in back and come sneaking around toward the gate. I saw him, but I couldn't warn you without giving myself away."

"Thanks. You saved my life," I say. "But I mighty near died of fright."

"He probably figured you were a post, and was just reaching to let down the bars when I fired."

My heart is still racing, and I can't hardly get my breath.

"He just let out a yell and jumped about six feet straight up before he collapsed," Neece says, walking me toward the gate and showing me the body of the Injun that looks like a dark lump on the ground.

"I don't think we'll be bothered the rest of the night," he says. "They know we're alert. Here, help me set these posts back in place. I'll have Lynch come out and relieve us for a spell."

I couldn't swear to it, but it sure sounded like Neece give a little chuckle as we headed back toward the station.

Chapter Nineteen

I got over my fright soon enough, but the Injun threat was real. I couldn't help but think their attacks had picked up because of Brown's scheme to give them guns and other stuff to do it. This awful secret just kept gnawing away at my insides, but I still hadn't figured out what to do about it. I had to tell somebody soon, or I was going to make myself sick worrying.

And I felt even worse, two days later, when the eastbound mail rider come in. He brought news that a small emigrant train was attacked in Egan Cañon a few days before. Every man, woman, and child had been murdered.

I grabbed the mochila and galloped off, hoping the cool night wind would blow the vision of this terrible massacre out of my head. There warn't no problems on this run, and, when I rode past Riverbed station, just before dawn, it was all dark and silent.

I got to Simpson Springs just as the sun was poking its head up over the low eastern mountains. Shad had seen me coming about three miles off and had a horse ready and saddled for Bob Haslam. As Haslam grabbed the mochila from me and threw it over his saddle, he asks: "See any Indians?"

I quick like told him what had happened to the emigrant train, and also about our brush with the Paiutes who were trying to steal the horses at Willow Springs.

"I'll keep my eyes peeled," he says as he mounts up and spurs away.

Shad and Barrington had finished the bathing pool at the spring, and I walk over to take a look at it. The sun is just starting to knock off the night chill, but it still ain't warm enough to be soaking in this spring water.

"It'd make a good horse trough," Barrington says, grinning and looking around to make sure Brown ain't within earshot.

"Has he tried it out yet?" I ask.

"Nope. But he'll probably be at it this afternoon when the sun gets good and hot."

"Is Brown inside, fixing breakfast?" I ask.

"You got to be joshing," Barrington snorts. "He's somehow got it in his head that station masters don't have to do anything but give orders."

We amble back to the station house where Shad is washing his hands in a bucket by the door.

"I's fixin' to fry up some bacon and hoe cakes," he says.

Barrington pitches the old coffee grounds out the door and rinses the pot with a dipper of water from the barrel.

"Don't be throwing out garbage right in front of the door!" Brown snaps.

I hadn't seen him when I came in, but he's sitting by the fireplace, his chair tilted back against the rock wall.

"Sorry, chief," Barrington says, not really sounding regretful.

Brown's presence in the room is kind of like something heavy setting on your chest, so breakfast is a pretty silent affair.

"Must be clouding up," Barrington says, glancing toward the door we'd propped open to let out the smoke of the bacon grease and to admit some fresh air. "I'd like to see a good rain."

I was finished eating, so I got up, went to the doorway, and looked off to the northwest.

"It ain't going to rain for a while," says I, eyeing a thick cloud that's hugging the ground and rolling toward us like a huge wad of dirty, brown cotton. It's spreading fast, growing wider and higher, sliding a haze over the sun. "Dust storm coming," I add over my shoulder, not able to take my eyes off the brown cloud that's boiling along on some silent wind, snuffing out the low mountains and the desert sage at a mighty fast pace. I'd been in a dust storm once before, and they warn't pleasant — all grit and grime and piles of powdery dust sifting through the cracks, reddening the eyes, and grating between the teeth.

Brown came over to the door and shoved me aside to take a look.

"Shall we get the horses inside?" Barrington asked.

"No," Brown says. "No time. They can ride it out where they are. They'll breathe some dust, but it won't hurt them. That storm will be on us in a minute or so."

Even as he spoke, the sky was turning a funny color, and the light begun to dim considerably. But it warn't like a cloud had gone over the sun; it was more like an eclipse, when you know it shouldn't be getting dark, but it is. The sun was just kind of a yellow ball I could look at now without hurting my eyes.

"Check that corral gate!" Brown yells at nobody in particular.

I was standing closest and went dashing out toward the penned-up ponies. They were beginning to snort and mill around as they smelled the dust coming on the first puffs of wind.

The corral gate was latched, and, as I turned to run back, my eyes were squinting at the pall of dust while the wind whipped up more of it from the ground around me. With my eyes mostly shut, I tripped over a clump of sage and went sprawling on my hands and knees, and my Colt fell out into the dirt. I grabbed it up and shoved it back into its holster.

By the time I reached the station, the storm was on us, with gusts whipping and the dust swirling. I couldn't see no more than a few yards in any direction, and it was mighty near dark. The smell of dust was everywhere, and the inside of my nose was coated with it, even after I got in the room. Barrington pushed the door shut and leaned his back against it.

Shad sneezed a time or two, while Brown soaked his bandanna in the water barrel and then tied it around his nose and mouth.

Barrington was wiping his eyes with the back of his hand, and none of us was talking. It'd got so dim with the door shut and all that dirt flying around past the two small windows, that I slid up the glass chimney and struck a match to the wick of the lamp on the table.

Just as I set back down to wait it out, I thought I heard a noise outside. But, before I could even move or say anything, the door was flung inward, sending Barrington flying.

I jumped up from the bench, my heart nearly stopping, because there, framed in the doorway against the opaque light outside, was Culbertson, a pistol in each hand. A shot blasted the lamp I'd just lighted, and I cringed as glass splattered the back of the room and flaming coal oil ran across the table and dribbled down onto the dirt floor.

That first shot froze all four of us. My Colt was at my hip, but I dared not reach for it with two guns covering me from only a few feet away.

"Now, all hands in the air!" Culbertson grates, his voice sounding like a rasp on a grindstone, I reckon from breathing so much dust. He steps inside and kicks the door shut behind him.

My stomach has dropped down into my boots as he looks at me and Shad and says: "It was a long, hard trail, but I've finally tracked you down."

"Who the hell are *you?*" Brown asks. He don't seem scared — only startled.

Barrington, who has got up as far as one knee, looks as blank as Brown.

"Shut up, old man!" Culbertson snaps. "Get over in the corner! You, too!" he adds, waving a gun at Barrington.

Brown edges toward the far corner near the fireplace, and Barrington, moving slow, joins him.

Barrington never wears a gun, and, if Brown carries one, it ain't no belt gun. Shad ain't wearing the .44 I'd left on his bunk a couple of days before. All our plans about being prepared have gone to smash.

"Shadrack!" Culbertson says, pointing one of the pistols at him. "Get your black ass over near the door. As soon as this storm passes, get out and saddle one of those horses. You and I have a long ride back to Kansas."

I can imagine what Shad is thinking, but his face is rigid as black marble. The burning coal oil is blazing up, throwing an eerie light on the inside walls of the stone room. Culbertson flings off his hat and moves to put his back to the door. Flames are catching the wooden table top afire, and the flickering light is reflecting off Culbertson's round, rosy cheeks and blond hair that's plastered by sweat across his forehead.

I'm hoping he'll forget about me, now that he's got Shad. Then I can go after them later. But I might've known better. He's probably been thinking and planning and scheming what he'd do to me for causing him all this trouble and embarrassment. To him, nigger stealing was probably worse than horse stealing. And horse stealing was a hanging offense.

If he'd shot me then and there, without no hesitation, he probably could've got clean away. But he had to enjoy seeing me squirm, I reckon. He'd come too far and worked too long on building up his hate just to gun me down, quick like. He wouldn't get no satisfaction from that.

I knew I was dead if I didn't try to do *something,* and that reckless, desperate feeling begun to come over me, like it had that night at the Hartz Farm. I eased around back of the big table that was blazing in the middle of the room, whilst I held attention by saying: "What're you going to do to me, you red-faced pile of cow crap?"

Like I figured, this set him off, and his rosy cheeks just went flaming red, and his jaw clenched. As soon as his hand begun to move, I was on the floor behind the table and yanking my Colt. There was a blast of gunfire, and the table must have stopped the slugs while I was getting my pistol into action. But the hammer fell and nothing happened. A misfire. In a panic, I yanked back the hammer to try again. But the works was jammed with dirt and the gun wouldn't cock.

Just then Culbertson jumps to one side so he can get a clear shot at me. I roll away to the right to get behind the table again and roll right through the burning coal oil on the floor. The room explodes with gunfire again, and I can't hear nothing, because my ears are ringing so loud.

Instead of catching fire, my body has smooshed out the small fire on the dirt floor, and I'm banging the Colt on my thigh to knock the dirt out of it when I finally hear Shad yelling: "Lance! Hold it! Hold it!"

I look up, and Shad's standing there with his .44 Dragoon in hand. "It's all over!" he yells, and I can barely hear him over the ringing in my ears. I look around, and Culbertson is on the floor near the door, not moving. I get to my knees, then stand up. Brown is down, too, kind of kicking and holding his stomach. There's a Derringer on the floor beside him. I don't see Barrington.

"What happened?" I ask.

"Dey each shot de other," Shad says. "Brown had a hide-out gun and got off a shot whilst Culbertson was tryin' to shoot you."

We go over to Culbertson, and Shad rolls him over with the toe of his boot whilst he holds the Dragoon at full cock. Culbertson has got a red stain spreading on his white shirt.

"Dead center," says I. But his face still looks so ruddy I fight down my queasy stomach and put my fingers to the side of his throat under the jaw. There ain't no heartbeat I can feel.

Then we check Brown. He's been gut-shot but is still alive and groaning in agony. I straighten up and look at Shad. As much as I have no use for this man, it hurts me to see the suffering he's going through. "There ain't nothing we can do for him, Shad," I say. "We ain't even got any laudanum."

I yank a blanket down that's hanging by Brown's bunk, roll it up, and tuck it under his head. Barrington comes out of the middle room, looking pale and shaky while Shad sets his gun on the mantle and scoops a bucket of water from the barrel by the door and sluices it across the burning table. It takes two more buckets before the fire is out. The room is full of smoke and steam and broken glass and the smell of burnt gunpowder and dust.

The storm is still blowing outside like nature don't give a hang that one man's been killed and another mortally wounded in this isolated station.

Shad and me crouch down by Brown. He's in terrible pain. "Barrington, ride to Salt Lake City for a doctor," I say.

"Don't bother," Brown gasps. "I won't last." His face, above the droopy mustache, is pale and clammy.

Shad motions me and Barrington into the next room. "I seen men shot like dis befo'," he says. "He be dead by to-morrow."

"He's right," Barrington agrees. "Even a doctor couldn't do anything now."

"Then there's something I got to do. Come on," I say.

We go back to Brown who's still lying by the fireplace, and the three of us lift him, gentle like, into his bunk. He cries out with the pain of moving him, but it can't be helped. I see he's going into shock, so I lean down close and say: "Brown, I know about your deal with the Injuns to wreck the Pony Express."

His face don't hardly change.

"You're going to die," I say, pretty blunt. But he already knows. "Is there anything you want to tell us before you go . . . like the names of the men who're in on this plot with you?"

He don't say nothing for a few seconds, only closes his eyes, and I'm afraid he's unconscious. But he's heard me and understands, because directly he opens his eyes, and looks right at me and says: "I'll tell you. What have I got to lose? I'm not giving my life for those fools. It was a crazy idea from the start. At least, I'll die with a clear conscience."

He pauses and takes a deep breath, like he's gathering his strength.

"Shad, hand me that paper and pencil off the shelf over there," I say. "Barrington, listen close. You're a witness to this." The stocky hosteler leans in close.

Brown's voice is weak, and he's lying on his side, kind of bent, with his hands on his lower mid-section like he's holding onto the lead that's gone through his bowels.

Then he starts talking and gives us the names of all his fellow-conspirators, from men in Congress who hatched the plot to rich planters who financed it, right on down to the men who had the keys to the Southern state arsenals. I hold back my surprise and get it all down on paper until Brown finally gasps that he's thirsty. I know it'll hurry his death, but it don't matter now. I hold a dipperful of water for him to drink. While he's drinking, I say: "Brown, I want to thank you for saving my life. That man was a slaver named Culbertson who was after me and Shad."

"I didn't do it for you," he gasps, mean and contrary to the end. "He wasn't going to leave any of us alive."

He don't say nothing else for a bit, like he's resting. Directly I see he's passed out, which is a blessing, because he ain't suffering for now.

Then I feel Shad dabbing a wet rag on my back. "Take off yo' shirt, Lance. You's got some burns on yo' back."

I peel out of my shirt that's all soaked and streaked with coal oil and dirt, and has holes scorched in it. I catch my breath at the pain as Shad treats the raw spots on my hide with some of Brown's Quaker Maid Whiskey.

"At least dis pain won't be de last you feel," Shad says. "Not like him." He nods toward Brown.

"You're right," I say, feeling ashamed. "I didn't like the man, but I feel sorry for him. All that work he was making up for us around here was just to keep us busy so we wouldn't have no time or energy to check on what he was doing, meeting with the Paiutes."

"Dat's all it was, sure enough."

In about thirty minutes the storm blows over, and we haul Culbertson's body outside in the clear sunshine, and lay him on his back. He looks like he's just asleep, except for the red stain on his shirt and his cherub cheeks ain't a rosy color no more. Culbertson did lots of bad stuff in his life, but I can't find no hate in my heart as I look down at the thing that used to be a man. It's like looking at a locust husk on a tree trunk after the locust is gone.

"I think I'd better ride up to Salt Lake and fetch Mister Egan," Barrington says, not asking for no explanations about all this.

I give him a brief one anyway. Then I say: "Shad and I'll

223

stay here and bury Culbertson. And we'll tend to Brown as long as he lasts."

Barrington takes off toward the corral, and Shad says to me: "You look a mite peaked. Stay out here in de air and rest in de shade. I'll clean up inside."

I nod, thankful I got a friend like him.

Brown died sometime that night after hours of moaning and muttering, without ever coming to again. He just drifted away on a wave that lifted and broke on some unseen shore.

"I reckon we won't never know what it be like till we passes ourselves, Lance," Shad says as he covers Brown with a blanket.

Well, I reckon Aunt Martha's favorite servant, Divine Providence, had done for us once again 'cause our two biggest problems was solved all at the same time. Culbertson was dead, and the plot to wreck the Pony Express was about to be busted wide open.

"Shad, I reckon things are going to work out," I say, thinking if I can put some time and distance between me and all this violence, the world is going to look like a mighty fine and sunny place.

Chapter Twenty

When Superintendent Howard Egan heard the whole story, he didn't waste no time. He right quick notified Mr. Majors and Mr. Russell who had eleven people arrested and charged with conspiracy and attempted murder and a host of other things. Me and Barrington had to put our signatures to sworn statements about what Brown had told us just before he died and about what I had overheard at Riverbed station. All this just added fuel to the fire that was already threatening to burn up the country. Indictments were brought against the arrested men. Three Congressmen were immune from prosecution while Congress was in session, but, before that assembly adjourned, the three just disappeared somewheres and warn't seen until a few months later when they turned up as officials of the new Confederate government.

Of course, there was a mighty ruckus in the newspapers when this plot to wreck the Pony Express was busted wide open. Shad and I warn't exactly heroes, but we got a good bit of the credit when all those headlines were slung across the country, and the men Brown had named were rounded up and jailed. I reckon it shouldn't have come as no surprise when a slick lawyer out of Mississippi was hired to defend the eleven men. It must have taken a pile of money to hire him, but nobody knew where it come from. Anyway, what with one legal trick and another, he was able to stall their trial for months. So, after a few weeks, interest in the scandal just kind of went flat, like a glass of beer that's been left set too long. It was a mighty big relief to me, because I warn't cut out to be famous, even for a little while, and I was getting wore out with congratulations by the company bosses and being joshed by the other riders and station keepers. The owners didn't offer us no reward. I reckon they figured we'd just done our job. Besides, there was lots of others who did more heroic deeds than ours every day.

But at least the Injuns warn't being supplied with no more guns and encouragement to kill off the Pony Express. The Paiutes did continue to raid stations off and on for a few more months, but they warn't near the threat they'd been before.

While all this was going on, the pony riders kept running the mail. Barrington was made station master at Simpson Springs to replace Brown, and Shad and I were reassigned to Willow Springs as a home station under Peter Neece, which suited us right down to the ground.

In between runs, Mr. Egan, Shad, and I rode over to the Riverbed station and made a close inspection of the place. The only way Shad would go along was if we went in the daytime, which we did.

We discovered that someone had rigged a wooden whistle under an eave of the stable roof. It was fastened on a corner and set so as to catch the prevailing wind and give off that weird wailing noise.

"Apparently Brown was just trading on the reputation this place has for being haunted," Mr. Egan said after we'd made our discovery. "He rigged this thing to make sure everyone would stay away so he'd have a private place to meet with the Paiutes."

I nodded. "It warn't desert fairies at all."

But Shad didn't seem totally convinced. "What about dem stories Deweese told us? Dey was station keepers seein' white shapes movin' in de moonlight. And dey was hearin' dose moanin' noises long before Mister Brown showed up."

"I wasn't able to keep station masters here," Egan admitted, kind of lame like. "Maybe those strange white shapes they

saw were due to the moonlight on the salt desert out there."
He waved his hand toward the arid desolation around us. "As
to the noises . . . I don't know. Had to have been the wind."

He didn't even sound convinced himself, so I reckon there
was something deep inside him that was conjuring up visions
of the fairies and gremlins from the misty bogs of Ireland.

The Riverbed station was never manned, but it didn't really
matter since it warn't that far to the stations on either side of
it. A much bigger problem for the company, after the Injuns
kind of slacked up, was money. Russell, Majors, and Waddell
couldn't get their hands on enough of it. Because of all the
wrangling in Congress between the Northern and Southern
interests, the company was never granted the contract to haul
the U. S. Mail. I reckon that was why Mr. Russell got into
some kind of trouble with the Secretary of the Interior and
the Indian Trust Fund Bonds. I didn't understand none of
it, even after reading about it in the newspapers when Mr.
Russell was arrested in December. I would have had more
luck unsnarling a fishing line than understanding the financial
tangle he'd got himself into trying to keep the Pony Express
afloat. I only know that a bunch of the riders and stations
keepers begun playing on the name of the Central Overland
California and Pike's Peak Express Company by calling it
"Clean Out of Cash and Poor Pay."

Out here on my run in the Utah Territory, I didn't have
hardly any need for money, but I had to borrow some when
I went back to see Jane twice during the next few months.
She and I took up where we'd left off, and directly we found
out this warn't no passing fancy and wound up engaged.

In November, Abraham Lincoln was elected President of
the United States, and the news was carried by the pony riders
from St. Joe to Sacramento in a record eight days. I was proud
to be a part of that run, which was the fastest ever.

The plotters eventually came to trial. Most of them got convicted and sent to prison. But by then nobody much cared because in April, 1861, the war started, which ruined a perfectly beautiful spring.

The Express just kept on running, even though the partners were pretty much bankrupt. I don't know how they managed it, but that warn't my problem, except for missing my pay a time or two. Finally, in October of that year, the telegraph was completed across the country and put the Pony Express out of business for good after only eighteen months.

We were all sorry to see it go, but in the spring of 1862 Shad and I took up adjoining homesteads of one hundred and sixty acres each in the Nebraska Territory where we raised horses and provided remounts and hay for the military posts in the region and the Union Army. We steered clear of the war, and that fall, when I was twenty-one, Jane and I were married. Before Shad could save enough money to buy his wife and child out of slavery, President Lincoln took care of that for him. But freedom for the slaves and the first cross-country railroad were a ways off in the future yet, and all that's another story.

THE END

Apache Law

The Lonely Gun

LUKE ADAMS

They call him half-breed. And a lot worse. The only time Mitch Frye has ever felt at home was as a scout for the 6th Cavalry. But when the scouts are cut loose, Frye is a man without a home. Then fate—or bad luck—draws him to Paxton, a wide-open boom town in Arizona, a town without a lawman. He thinks he is only passing through, but the mayor has other plans for him. He gives Frye a hard choice—pin on a star or stand trial for murder. And it isn't long before Frye regrets his decision. Somebody is killing off miners in the area, and it is up to Frye to find out who is behind it . . . even if it looks like that someone is the mayor himself.

___4631-8 $3.99 US/$4.99 CAN

Dorchester Publishing Co., Inc.
P.O. Box 6640
Wayne, PA 19087-8640

Please add $1.75 for shipping and handling for the first book and $.50 for each book thereafter. NY, NYC, and PA residents, please add appropriate sales tax. No cash, stamps, or C.O.D.s. All orders shipped within 6 weeks via postal service book rate. Canadian orders require $2.00 extra postage and must be paid in U.S. dollars through a U.S. banking facility.

Name_____
Address_____
City_____ State_____ Zip_____
I have enclosed $_____ in payment for the checked book(s).
Payment <u>must</u> accompany all orders. ❏ Please send a free catalog.
          CHECK OUT OUR WEBSITE! www.dorchesterpub.com

A BALLAD FOR SALLIE

JUDY ALTER

Longhair Jim Courtright has been both a marshal and a desperado—and in Hell's Half Acre, the roughest part of Fort Worth, he is a living legend. His skill with a gun has made him a hero in some people's eyes . . . and a killer in others'. As soon as young widow Sallie McNutt steps off the stage from Tennessee, her refined manners and proper attire set her apart from the other women of the Half Acre. And it isn't long before something else sets her apart—someone wants her dead.

___4365-3 $4.50 US/$5.50 CAN

Dorchester Publishing Co., Inc.
P.O. Box 6640
Wayne, PA 19087-8640

Please add $1.75 for shipping and handling for the first book and $.50 for each book thereafter. NY, NYC, and PA residents, please add appropriate sales tax. No cash, stamps, or C.O.D.s. All orders shipped within 6 weeks via postal service book rate. Canadian orders require $2.00 extra postage and must be paid in U.S. dollars through a U.S. banking facility.

Name_____
Address_____
City_____State_____Zip_____
I have enclosed $_____ in payment for the checked book(s).
Payment <u>must</u> accompany all orders. ☐ Please send a free catalog.

WILL CADE

Larimont

John Kendall doesn't want to go back home to Larimont, Montana. He has to—to investigate the death of his father. At first everyone believed that Bill Kendall died in a tragic fire... until an autopsy reveals a bullet hole in Bill's head. But why is the local marshal keeping it a secret? John isn't quite sure, so he sets out to find the truth for himself. But the more he looks into his father's death, the more secrets he uncovers—and the more resistance he meets. It seems there are a whole lot of folks who don't want John nosing around, folks with a whole lot to lose if the truth comes out. But John won't stop until he digs up the last secret. Even if it is one better left buried.

___4618-0 $4.50 US/$5.50 CAN

UNDER THE BURNING SUN
H. A. DeRosso

Of all the amazing writers published in the popular fiction magazines of the 1940s and '50s, one of the greatest was H.A. DeRosso. Within twenty years he published nearly two hundred Western short stories, all noted for their brilliant style, their realism and their compelling vision of the dark side of the Old West. Now, finally, for the first time in paperback, we have a collection of the best work of this true master of the Western story. This collection, edited by Bill Pronzini, presents a cross-section of DeRosso's Western fiction, spanning his entire career. Here are eleven of his best stories and his riveting short novel, "The Bounty Hunter," all powerful and spellbinding, and all filled with the excitement, the passion, and the poetry of Western writing at its peak.

___4712-8 $4.50 US/$5.50 CAN

Genevieve of TOMBSTONE

John Duncklee

Tombstone in the 1880's is the toughest town in the West, and it takes a special kind of grit just to survive there. Ask the Earps or the Clantons. But among the gunslingers and lawmen, among the ranchers and rustlers, there is Genevieve, a woman with the spirit, toughness—and heart—the town demands. Whether she is working in a fancy house or running her own cattle ranch, Genevieve will not only survive, she will triumph. She is a woman who will never surrender, never give in—and one that no reader will ever forget.

___4628-8 $4.99 US/$5.99 CAN

Dorchester Publishing Co., Inc.
P.O. Box 6640
Wayne, PA 19087-8640

Please add $1.75 for shipping and handling for the first book and $.50 for each book thereafter. NY, NYC, and PA residents, please add appropriate sales tax. No cash, stamps, or C.O.D.s. All orders shipped within 6 weeks via postal service book rate. Canadian orders require $2.00 extra postage and must be paid in U.S. dollars through a U.S. banking facility.

Name_____
Address_____
City_____ State_____ Zip_____
I have enclosed $_____ in payment for the checked book(s).
Payment <u>must</u> accompany all orders. ☐ Please send a free catalog.
CHECK OUT OUR WEBSITE! www.dorchesterpub.com

OUTCASTS
THE OUTCAST BRIGADE

JASON ELDER

They are not wanted where they come from. They are not welcome anywhere. They are outcasts, rootless and friendless, until luck or destiny throw them together. A former Apache scout shunned by his tribe, an ex-Union Army major, a former Confederate captain, and two army deserters, all forced to band together to stay alive—as long as they can avoid killing each other. Can they bury their anger and work together long enough to do what they have to do? Can they make it to Mexico to rescue a band of friendly Apaches who have been captured and sold into slavery? It is no easy task, because even if they manage not to kill each other, there are plenty of others eager to do it for them.

___4699-7 $3.99 US/$4.99 CAN